Praise for *Principal Investigation*—

The shocking debut novel featuring Dr. Celeste Braun and written by B. B. Jordan—professor of immunology and head of a research laboratory studying molecular biology at a major California university. This authentic and exciting new series takes readers behind the scenes of the latest medical breakthroughs—and reveals that the search for new cures is not unlike the search for criminal justice.

"I was captured by the book and read it rapidly to its conclusion. It is a very imaginative and compelling story that reflects well the activities of a scientific lab."
—David Baltimore, Ph.D., Nobel Laureate

"A stunning new talent . . . great insights into how the hottest science is done . . . B. B. Jordan is a dazzler!"
—Jon A. Jackson, author of *Dead Folks: A Detective Sergeant Mulheisen Novel*

"*Principal Investigation* is a wonderful biomystery. The characters are lively and humorous. The gripping plot, centered on the immune system, rings true. I could not put it down once I started reading it."
—Lubert Stryer, M.D., Professor of Neurobiology, Stanford Medical School

MORE MYSTERIES FROM THE
BERKLEY PUBLISHING GROUP . . .

CAT CALIBAN MYSTERIES: She was married for thirty-eight years. Raised three kids. Compared to that, tracking down killers is easy . . .

by D. B. Borton

ONE FOR THE MONEY	TWO POINTS FOR MURDER
THREE IS A CROWD	FOUR ELEMENTS OF MURDER
FIVE ALARM FIRE	SIX FEET UNDER

ELENA JARVIS MYSTERIES: There are some pretty bizarre crimes deep in the heart of Texas—and a pretty gutsy police detective who rounds up the unusual suspects . . .

by Nancy Herndon

ACID BATH	WIDOWS' WATCH
LETHAL STATUES	HUNTING GAME
TIME BOMBS	C.O.P. OUT
CASANOVA CRIMES	

FREDDIE O'NEAL, P.I., MYSTERIES: You can bet that this appealing Reno private investigator will get her man . . . "A winner."—Linda Grant

by Catherine Dain

LAY IT ON THE LINE	SING A SONG OF DEATH
WALK A CROOKED MILE	LAMENT FOR A DEAD COWBOY
BET AGAINST THE HOUSE	THE LUCK OF THE DRAW
DEAD MAN'S HAND	

BENNI HARPER MYSTERIES: Meet Benni Harper—a quilter and folk-art expert with an eye for murderous designs . . .

by Earlene Fowler

FOOL'S PUZZLE	IRISH CHAIN
KANSAS TROUBLES	GOOSE IN THE POND
DOVE IN THE WINDOW	MARINER'S COMPASS

HANNAH BARLOW MYSTERIES: For ex-cop and law student Hannah Barlow, justice isn't just a word in a textbook. Sometimes, it's a matter of life and death . . .

by Carroll Lachnit

MURDER IN BRIEF	A BLESSED DEATH
AKIN TO DEATH	JANIE'S LAW

PEACHES DANN MYSTERIES: Peaches has never had a very good memory. But she's learned to cope with it over the years . . . Fortunately, though, when it comes to murder, this absentminded amateur sleuth doesn't forgive and forget!

by Elizabeth Daniels Squire

WHO KILLED WHAT'S-HER-NAME?	REMEMBER THE ALIBI
MEMORY CAN BE MURDER	WHOSE DEATH IS IT ANYWAY?
IS THERE A DEAD MAN IN THE HOUSE?	WHERE THERE'S A WILL

SECONDARY
Immunization

B. B. JORDAN

BERKLEY PRIME CRIME, NEW YORK

This is a work of fiction. Names, characters, places, and incidents are either the product of the author's imagination or are used fictitiously, and any resemblance to actual persons, living or dead, business establishments, events, or locales is entirely coincidental.

SECONDARY IMMUNIZATION

A Berkley Prime Crime Book / published by arrangement with the author

PRINTING HISTORY
Berkley Prime Crime edition / October 1999

The Penguin Putnam Inc. World Wide Web site address is http://www.penguinputnam.com

ISBN: 0-425-17118-3

Berkley Prime Crime Books are published by The Berkley Publishing Group, a division of Penguin Putnam Inc., 375 Hudson Street, New York, New York 10014.
The name BERKLEY PRIME CRIME and the BERKLEY PRIME CRIME design are trademarks belonging to Penguin Putnam Inc.

PRINTED IN THE UNITED STATES OF AMERICA

10 9 8 7 6 5 4 3 2 1

ACKNOWLEDGMENTS

The alliterative angels continue as muses and I thank my agent, Cynthia Cannell; mentor, Jon A. Jackson; and my partner, Peter Parham; as well as my editor, Natalee Rosenstein, whose support, encouragement, and excellent advice are largely responsible for the appearance of this sequel. I would also like to thank Michael Lemonick for his continued help in the world of publishing; Roger Brent for sharing material about the QHMP; Shu-Hui Liu for drawing the Chinese characters in Chapter 13; and Analisa D'Andrea for advice on Italian expressions. I acknowledge the inspiration of *Courier to Peking* by June Goodfield and *A Literary Companion to Science* by Walter Gratzer for providing ideas relevant to the plot of this novel. The scenes in Puerto Rico were made possible by the funding of a scientific conference in San Juan by the Pew Charitable Trusts, and the scenes in Taiwan evolved from the enthusiastic hospitality of my colleagues, Alice and C. C. Wang during a visit to the Molecular Biology Institute of Taipei.

This work is entirely fiction and any resemblance to reality is purely coincidental.

To Peter

SECONDARY
Immunization

1

Crise de Foie

Celeste Braun could count on one hand the number of times in her adult life that she had thrown up. She sometimes declared that she had an iron stomach. From her early training as a biologist, Celeste had long overcome natural squeamishness about blood and guts. She never got stomach flu. The times that she had "tossed her cookies" in "a technicolor yawn," as an Australian colleague would say, were unquestionably her own fault. Once, in London, she had disgraced herself by being sick on the steps of a government official's townhouse where she had incautiously swilled too much single malt at a reception for visiting scholars. Years later, again in London, returning from Paris, she had endured a *crise de foie,* the French euphemism for indigestion from overindulgence. The crisis peaked at the Selfridge's cheese counter, which, unlike Monty Python's absurdly empy *fromagerie,* was well stocked, and its heady aroma overwhelmed Celeste's abused stomach. She just made it outside the store, to the Oxford Street pavement, before she emptied her guts in front of the Easter display windows. But those events were years ago, in staid old England. This was musty San Juan. Perhaps for only the third time in her adult life, Celeste, having completely lost her composure, had lost her lunch. And what had led to this rare event was certainly not overindulgence.

Celeste had been touring the military museum in the El Morro Fort with a group of scientists. It was the last stop of the "field trip" to the historical sites of old San Juan, an afternoon off before the conference banquet that evening. Celeste was undeniably bored. In fact, the whole trip had been a tedious disappointment. When the Instituto de Medicina Botánica had invited Celeste to speak at the conference, she had jumped at the chance to visit Puerto Rico for the first time. It would be spring, before the interesting birds migrated north. She had recently developed a passion for birdwatching. But except for today's excursion, she had seen little of the country or its birds.

Celeste was the virologist in a diverse panel of four international guest experts that included a neurologist, an oncologist, and a cardiologist. The conference organizers had arranged a role for the outside panel in every session, leaving them no free time. Celeste had shortly realized that it was a thinly disguised scam to use the panel as consultants for the Instituto's nascent venture into commercializing their herbal remedies. Ironically, she had perhaps contributed more than they'd wanted in terms of scientific criticism, being the only Ph.D. among the invited medical experts. So her participation in the conference had been a rather thankless experience. Meantime, her sighting of a red-legged thrush in the hotel garden was about as thrilling as seeing a robin at home in San Francisco.

It wasn't as if San Juan was lacking historical glamour. Three hundred years as the strategic naval command post of the Spanish empire in the New World had left a powerful romantic legacy. The fortified walls of old San Juan were punctuated by *garitas,* cylindrical stonework sentry boxes capped with conical roofs, like fairy-tale turrets suspended precariously over the brilliant blue sea. The old city itself was a pastel stucco refuge, decorated with lacy wrought-iron balconies. It was perched on a promontory above the sweltering concrete bustle that comprised most of San Juan, an historic heaven above a modern hell. Celeste could understand why the Instituto had decided to convert a block of these beautiful old buildings into their privately funded laboratories and clinic rather than choose a location in downtown San Juan.

Their tour guide was an insufferably officious pedant, wearing an eighteenth-century Spanish military uniform. He had trapped the scientists in his charge with an enthusiastic and lengthy account of the prolonged struggle between the Spanish Armada and the British Navy. He spent a particularly long time describing the extensive underground catacombs, which had been used for hiding gunpowder during sieges and probably as escape routes. They apparently connected to a honeycomb network under the residential part of Old San Juan. The street plan, the guide told them, reflected a prescribed grid pattern that was codified in the Royal Ordinances of Philip II in 1573, and formed the basis for the design of many colonial Spanish cities in the Americas.

Were the catacombs still usable, one of the scientists had asked? Surely, the guide responded, but the police had closed them off in the early 1970s to discourage hippies who had tried to squat there.

The guide herded his group into the interior of the fort, where they were permitted a private viewing of military paraphernalia from the sixteenth through the nineteenth centuries. Celeste had followed, sheeplike, at the rear. In the fourth of these interminable exhibition rooms, the guide indicated a barred iron gate that sealed off an entrance to the catacombs.

Celeste idly pushed on the gate when the guide's attention was directed elsewhere. To her surprise, it gave way to her touch. She peered into the dark passageway. By the dim light infiltrating from the exhibition room, Celeste could just make out what seemed to be an intersecting cross tunnel about fifteen yards away from where she stood. Thinking it would be interesting to peek around the corner to see the catacomb network, Celeste stepped into the corridor, leaving the gate slightly ajar behind her.

She walked cautiously toward the end of the tunnel, glancing back to be sure she hadn't been noticed. This caused her to blunder straight into an extensive network of spiderwebs. But, after a brief panic at the sticky touch of the webs on her face, she recovered her composure and went on.

It was cool in the passageway and oddly dry. At the intersection, Celested halted and peered into the cross tunnel that stretched before her. As her eyes adjusted, she saw that uncomfortably close to where she stood, the passageway was blocked by a body-sized heap. If it was human, it was horribly contorted and seemed to be writhing unnaturally. It was the realization of what she was looking at that had caused Celeste's lunch to reappear.

The odd-shaped pile in front of her *was* a body. It was definitely dead, and it was crawling with live rats. There had been no cautionary odor revealing the presence of the corpse and Celeste had nearly stumbled over it. So it was not long dead. But it was rapidly deteriorating. The perpetrators of the disassembly scampered into the darkness beyond as soon as Celeste's reaction revealed her presence.

Celeste tried hard to recover her nerve, to look at the cadaver with the attitude of an observant scientist. It was naked and appeared to have been a man. Above the groin rose what was left of a beer belly, perhaps a Bacardi belly. It had been slashed open with a sharp object, surely a knife, in a crudely V-shaped incision. The exposed guts were undoubtedly what had attracted the rats.

Celeste clenched her lips and wiped off her face with a tissue from her shoulder bag. She closed her mind to the horror and turned purposefully back, willing herself to walk, not run, the short distance to the gate. When she reached it, Celeste seized the bars too forcefully, so that the gate struck the stone wall of the tunnel with a clang. Catapulted by the rebound, she nearly leapt into the exhibition room that she had left a few minutes earlier.

Back in the bright artificial light, Celeste stood for a moment, breathing hard and blinking. The guide, disturbed in his harangue of the captive visitors, heard the clang from the adjoining room and darted back to investigate.

"There you are," he declared with an annoyed tone. He eyed Celeste suspiciously. What had she broken? He hoped it wasn't something valuable and waited imperiously for her to apologize, to explain herself.

After a moment of conscious effort at control, Celeste stated in a too-loud voice, "There is a dead body in the catacombs. You must get help. The police."

Señor Raul de Leon was the head of the homicide squad and the chief of the San Juan police. He sported a neatly trimmed, chestnut-brown beard that completed his spotless uniform, and had the naturally disdainful features of a Spanish aristocrat. His behavior toward Celeste was impeccably polite. He had met plenty of professional women in his day. Although there were none on the police force, several of the lawyers working with the San Juan police were women. But this particular professional woman in front of him looked nothing like the elaborately made-up, elegantly suited, and high-heeled lawyers of his acquaintance. She was wearing belted, khaki trousers and a black T-shirt with a crumpled linen jacket and flat, closed-toe sandals. In fact, her outfit was rather androgynous. But her face was very feminine in a sort of ethereal way. She reminded him, partly because of the way her hair was done and partly because of her long straight nose, of a particular photograph of Virginia Woolf that he remembered seeing on a book jacket in his mother's collection of English novels. She exuded the same thoughtful dignity as that photograph. Her apparent indifference to dressing to please the opposite sex was intriguing to him.

Señor de Leon was a descendant of the de Leon family in San Juan that orginated with the fabled explorer. He had been well-educated at New York University and spoke American English with almost no accent. The interview had been very straightforward, and it was time to draw it to a close.

"Is there anything else, Professor Braun, that you can think of that you have not mentioned already? Any extra detail might be important. I understand you are a scientist. Your powers of observation could be very helpful."

Celeste did not feel like a coolheaded, detached scientist at that moment. "No, I really can't think of anything else. I'm sure I must be forgetting something, though." She paused, casting her thoughts back over the scene. "I can still picture the body so vividly." Her stomach turned again as she brought it to mind, and she shuddered visibly. "Just as I described it in the statement that your colleague recorded. It's an image that I'm afraid will haunt me for a while. I simply can't remember much before or after seeing it."

Señor de Leon was getting just a little restless in spite of his mild curiosity about Celeste. He was anxious to return to the scene of the crime to make sure that the photographers didn't disrupt more than necessary. "Well, we will check for footprints, of course, but yours or the rats' may have made it difficult to see anything else in the dust. And, please, if you think of anything at all, professor, call me." He stood up and handed Celeste an elegantly printed card, which she inspected. It seemed incongruous to Celeste that this Spanish gentleman could be contacted using an American area code and phone number. It also always seemed incongruous to be called professor. In reality, she was only an assistant professor. And, she felt she certainly hadn't been of much assistance.

The door to the interview room opened. "Ah, here is Pedro," said Señor de Leon. "The statement is ready for your signature. I will leave you to read it over and check back in a few minutes."

Pedro silently laid the typed statement on the wooden table in the interview room and set beside it an old-fashioned fountain pen. He followed Señor de Leon out of the room and began to speak to him quietly in Spanish as they shut the door behind them.

Celeste looked over the transcript of her earlier interview with de Leon's deputy. It seemed accurate, if regrettably sparse. She signed the statement and then sat back to wait for her dismissal. This was the first moment she had been alone since finding the body, except for a hasty clean up in the minimal ladies' toilet at the police headquarters.

Save for two empty wooden chairs and the table in front of Celeste, the room where she sat was bare with walls of whitewashed stucco. It resembled a monk's cell that could have been transplanted from any one of the mission museums on California's El Camino Real, except that it was missing the requisite straw sleeping pallet in the corner. Celeste supposed that the police used a room free of distractions to try to reduce the chance that someone being interrogated would be influenced by suggestive objects. However, the overall impression was one of bleak intimidation of the kind that might have been experienced by a political prisoner in South America.

Feeling somewhat intimidated herself brought Celeste a flood of memories that continued to plague her. What plagued her the most about them was that she always began by thinking how fortunate she was to be alive. It had been only nine months earlier that she had sat in a wooden chair like the one she was currently occupying and was being threatened at the needlepoint of a syringe full of deadly poison. She had been unbelievably stupid to have got herself into that situation, all because she thought logic would save the world from a killer epidemic. Who did she think she was? Nancy Drew? But to be fair, if she hadn't interfered the result would have been a global nightmare. Had she been a real PI in the "private investigator" sense and not merely a lab PI or "principal investigator," she surely would have handled the whole affair better. She had been damn lucky to escape. Still, deep down, Celeste wondered if she had learned anything from the experience and whether, if pressed into action again, she would be better at it.

"Don't even think about it," she said out loud to herself. This horrific brush with a murder victim should be a warning and a reminder to steer clear.

A polite knock on the door followed by the entry of Señor de Leon and Pedro brought Celeste back to reality. She stood and picked up her shoulder bag, ready to say her farewell and definitely ready to pack her bags for the home-bound flight in the morning. She could tell earlier that Señor de Leon was in a hurry to get on with his investigation, and she certainly wasn't about to keep him. But instead of ushering her out, he gestured for her to sit back down and instructed Pedro in Spanish to take the signed statement away. When the silently compliant Pedro had left, Señor de Leon closed the door behind him.

"Well, Professor Braun," said Señor de Leon clearing his throat. "It appears that you have discovered an important corpse. I have just had the FBI from Miami on the phone. They tell me to request two things from you. First, we ask that you not discuss this incident with anyone. It is already unfortunate that your colleagues who were at the museum know it happened. But it is still important that the details that only you saw remain confidential."

Great, thought Celeste. That will guarantee that I'll keep it bottled up inside. Not very therapeutic for dispelling "the creeps." Out loud she said, "And the other request?"

"You may be asked to travel to Miami to be interviewed should the case prove difficult."

"Fine," said Celeste, slightly sarcastically. "Anything to help the FBI. After all, they consider me clean. I'm sure I was thoroughly checked out before I was asked to serve on the National Institutes of Health grant review committee. They know they can rely on me."

"It should not be too big a demand. And perhaps the case will be solved before they need to ask for your help," said Señor de Leon, trying to be gracious in the face of Celeste's attitude. "Also, it might give you an excuse to visit us here in Puerto Rico again."

"Well, I would like another chance to see the birds sometime. But I don't think I'll go out of my way to revisit the police headquarters." She finished this last statement with a smile.

In kind, Señor de Leon responded, "Oh, you offend our hospitality, Professor Braun. Please be sure to get in touch if you return. I'd be honored to show you some of the more pleasant sights." If she did come back, he would need to keep an eye on her. He had his reasons for keeping the catacombs off-limits.

"No offense meant, Señor," said Celeste. "I could look forward to that." There was a challenge to be met in his chilly politeness.

Celeste picked up her bag, stretched out her hand for a departing handshake, and made her way out of the police station into the cooling dusk. In spite of her resolution to steer clear of the world of crime, she knew she would say yes if the FBI needed her.

She just could not shake those disturbing thoughts. How did she know she could believe de Leon? He could be telling her to keep quiet for all kinds of reasons. It certainly never reflects well on a place when tourists can run across dead bodies. There is also plenty of drug traffic in and out of Puerto Rico, and the police are not necessarily above corruption. Celeste was too drained to give full vent to her suspicions. She would have to wait to see what transpired and, as a scientist, then assess the evidence.

2

Hippocratic Headache

Washington society had become boring again. Buffy felt another one of her headaches coming on as she mentally reviewed the conversations she had just left behind. She let herself into the house and turned off the burglar alarm. The luncheons had almost been fun during the six months that Austin had left her for Jill. Buffy had been the center of attention, then. But now that Austin had returned with his tail between his legs, things were back to normal. Not only that, but Jill had inexplicably been brought into the fold once she'd dumped Austin. She had been at the book club luncheon today, looking prettily pregnant and very self-satisfied. However, despite her appearance, rumor had it that Jill's new husband was spending most of his time at his job in Virginia and that Jill refused to move out of her house in Georgetown to join him.

Buffy walked across the huge expanse of remodeled kitchen that had been her reconciliation present and opened the camouflaged refrigerator to pour herself a glass of sparkling water. The door fell closed with an expensive thud as another jab of pain pulsed through her forehead. Seeking relief, Buffy laid her cheek on the cool granite countertop and was thankful that the cook was off today so there was no need for small talk. Then she kicked off her pumps and unzipped the tight skirt of the suit she had worn to the luncheon. Her waist expanded gratefully. Carrying her skirt and glass of water, Buffy dragged her way up the thickly carpeted staircase to lie down in the master bedroom. As her head hit the pillow, the phone rang.

"Buffy, it's Cynthia," said a conspiratorial voice in response to Buffy's unenthusiastic "hello."

"Hi, Cyn," said Buffy with a sigh. "I'd love to talk about the luncheon but I've got another one of my headaches again. Can I call you back later?"

"Okay," said Cynthia, sounding disappointed. "I was hoping to hear what you thought about Jill." She paused, not wanting to get off the line. "But you just reminded me of something. I keep forgetting to tell you about this headache clinic that Rhonda told me about. You're supposed to go over there while you have a headache so they can do some kind of analysis. Rhonda gave me the card. Hold on while I find it."

"I'm not going anywhere," said Buffy from her prone position on the bed. She heard sounds of rustling from the other end of the line. Probably searching her handbag, thought Buffy.

"Here it is," said Cynthia. "Dr. Sandra Lovett, Neurology/Oncology Clinic, 2224 Eye Street. Look, I have to do an errand in Dupont Circle, so I'll take you down to the clinic if you can't drive."

Boy, she really wants to gossip, thought Buffy, but the possibility of some relief from her headaches was sufficient inducement.

An hour later Buffy and Cynthia were sitting on a leather couch in Dr. Lovett's waiting room, leafing through out-of-date fashion magazines. Sandra Lovett inspected them through the peephole in her office door.

They both looked like perfect candidates. Maybe her luck was changing. She always felt guilty "treating" the elderly and terminally ill. So it was a relief when patients came along who looked liked they had nothing better to do with their time or money than seek cures for boredom and anxiety.

Sandra glanced quickly at the name on the clipboard her nurse had brought in. She opened the door and looked at the women sitting on the waiting room sofa. "Margaret Buffum?" she inquired.

Buffy was surprised by the doctor's striking appearance. In her experience, women doctors were either motherly and plump or stern and schoolteacherish. Dr. Lovett looked like a fading Italian movie star playing the role of a sanatorium doctor. Buffy wondered if Lovett was a name acquired by marriage, but she saw no rings on the doctor's fingers. The doctor's remarkable beauty was only slightly diminished by what looked like a permanent expression of tension, giving her a fierce aspect.

"That's me," said Buffy in a small voice, rising from the couch.

"Okay," said Cynthia, also rising. "I'll be back in about an hour. See you later."

Sandra ushered Buffy into the office and motioned for her to sit down in a chair opposite a large mahogany desk, behind which Sandra took her seat. She then, quite professionally, extracted the history of Buffy's headaches. Apparently they had begun during a period of neglect by her husband, but had disappeared when he had left, only to return when he rejoined the household. Sandra had figured it would be something like that. Then she came around the front of the desk and pressed Buffy's head at various points, asking her where she felt pain and to describe the nature of the pain. Was it jabbing, pulsating, chronically searing? Buffy noticed that

Dr. Lovett's fingers were cool and soothing, undoubtedly a sign of professional competency.

Finally, Sandra sat back down behind the desk and
put on a pair of severe black-framed reading glasses. She
picked up a pen, making a few notes while she spoke.
"I can understand your distress, Ms. Buffum. You have
a classic phenotype. Fortunately, we have had some success with your kind of case. The treatment, however,
must necessarily extend over a period of six months
and," she added, looking over her glasses, "it is not
inexpensive."

"At this point, I'll do anything to get rid of these
things, Doctor Lovett. And," Buffy declared, "I'm not
worried about the expense."

Applauding her own instinct, Sandra replied, "The
protocol is a combination of topical herbal therapy and
injections, in three phases about two months apart. The
expensive part is that the clinics for the second and third
phases are in San Juan, Puerto Rico, and Taipei, Taiwan.
There are almost no insurance plans that cover this type
of international care. It's possible though, that your initial treatment here in the U.S. may be partially covered."

"The way I look at it," said Buffy, "is that Austin
owes me this, one way or another." And suddenly she
realized that her present headache had already subsided
into only a minor migraine. "You know, I feel better
already. When can I start for real?"

For a fraction of a second Dr. Lovett looked a little
startled. "Uh, sorry," she said, snapping back to her
expression of being in control. "I'm, um, used to having
my patients go away and think about it for a few days,
which gives me time to check when the clinics abroad
have openings. That will determine the date when we
can start here."

"Well, okay," said Buffy, a little disappointed that

she couldn't start spending Austin's money immediately.
"I'll wait for your call, but consider me signed up."

"I appreciate your confidence, Ms. Buffum. I certainly hope I can do something for you," said Sandra, removing her reading glasses and looking sternly at Buffy. "You'll hear from me in a few days."

After Buffy left her office, Sandra used the intercom to confirm with her nurse that there were no more patients waiting. She then lit a cigarette, inhaling deeply, and connected to an outside line. She tapped out the seven-digit number that she had been instructed to commit to memory.

She heard a tinny ring and a recorded male voice came on the line, "The number you have called cannot be connected as dialed. . . ." Annoyed, Sandra punched the receiver cradle to hang up. She kept forgetting that dialing even local calls in the District now required an area code. She tried the number again, this time prefaced with 1-202. Again a tinny ring and again a recorded male voice, but this time one she expected. Sandra waited for the tone to indicate that the machine would be recording.

"Pigeon in the coop," she said. "Anxious to fly." Then she pressed the pound sign and hung up. Sandra knew that the time, date, and origin of her call would all be communicated automatically.

Sandra contemplated the piles of folders on her desk. The financial juggling pile had been steadily growing while the patient pile was steadily shrinking. She was well aware that she would be begging to be even part-time staff in an HMO were it not for her extramural connections. And occasionally she longed for the anonymity. But today, Mrs. Margaret Buffum, wife of the philandering Austin, had postponed Sandra's day of reckoning once more. Sandra intended to use the situation to her advantage.

Neurology was a difficult specialty for someone to
maintain as a thriving private practice these days. Sandra
had established her reputation by capitalizing on her fa-
miliarity with herbal therapy. She'd been able to survive
by attracting open-minded patients who felt that she had
something new to offer when the headache treatments
of her more conventional colleagues had been exhausted.
But patients with money for alternative therapy were
getting harder to come by as the HMO culture infiltrated
the lives of even the well-to-do. It was while attending
a course at the San Juan clinic a few years earlier that
Sandra got the brilliant idea that was now keeping her
clinic afloat, though only barely. Initially it was her family contacts that made it worth her while to develop the
courier business. But Sandra knew that long-term de-
pendence on them would mean nothing but trouble, and
her secret, personal goal was to break free of their hold
over her. Hopefully this new patient would help her toward that goal.

Stubbing out the remains of her cigarette, which she
had smoked down to the filter tip, Sandra craved relax-
ation. She contemplated a swim at the George Washington University pool and then a nice quiet solo dinner in
Georgetown. She stood up to remove her white doctor's
jacket in preparation for going out and was startled by
the telephone. That was quick. There was usually a day's
delay in response to her messages. She picked up. "Dr.
Lovett speaking."

"Alessandra, *cara*." The voice on the phone was
raspy and hissed the *S*s in Alessandra." It wasn't a response to her message. And this unwelcome call would
probably mean she had to change the message, against
her better judgement. It never rains, it pours, she
thought, and was not inclined to be pleasant.

"You shouldn't call me here. Where are you phoning
from?"

"Don't worry, *cara*." This time her caller rolled his *R*s. "No one can trace the line. I'm at the bar with Gianni, at La Fontana. Business is a little pressing." Again, the hissing *S*s.

"What is it?" asked Sandra, none too graciously. At least he was in Florida so there was no question of an office visit.

"*Cara*, don't sound so angry. I call and invite you to a nice dinner at Luigi's Ponte Vecchio in Baltimore. It should be a pleasure. They tell me Carlo's carbonara is to die for. Luigi make a special reservation for you at 9 P.M. tonight."

"What's the hurry?" asked Sandra. "You know I haven't been getting so many new patients." She had just done a job for the family and needed to make other plans for her next patient if she was going to expand the legitimate side of her business and get away from them. Of course, some might not think there was a legitimate side to transmission of coded information, but Sandra already had a few select clients interested in passing trade secrets and one even for national security. And she could guarantee complete privacy as part of her clients' privilege.

"Ah, *cara*, we are not so happy about the operation at the Puerto Rico clinic. Someone was getting a little too close to the family business, and we had to discourage him. We need to transfer some business to the Taiwan clinic until things quiet down in San Juan. I am sure your next patient could take the information for us."

Sandra did not like the sound of the word *discourage*. Any violence associated with her extracurricular activities could jeopardize the patronage of other clients. "Do I have a choice?" she asked.

"*Cara*, when would you ever choose not to help the family?"

Evidently it was a rhetorical question. The line went dead before Sandra could answer.

Sandra parked in an unpaved lot on the far side of the sunken highway that cut through the center of Baltimore. Her jet black hair hadn't completely dried during the drive to Baltimore, but the swim was worth the hassle of figuring out what to do with her hair now. She opened the glove compartment of her maroon Alfa Romeo Spider and took out a comb, a bottle of brilliantine, and the necessary hairpins. As she checked the rearview mirror to smooth the slick chignon she had produced, she noticed that the black Thunderbird that had followed her from D.C. had parked at the opposite end of the parking lot. She assumed that the lack of discretion was intended to keep her on track.

Toilette completed, Sandra crossed the footbridge over the highway. The footbridge wasn't exactly the Ponte Vecchio, but it did lead to the street where the restaurant was located on one of the older boulevards remaining in Baltimore's Italian neighborhood. There was a small-town friendliness about the redbrick buildings and warehouses lining the side of the street that had survived the indiscriminate demolition for the highway. The fading, summer evening light contributed to the illusion.

Luigi, Jr. was maitre d' for the evening and was evidently pleased to see Sandra, if not surprised. In his snappy dinner jacket, he was a gorgeous thirty-five year old, almost a decade younger than she. Sandra had heard that he was recently divorced and on the prowl. She considered how scandalized her family would be if she had a flirtation with him. It would be tempting if she weren't so tense and tired out. It was incredible that in this day and age her family considered themselves too aristocratic to be socially involved with restaurant owners, even if they *were* Italian. Business relationships were fine, however. And that was why she was here.

Luigi, Jr. led her to a table for one in a dark corner of the restaurant. The decor hadn't changed since Sandra had been a child. She wondered how faded and dusty the plush, red velvet chairs and empty chianti bottles hanging from the ceiling would look in broad daylight. Luigi lit the candle on her table with his lighter and waited to light her cigarette while she removed one from the pack.

"Hard to give up, huh? Especially after a good time in bed, no?" He smiled wolfishly.

"No," she said, definitively.

"Would you like to see the menu?"

"No, just tell Carlo I'll have a half Caesar salad and the carbonara."

"Thought that's what you might order," said Luigi smugly. "But they didn't specify dessert did they?"

"Only that it can't be with you, sweetheart."

"Just my luck," said Luigi, shrugging carelessly. "I'll let Papa know you've arrived."

The carbonara alone almost made the drive up to Baltimore worthwhile. The eggy sauce was a perfect blend of pancetta and fontina; Carlo never had to use cream. After her second glass of chianti Sandra began to feel human. This was the first leisurely meal she'd had in weeks and certainly the most delicious. She idly speculated whether Luigi, Jr. was really any good in bed or just a lot of hot air. But the thugs in the Thunderbird would report back, and she didn't want to deal with the fallout.

As the restaurant was closing down for the evening, Sandra went through the charade of paying for the meal with her credit card. She slipped the customer copy into her purse and, with a quick glance as though checking the balance, confirmed what she had anticipated. Instead of credit card digits there was a string of letters.

During the drive back to D.C., Sandra wondered whether it was technically feasible for her couriers to do double duty and carry two messages at once. She thought that it probably was, but the risk of mixing up the information was too great. This latest demand confirmed the necessity and urgency of extricating herself from a situation where family business always took precedence. It wasn't just a matter of ego and wanting to shake their domineering control. Family demands were obviously threatening her reliability to other clients. And frankly, she wouldn't be surprised if revealing her association with the family could be used by other clients as leverage against her. She continued to believe that her other clients weren't aware of her connections, but she couldn't be sure and it worried her.

Sandra could almost taste her desire for legitimacy. But when she got back to her apartment she was compelled to redial the recording she'd contacted earlier in the day, remembering to include the area code this time. On a desk in an obscure office in the Department of Foreign Affairs, the machine recorded her message. "Pigeon unexpectedly grounded. Ignore previous call."

3

Langley Lament

Four months after Celeste had discovered the body in the El Morro catacombs, the telephone rang on Raul de Leon's desk in the San Juan police station. That incident had been supplanted by many more pressing ones, and as far as the San Juan police were concerned, the crime had transmuted into unsolved *basura,* the word written on all the city trash baskets.

Raul picked up the phone. *"Si?"*

"Uh, hi, is that Señor de Leon?" The voice was deep, slow, and mainland American.

Raul recognized Jack Minot's flat Midwestern accent. It was the perfect accent for a career FBI agent. But he said, noncommittally, "Yes, this is Raul de Leon speaking."

"Raul, buddy, it's Jack over here in Miami. I hate to keep bothering you with our problems, but I could use some advice."

Raul's heart sank at the sound of a request like this. *"Si?"*

"Well, I think I've finally got a new idea about how to nail the Valentino mob for their drug operation that's coming out of that clinic you have over there."

Raul's heart sank even further. Minot's last brain-storm on this case had ended in the death of one of the FBI's own agents. Granted, the guy must have been in-ept to get himself caught, but it looked bad for Raul's force. He had enough of his own problems without having to take responsibility for the FBI's incompetence. Besides, his own men had just got wind of a new ship-ment and thought they might be able to make a bust before the drugs even got over to Miami. If Puerto Ri-cans were ever going to have a shot at independence, they needed to show they could take care of their own.

Raul hadn't jealously guarded the privacy of the cat-acombs for nothing. So, he should at least find out how Minot intended to stomp all over their territory again. He tried not to be too encouraging when he asked, "What did you want to know?"

"I can't tell you too many details, for obvious rea-sons," said Minot, "but I'll tell you what you need to know to answer my question." Minot was also treading on thin ice. He needed Raul's advice and would likely need his cooperation, so he didn't want to piss him off. But he was beginning to smell a mole interfering with the whole Valentino investigation. He didn't think it had anything to do with Raul, but you could never be too careful.

Minot took a deep breath and began his edited tale. "We've been tracking the pattern of mob-grade heroin distribution in Miami. We know, thanks to you guys, that it's coming from San Juan. Well the same pattern is showing up for the distribution of similar junk in LA. Junk that's coming from Taipei. The distribution instruc-tions seem to be coming from a clinic over there, too, just like the situation in PR. We know both clinics them-selves are legit, with real patients, docs, and everything. But we think that the drug operation has something to do with the patients. We need to get someone inside the clinics to check out what goes on there. And it's gotta be someone with some understanding of their treatment programs, which leads me to my question."

"*Si?* Uh, yes?" prompted Raul.

"I know this is gonna sound crazy, but I'm thinking about contacting that woman, Dr. Braun, who found our corpse in your fort over there."

"Yes, it does sound crazy," said Raul. "She was not much help at the time. I don't see how she could be useful now, so many months later."

"Yeah, yeah. I know you can never be too careful in recruiting a spook with no training. But we've been doing some homework, and there are two things in her favor besides the fact that she already saw the body. We need help from someone who knows the medical field, who has a good excuse to get involved with the clinics, and she's got the right expertise. That's why she happened to be over in PR in the first place. The second is that she's already had crime busting experience, so she's not chicken, and she's on the right side. You probably didn't hear about it over there, but last year she uncovered a biotechnology scam on a Japanese company that could have been major-league dangerous."

Raul had heard about it. They weren't as isolated in Puerto Rico as the mainland seemed to think. And having heard of Celeste's previous escapade, he liked the idea of involving her even less. "Wasn't that the case that caused a shake-up in the Pentagon?"

"Yeah, that's it. That's her."

"I think she is probably a first-class troublemaker," said Raul. "Besides, I was not impressed by her powers of observation at the scene of the crime. She did not even mention the telltale cut on the corpse. My men figured that one out. That's why we called you."

"Raul, buddy, I'm sorry to hear you're so down on this. I'm not sure we have a choice. If our guys in Japan confirm that she's clean, she's the best chance we have to get at the technology involved here. Besides, I saw a picture of her. Not a bad-looking babe, if you like the intellectual types. You've always been a ladies' man.''

''As you say, if you like the intellectual types,'' said Raul. ''Anyway, aren't you asking me to be a baby-sitter and not a date.''

''I'm not asking you to be anything,'' said Minot. ''I'm just checking that you have no professional reason to object to this recruitment.''

''Well,'' said Raul, hesitating. Now was his chance to try to keep Minot off his turf. ''It's likely she would be recognized here, since she was at a clinic conference when she found the body. Does she know, by the way, that the corpse was one of your agents?''

''Not if you didn't tell her.''

''Certainly not. I just warned her to keep her mouth shut and that you guys might get in touch.''

''Good, then she should be expecting it,'' said Minot. ''But,'' he hesitated, apparently considering Raul's objections, ''Maybe you have a point there about Dr. Braun being too recognizable.''

Nothing Raul had said was sufficiently compelling to dissuade Minot from his idea of approaching this Dr. Braun for help. Her expertise was just too valuable, seeing as Minot was convinced that the medical business of the clinic itself held the clue to his case. But Raul had raised several of the concerns that Minot's boss had also raised. They both pegged her as a troublemaker, and neither liked the idea of her returning to San Juan. It occurred to Minot that this could possibly make his investigation smoother. He could pretend to reject the idea of recruiting the doctor, after all. Then he could actually recruit her, provided the Japanese references checked out. This way, as an agent known only to himself, she would be invisible to potential mole activity. If he sent

her to the Taipei clinic intead of San Juan, no one would
be the wiser.

"Since you've brought up the catacomb murder,"
said Raul, recapturing Minot's attention, "I should mention that I was kind of put out to hear from your Virginia
cousins right after your man's body was found. Haven't
they figured out yet that what goes on here isn't a foreign affair?"

"Oh, them," said Minot. "They don't know their ass
from a hole in the ground. My boss did mention something about them snooping, too."

"Well, I told them to call your boss and that it was
none of their business."

Man, thought Minot, these PR guys are so touchy.
He decided that it would definitely be a good move to
appear to buy Raul's negative recommendation about
Celeste. It wasn't like Raul was falling all over himself
to be helpful and if Minot needed help in the future, it
would be a good idea to keep him sweet.

"Well, we certainly respect your territory, which is
why I called you," said Minot. "And as a matter of
fact, you've made me think twice about recruiting this
Dr. Braun. Your advice is much appreciated, and I will
take it under serious consideration."

"Glad to be of service," said Raul, relieved that Minot was going to leave him alone, at least for now. He
had no evidence, however, from past experience that
logic penetrated very far into their operating decisions.

Oblivious to government concerns about her, Celeste
Braun pursued life as an academic scientist. This life had
its own trials and tribulations. Not long after Minot
quizzed Raul, Celeste was attending another scientific
conference, this time in the Virginia countryside. It had
been a late night and Celeste resisted awakening. But
there was another reason she wanted to stay asleep.

When she could fight it no longer, she carefully opened one eye and immediately saw the reason. At close range it took the form of a hairy shoulder. It was accompanied by faint snores. She was very careful not to move. Recollections obligingly moved to her brain instead.

Her situation undoubtedly had something to do with the bottle of malt whiskey that had circulated among the diehards after the conference bar had closed in the evening. She was pretty sure it was Milt Stevens who lay next to her. If she'd known he was that hairy and that inept, she wouldn't have bothered. They had met at conferences a few times before, and he always struck her as a solid family man. This time he had been obviously flirtatious, in a sort of overgrown preppie way. Probably hadn't flirted since his college days and was suffering something like seven-year itch. Celeste seemed to be in the business of scratching those itches lately. Logically, it was the safest way to sleep around. Married men were less likely to carry nasty infections, though she did insist on condoms. Unfortunately, they were uniformly mediocre in bed, which is probably why they were seeking relief from bored wives who had long since given up on them. Sex with these guys was totally predictable. It started out all right, with high school style foreplay, but once clothes were shed it was all business, with very little finesse and absolutely no concept of or interest in female pleasure. Celeste should have known better by now, but alcohol had a way of inducing temporary amnesia.

For an intensely lonely moment Celeste missed Mac. They'd been living on opposite sides of the country for almost a year now and when she'd seen him in June, she knew it was the last time as a lover. It would be a long time until she could comfortably see him later as a friend. And she wasn't even sure she wanted him as a friend. At least she could always count on Harry, her longtime buddy and occasional bed partner, but he too was on the East Coast, still working for *The New York Times*. Get a life, woman, she had been saying to herself lately. But it was easier said than done.

And here she was in the middle of nowhere, attending a conference on a topic that was only peripherally related to her own research. And why was she here? Well, that was a good question. Certainly the invitation had surprised her, and she had been sort of flattered. She didn't know the organizer but he had said that they always included one session with guest speakers who did research in outside areas that might become relevant to the scope of the field in the future. In her darker moments, this being one of them, Celeste thought she had been invited because they needed more women on the program in order to get funding for the conference from the National Science Foundation. But, hey, publicity was publicity, and it didn't matter why you were invited as long as you delivered the goods. Besides, pretenure faculty shouldn't turn down any invitations to lecture.

Celeste slowly turned her head to glance at her watch on the bedside table. She knew she had to make a move if her indiscretion wasn't going to be common knowledge among the conference participants. Her morning-after soul-searching was getting too intense, anyway. She tried a gentle shove, inducing the sleeping Milt to roll away from her and simultaneously giving her leverage to get out of bed. He snorted and settled down into a different snoring pattern. No wonder his wife wasn't enjoying his company these days.

Celeste was free and clear. She quickly donned her scattered clothing and let herself out the door into the corridor, turning to shut it carefully behind her. She had to think about where her own room was and stayed in front of Milt's door for a moment too long. At the far end of the corridor was a staircase vestibule, and she could hear rapid steps descending. She stood very quietly, hoping that whoever it was would not look into the corridor while rounding the bend to the next set of stairs.

A blond man appeared, accompanying the footsteps. He paused and looked straight at her.

Celeste smiled at him with relief. It was the manager of the conference center, not one of her colleagues.

"Good morning," he said, returning her smile. "Nice morning to be up early." He turned without waiting for a response and continued his descent.

Celeste walked slowly toward the staircase where the man had disappeared. By the time she reached the ground floor and emerged into the dewy morning, the manager was nowhere to be seen.

The conference center was a converted colonial estate, and the grounds were dotted with yellow clapboard buildings of plantation vintage. Celeste figured that the building she had just left must have been modified servants' quarters. It was too spacious to have been slave quarters. Off to one side, at the base of a rolling hill that bordered the extensive grounds, a more modern hotel-like building had been added to expand the center's capacity for guests. Celeste headed toward this building, where her room was located along with accommodation for the other female guests. Being a woman had some advantages.

As she walked, Celeste felt the rays of the early morning sun trying to get a hold on the day. This late in August, it was sufficiently cool at night to cause complete precipitation of the previous day's humidity, which contributed a newly washed aspect to the atmosphere. Celeste's path took her toward a diminutive two-story house with a sign in front that read GROOM'S QUARTERS. Someone had told her that the manager lived there. It could have been her imagination, but Celeste thought she saw a curtain being pulled to one side and then let fall as she passed by. She shivered in the chilly damp.

It was the last day of the three day conference and the topic for discussion was neural networks. Celeste sat at the back of the lecture hall, feeling rather detached from the proceedings and nursing her hangover. She appreciated the amenities of small conferences. They usually had long narrow tables, parallel to the lecture stage, for the participants to sit at and take notes. And, if necessary, lean their heads on their hands while listening to a talk.

The Society for Self-Assembly in Biology was interested in any biological system that spontaneously established itself. Until recently they had primarily focused on the so-called cytoskeleton, or internal structural elements of a cell. These elements are composed of single units of protein that polymerize into fibers and lattices, forming an internal scaffold for components to move around inside a cell and that helps the cell itself move. Much of the society's interest was in making models of the dynamics of assembly and disassembly of these cytoskeleton structures, attempting to understand the biophysics of the process. Celeste had presumably been invited to lecture because many of the same principles operate in the self-assembly of viruses as they reproduce inside cells, a process that she had been studying for most of her research career. The discussion going on at the front of the lecture hall revolved around whether self-assembly principles might also operate during the learning processes that establish connections between nerves in the developing brain. It was far afield from Celeste's usual preoccupation with virus biology, but her attention was captured by the speaker who had just approached the podium.

"I'd like to begin," he said, "by taking a poll. How many of you in the audience think that eventually all emotions and intellectual processes will be able to be explained by molecular interactions?''

About fifteen conferees, scattered among the one hundred or so participants, raised their hands.

''And how many of you think that such things will never be able to be explained in scientific terms?''

Only about half a dozen hands went up.

''How many of you don't really care?''

At least thirty hands went up in response. Thus proving once again, thought Celeste, that the majority of scientists are not philosophers.

Interestingly, the speaker wasn't much phased by the reaction of the audience. It was evidently just a device to get attention. He then launched into a detailed technical discussion of his own work and lost Celeste.

A nap during the free time after lunch, followed by a sweaty jog around the back roads of the conference grounds restored Celeste's equilibrium. And, by the pre-dinner session she felt human again. Milt had allayed Celeste's concern about trying to avoid a repeat performance of the previous night by leaving the conference in the early afternoon. He had dragged into the session just before lunch, looking pretty fragile, and told Celeste that one of his kids was sick and he needed to get home to help his wife. Celeste thought that the excuse was a little heavy-handed, but was relieved nonetheless.

There were no evening lectures scheduled after the conference banquet. Instead, entertainment was provided by a bluegrass band in celebration of the society's twenty-fifth anniversary. Celeste was not in a hurry to follow the crowd over to the large gazebo behind the dining hall, where the band could be heard tuning up. She wandered out to the edge of a small pond on the grounds at the side of the dining hall, attracted by the musical croaking of the resident bullfrogs. She stood quietly, watching the fireflies flicker, hoping to see a frog reveal itself. Fireflies were one of the few things about an East Coast summer that Celeste missed in the West.

As she stood, Celeste could sense that someone had come up behind her, so she was not startled to feel a warm hand laid on her shoulder. She turned to look at the owner of the hand. It was the conference center manager.

"Are you going to listen to the bluegrass band, or could I interest you in a nightcap in the groom's quarters?"

Celeste was not a big bluegrass fan and was even less a fan of pretending to know how to dance to it with men she didn't want to dance with. "Well, maybe a beer would serve as 'hair of the dog,' " she said. "But don't you have to play *mein* host?"

"Not at this point. My work is over. The band showed, they're all set up, and the staff will clean later," he said, ticking these items off on his fingers. "I'm off duty until the next conference starts on Monday. Besides, I'm not really the host, just a behind-the-scenes man, to make sure everything runs smoothly. Even though I make a point of showing up at the opening receptions, it doesn't register with most conferees that I exist."

"Our powers of observation are better than that. I certainly recognized you." And what red-blooded woman wouldn't, thought Celeste. It momentarily slipped her mind that most conference participants were male, who would not necessarily notice a good-looking blond man in their midst.

"Yes, you looked pretty relieved when you saw me this morning. I guess you were glad I wasn't gonna be a source of gossip."

"Was I that transparent?"

" 'Fraid so," said the manager cheerfully. He gently

took Celeste's arm and led her in the opposite direction from the crowd.

"I'm sorry," said Celeste, as they started to walk through the conference center grounds. "I don't remember your name. I'm Celeste Braun, from Bay Area University, San Francisco."

"The name's Stash, Dr. Braun. Short for Stanislaus, which goes with my last name, pronounced Romanitch, spelled with a *cz* at the end."

"Polish?" asked Celeste.

"The best Detroit neighborhood," said Stash.

"Anyway, I'm off duty, too. Call me Celeste."

They had reached the groom's quarters and Stash opened the front door, gesturing for Celeste to enter ahead of him. "You could call me Dr. Romanicz, if you like," he said. "I did earn my Ph.D. in immunology, many years ago."

"So what are you doing here?" asked Celeste, pausing in the entryway.

"It's a long story. Let's get a beer. Then, I'll tell you about it."

Stash led her down a brightly lit hallway in the direction of his sitting room. At eye level, on both sides of the walls, hung a row of striking black and white photographs extending the entire length of the hallway. Celeste was compelled to stop and look at them. There were portraits, landscapes, and some very evocative photographs of city neighborhoods. Probably Detroit.

"If these are yours," said Celeste, "I'm not surprised you're not doing immunology any more. But it still doesn't explain what you're doing here." Stash was already out of the hallway, having turned right, ahead of Celeste. Judging from the sounds of a refrigerator opening, followed by the hiss of a lifting bottle cap and pouring, he was in the kitchen.

Before joining him, Celeste paused in front of the last

portrait to her right. It was an incredible study of a very pregnant, naked woman in profile. She was the image of wholesome fertility with swollen breasts protruding over a swollen belly in which her belly button looked like a valve. Her shoulder length hair was girlishly parted in the middle and was tucked behind her ears. The woman's eyes were focused inward, and she had an air of complete self-sufficiency.

Stash came out of the kitchen, holding two glasses of beer, and stood beside Celeste. "My wife," he said. "Two months ago."

"Oh," said Celeste. "You must be a new father by now."

"Not exactly. The baby was born, but I'm not its father. In fact, I don't really have any part in it," said Stash, rather bitterly. "When we met, she was already pregnant by somebody else, in a soured relationship. I wanted to share the pregnancy. But as she became more and more pregnant, she withdrew from me more and more. I had hoped that once he was born, he would become ours and not just hers. But that doesn't seem to be happening."

"Where is she?" asked Celeste.

"In our house in Georgetown. She didn't want to move out to what she considers the boonies." He sounded sad and disappointed. Then he made an instant switch to a heartier tone. "Hey. You didn't come here to listen to me complain. You came here for a beer. So drink up." He handed her one of the beers he was holding and led her away from the portrait into a cozy sitting room, lined with books and more photographs. Celeste sat down in an inviting looking armchair, and Stash took a seat at one end of the sofa, lounging back into the cushions and extending his legs.

Celeste had a good look at him from this angle while she sipped her beer. His blond hair was slicked back from a high forehead, a style that bespoke his Detroit heritage. He had a nice rectangular face with smile lines, suggesting he was fortyish. He looked relaxed and happy to have company. Celeste had the feeling that he was lonely, in spite of the constant contact he must have with conference center users.

"Now, are you going to tell me how you got here?" asked Celeste. "Or is it top secret?"

"Why do you say that?" He looked at her curiously.

"Just a manner of speaking," said Celeste. "But it looks like I hit a nerve."

"Not at all," said Stash. "You just have an amazing instinct. I used to be, you know, 'in the business.' Retired now, though. There wasn't enough work to go around in these post–Cold War days. In fact, did you know this place used to be a safe house before they made it a conference center? Kind of adds a little spice to the atmosphere, don't you think?"

Celeste was intrigued. Was he telling her that he had been with the CIA? She thought that's what "in the business" meant. They also called it "the company," didn't they? She decided to give it a try. "I thought you said that you had a Ph.D. in immunology. Did that have anything to do with your work for the company?"

Stash smiled at her amateurish probing. "In a way," he said. "They supported me through graduate school at the University of Michigan. You see, I was recruited when I was an undergraduate at Wayne State for my photography skills. It was a fantastic first assignment. They needed someone to go up to Alaska for reconnaissance work. I was totally hooked. Later, when they wanted personnel trained in biological affairs, I volunteered. It was a terrific sense of belonging to something bigger. I miss it, frankly."

"I can understand that," said Celeste, with feeling.

"But . . ." She had a million questions. "How is it that you can tell me this?" she asked first.

"I didn't actually tell you anything," said Stash.

"I guess not," said Celeste, raising her eyebrows. "For a start, you haven't explained how your work for the business led you here."

"It's a typical redundancy scheme," said Stash. "The property was theirs, they needed to do something with it and with all of their now-superfluous staff. They're even going to send me to hotel management training."

"Like they sent you to graduate school?"

"Well, this time for an alternative career."

"I'm not a connoisseur, but it seems to me that you're good enough to go into professional photography," said Celeste.

"Strictly a hobby," said Stash. "I enjoy it too much. In fact, I'd love to take some shots of you sometime. Your face has great potential."

"Gee, thanks," said Celeste, sarcastically. "That's quite a compliment, but I'm really not up to it right now."

"I didn't mean now," said Stash. "It happens that I'll be at a hotel management course next month in San Francisco. I was hoping you wouldn't mind if I gave you a call. I'd really like to photograph some of the coastal scenery, and you in it if you're willing."

Celeste was a little taken aback. Was this some kind of come on? Was he just being friendly since his wife was so preoccupied with the new child that was not his? Did she really appeal to his artistic sensibilities as a photographer? Or was he assuming that she might be an easy lay from what he saw this morning? Did it matter? It wasn't every day that she was befriended by an ex-CIA agent, and that interested her. She liked his easy manner and his openness about his vulnerability. He had been frank about his wife, and he had been honest about missing the action of his CIA duty. She saw him as a kind of lost soul. After all, he was only proposing an excursion along the coast—not asking her to go to bed with him. But maybe she wouldn't mind if he were. She certainly found him attractive.

"You're welcome to give me a call," she replied. "As far as I know, I don't have any trips planned next month. I'd be happy to go up to Point Reyes with you, if that's where you have in mind. The break would do me good."

"Terrific, I'll look forward to it," said Stash as though he'd conducted a successful piece of business. He swung his legs down from the couch. "Now, let me see you back to your dorm."

4

Slaves of Duty

Total immersion was the only way Sandra Lovett could relax. A decent sex life was completely out of the question while she was still a slave to her family. The shock of the cool water on her body and the feeling of its sleek caress as she dove into the pool transformed her. For the next thirty minutes, churning up and down in the dark, green, chemical world of chlorinated water, her mind roamed freely and productively. Things had been looking up since Buffy Buffum had signed on as her patient. Buffy's headaches were already subsiding and she'd only just reached the stage where she would receive treatment at the clinic in Taiwan. Buffy was so pleased with the therapeutic effect of spending her husband's money that she had recommended Sandra's practice to three other friends. Sandra thought that this must be pretty close to what it feels like to really cure someone.

The new patients didn't hurt her prospects either. Sandra was able to get her family off her back by promising them the services of one of them. The other two she was finally able to make available to one of her more legitimate clients. In the course of their treatment, the patients would be used to carry separate coded messages, either to Taipei or San Juan. Sandra liked the idea that even she could not decipher the content of the messages her patients carried. She simply provided the courier service and was therefore able to operate with complete discretion. The transmission method itself had evolved and improved over the past couple of years thanks to the input of this latest client whose business she was trying to develop. The method, already completely harmless, was practically undetectable without knowledge of what to look for. Hopefully, with every successful transmission for a nonfamily client, the day when she could run her own show was getting closer.

Sandra had finished her half mile and felt contentedly spent as she glided to the side of the pool. She placed her hands on the edge and heaved to hoist herself out. The water seemed to hold on to her, and she realized suddenly that she was being pulled back into it. As she lost her grip on the pool edge, she felt a strong hand on her head shoving it below the water surface. Sandra hadn't yet taken off her goggles, and as she began to struggle for air, she could see the curly black hair on the chest of her assailant in front of her. She could also see the bulge below it, hanging conveniently in range in a skimpy Speedo sack. Swimming a half mile every day was better than water aerobics for developing a rapid underwater kick, which Sandra demonstrated with effective force. They both popped up for air.

"Cazzo!" swore Luigi, Jr., gasping. "Jesus Christ, Sandra, you wouldn't have done that if you knew how good I was in bed."

"Oh, stuff it, Luigi," said Sandra. She was outraged that her refuge had been violated. "Since when have they got you doing dirty work?"

"I wouldn't call delivering a message to the Principessa dirty work."

"Well, you should have chosen somewhere else for your delivery. If I ever see you here again, I'll do permanent damage to your precious jewels," she hissed. "Now, tell me what you came for so I can have some peace."

They didn't call her La Principessa di Ghiaccio—the Ice Princess—for nothing, thought Luigi. "They sent me to warn you about the possibility of someone poking around in the clinic. You might not believe it, but there's another smart lady out there who's smart enough to figure out what you're up to."

"Does she have a name, Luigi?" asked Sandra condescendingly.

"Dr. Celeste Braun," said Luigi.

"Sounds familiar," said Sandra, thinking a moment. "Puerto Rico, right? Wasn't she on the program at that clinic conference last spring?"

"You are as smart as they say," answered Luigi. "Apparently she discovered our little indiscretion there."

Sandra was becoming increasingly irritated. The pool was beginning to feel chilly. "I'd hardly call that a little indiscretion, disposing of an FBI agent."

"Well, how were we supposed to know?" asked Luigi, shrugging his shoulders so that water rippled off, back into the pool.

"So why are they worried now? That was months ago."

"A little bird told us she might be recruited to help them investigate the clinic," said Luigi. "I'm here to warn you to keep an eye out."

"Well, you did. So get the hell out of here."

"You'd be nicer if you were getting it more regularly," said Luigi, and he ducked underwater, swimming half the length of the pool before surfacing and giving her a jaunty wave.

Another slave in the making, thought Sandra, against her will, as she admired his lithe body.

Two weeks after her return from Virginia, Celeste went into the laboratory exceptionally early. She had woken up around five A.M. to extricate herself from a horrible nightmare and hadn't been able to get back to sleep. In her dream, rats were running all over her body and nibbling at her. She had been incapable of moving or speaking to indicate that she wasn't dead. They were brown rats like those she had seen in the tunnel in San Juan, not white laboratory rats. It was the first dream she'd had about the incident for a couple of months, and there was nothing in her recent experience that she could think of that would have reminded her of it.

As Celeste stood outside the door to her laboratory fishing through her handbag for her keys, she wondered again what had triggered the dream. She had long since recovered from the disappointing realization that she was not going to be contacted by the FBI for further information. And Celeste was well aware that she was better off without this distraction. This was a critical period for productivity in the laboratory, and it was advantageous for Celeste to be available to supervise the progress of her lab personnel.

A renewal application for the National Institutes of Health grant that funded most of the research in Celeste's laboratory would be due at the beginning of March, in just six months' time. That application would be reviewed in June for funding to be continuous from the following February for the next five years. Evaluation of work that was completed within the next six months would therefore influence her lab's funding more than several years into the future. It was important not only for the projects to be completed, but they also had to be written up and minimally submitted for publication by March. They would need to be accepted for publication by next June to have a major impact. In scientific research, it was still publish or perish.

Therefore, when Celeste finally managed to unlock the laboratory door and saw that the lights were on, she was pleased that someone in the lab was already at work. Her pleasure rapidly converted to dumbfounded amazement when she saw who the early bird was.

Although the personnel in Celeste's laboratory were there because they specifically elected to work with her, there was always one who made a point of trying to prove that he or she knew best. Celeste had learned not to take it personally as almost every laboratory was equipped with at least one assertive ego. This particular one had been working hard to gain the title of nemesis since he'd joined the laboratory. What made it difficult for Celeste was that Eric was only a third year graduate student and at a relatively early stage in his career to be able to benefit from intellectual rebellion. The students at BAU were encouraged to think that they were God's gift to science from the moment that they were offered admission, which didn't help the situation much. It also didn't help that Celeste had a particular interest in Eric's project and was relying on him to produce some data that was critical for at least two other lines of investigation in the laboratory. Celeste wondered hopefully whether this early morning diligence indicated some kind of new community spirit on Eric's part.

Eric's shaved head was covered in a tied, red bandanna, and the back of it faced Celeste as she entered the lab. He was staring intently at the computer screen on the desk next to his lab bench. The lab bench was covered with the debris of sloppy experiments and in the middle stood two Lucite boxes with liquid in them and wires attached to the lids. The wires connected to a power supply with a glowing red light, signifying that it was in use. The strange noises emanating from the computer and the fact that Eric evidently did not hear Celeste come in indicated that he was absorbed in playing a computer game. Celeste was not encouraged by this scene. In precomputer days, lab personnel might use an incubation or waiting period to read an article or at least browse through an issue of a scientific journal. Now the browsing was done on the Internet and, more often than not, people would use their experimental downtime to read E-mail from friends or play computer games. Celeste tried to make the best of the situation.

"You're in early, Eric. Big experiment?"

"Oh, hi, Celeste," said Eric, doing a quick trick with his hand on the keyboard to obscure what had been on the screen. He gave her the goofy student look that she had initially mistaken for innocence but now knew as defiance against growing up. "Well, there's a mountain-bike race that starts at noon today. And you had asked me last week to have this stuff analyzed for the California Serum Company pickup this afternoon, so I wanted to be sure it would be ready."

Celeste tried to swallow the temptation to point out that he had known for five days about this deadline and that it was pushing it to assume that the analysis would work the first time. She knew she shouldn't comment about the precedence of the mountain-bike race, particularly since Eric was in early and lab personnel had the inviolate academic privilege of working on their own schedules. Celeste chose the lesser of two evils. She was, after all, the supervisor of Eric's Ph.D. research.

"What if your gel analysis doesn't work? You won't have time to repeat it before the pickup so we will have lost another week. And you can't afford it with your oral examination coming up next quarter. Remember, the immunization schedule involves at least two injections, one month apart."

Eric sighed as if he had to explain something to a difficult child. "I've never run a gel that didn't work," he said petulantly. "Anyway, even though we talked about it last week, I still don't see the advantage of immunizing rabbits to get antibodies. I know I don't actually have to handle the animals and that the Calfornia Serum Company follows all the regulations about humaneness for injecting and bleeding the rabbits, but it's against my principles if there's an alternative strategy. And I really think that the phage display technique will be just as good for getting us the antibodies that we want." Eric was a vegetarian, though his mountain-biking shoes were made of leather.

Celeste was patient. "Let's talk through it again, Eric," she said. "I'll just leave my stuff in the office, and we can sit out here so you can keep an eye on your gel."

Celeste pulled a second chair over to Eric's desk and began to draw a diagram on a blank pad of paper. "All right, let's consider the advantages of injecting rabbits and having them make the antibodies that you want, versus the phage display technique that you think would be just as good. The discriminating properties that allow antibodies to bind to specific pathogens and signal their elimination by the immune system are so good they can discriminate between different strains of virus. Such antibodies are exactly what you want to use in the experiments for your thesis work. Of course, the antibodies are actually binding to characteristic proteins on the virus surface."

"Sure," said Eric. "That's obvious. What's not obvious is why I can't get discriminating antibodies using the phage display system."

"In the phage display system, you use molecular biology to produce antibodies on the surfaces of the phage, which have been genetically engineered to contain ran-

ANTIBODY PRODUCTION BY PHAGE DISPLAY

200 million phage each with potential to make one kind of antibody to display on its surface

Bacteria are grown in a petri dish and infected with phage

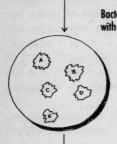

Each phage establishes a colony in the bacteria, so that 200 million colonies have to be tested to find the one that displays Antibody C

One colony in 200 million is a source of Antibody C

dom, cloned, antibody genes. Remember, phage are parasites that grow inside bacteria and form colonies . . .''

''I know what a phage is,'' interupted Eric.

''I know you know, but I was just trying to emphasize the randomness of the process. The random collection of antibodies made by the phage colonies can only mimic the early stage of an animal's immune response. But it has none of the advantages that are inherent in the immune system of an animal. Do you know what they are?''

''Well, both systems start out with a random array of antibodies.''

''Right, but that's all you ever get from the phage. So you have to test millions of phage to find the single antibody that binds uniquely to the particular virus strain you want to identify. The probability of finding that is extremely low. However, in an animal, the immune system works to increase the probability that the antibodies

ANTIBODY PRODUCTION BY RABBIT IMMUNIZATION

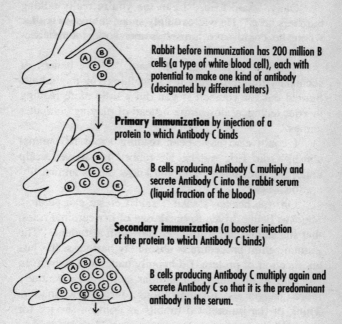

Rabbit before immunization has 200 million B cells (a type of white blood cell), each with potential to make one kind of antibody (designated by different letters)

Primary immunization by injection of a protein to which Antibody C binds

B cells producing Antibody C multiply and secrete Antibody C into the rabbit serum (liquid fraction of the blood)

Secondary immunization (a booster injection of the protein to which Antibody C binds)

B cells producing Antibody C multiply again and secrete Antibody C so that it is the predominant antibody in the serum.

Rabbit serum is used as a source of Antibody C

you want will be produced. This occurs for two reasons. Once the animal is 'immunized,' or exposed to a protein from a pathogen that stimulates antibody production, the cells that make the antibodies that bind to the pathogen multiply, so there are more of them. Also, after secondary exposure to the protein, so-called secondary immunization, the number of cells producing antibodies binding to the pathogen increases even further. These cells are also stimulated to mutate slightly, resulting in stronger binding antibodies. These stronger antibodies will, of course, be more useful in a diagnostic test."

"Okay," said Eric. "I can see you're really talking numbers here." He was certainly smart enough to realize where he could save himself some work, thought Celeste.

"The key difference," she said, "is the benefit of secondary immunization. It's something you might have figured out for yourself if you did a little more reading in your technical downtime instead of playing computer games."

"I could also have been reading about lab animal abuse," said Eric rudely. He rubbed his shaved scalp under the bandanna. "Did you know this is animal liberation week?"

"Oh, for heaven's sake," said Celeste exasperated. She was being driven to break one of her cardinal rules, that she should never lose her cool with a student. "The immunization procedure is absolutely harmless. It's just an injection of protein. I'd happily undergo it myself. In fact, we've all undergone similar, and even potentially more dangerous immunizations during vaccination. Think of the immunized rabbits as doing a service for mankind."

"What about womankind?" asked Eric.

Celeste just smiled and said, "Let me know when you have the gel finished so I can have a look at your protein preparations."

Celeste retreated to her office. A message was floating across the top of her computer monitor telling her to "wake up" to collect her E-mail. She'd finally been connected to the Internet, several years after the rest of the world thanks to the not-so-speedy campus electricians. It wasn't something Celeste had looked forward to, but it had turned out to be remarkably convenient; particularly for communicating with her colleagues abroad. There was, however, a Pavlovian aspect to the urge to read incoming messages that was hard to control.

There were three messages. The first was from Milt Stevens, saying that he had enjoyed getting to know her better in Virginia and asking whether she planned to attend any other conferences in the near future? She deleted it. The second was from Kazuko Hagai at Fukuda Pharmaceuticals in Japan, asking her to call and leaving a home telephone number. Celeste calculated that if she phoned now it would be almost three in the morning. She would have to wait until early afternoon to catch Kazuko before she left for work the following morning. Although Kazuko's English was excellent, she was usually hesistant to speak on the telephone. Celeste wondered what required that they speak in person.

The third E-mail was from Celeste's friend Harry at the *New York Times*. This message, too, was uncharacteristic; not one of Harry's typical, ironic one-liners. It was a gushing description of how he had finally fallen in love.

This is all I need, thought Celeste. Apparently Harry had interviewed Rutgers' top mathematician as part of an article he was doing, and it had been mutual love at first sight. Her name was Cammy (Camilla) Polson, and she had a "sweet Southern accent." He couldn't wait to introduce her to Celeste and, luckily, would have the opportunity to do so in October when he planned to accompany Cammy to a conference in San Francisco. Celeste thought that, for her part, she could easily wait to meet Harry's Southern belle. Though she should have been happy for him, she surprised herself with a possessive wave of jealousy. Then, she berated herself. There had never been a commitment between her and Harry, just a long-standing friendship. Celeste would be the first to admit they had never been in love. She would have to be more generous spirited. So Celeste responded, electronically, that she was thrilled for Harry and looked forward to their visit.

Celeste didn't have to be at her departmental faculty meeting until ten, or really until ten past ten, which gave her time to get a cup of coffee en route. As she passed through the lab on her way downstairs, she noted that neither Eric nor anyone else was there. But there was a tupperware container of a sloshing blue liquid on a small rotating platform on Eric's bench. This was a sign that the gel analysis of the protein was completed. The blue liquid would dye the proteins so they would become visible, and Celeste could determine whether they could proceed with the rabbit immunizations. Celeste pulled the laboratory door shut behind her and listened for the lock to click. Anyone could wander into the BAU buildings and, given that it was animal liberation week, a little extra security consciousness was called for.

The BAU campus, if its odd collection of hospital and laboratory towers could be called that, sat on top of the hill overlooking Golden Gate Park. Celeste thought that the prestigious address on Olympus Avenue was suitably descriptive considering that whenever the San Francisco fog was in, the BAU buildings were bathed in cloud. The address was also eminently appropriate to the godlike self-image of some of her fellow faculty members, a subset of whom Celeste was about to encounter at the faculty meeting.

Mid-September began one of the nicest seasons in San Francisco. The days were warm and clear even at BAU in the so-called Sunset district, where the sun typically made a token appearance as it sank below the horizon. Celeste appreciated the sunshine as she crossed the small patch of grass twelve flights below her laboratory and over to the café on the ground floor of the nursing school. The café was bustling with newly arrived students and almost festive with the optimistic beginning of an academic year.

Celeste stood in line for her double cappucino and tuned out the surrounding activity to think, with frustration, about her confrontation with Eric. It was ironic that they were haggling not about work that Eric had to do himself, but about rabbit immunizations that were contracted out to the California Serum Company. The first day of her very first laboratory experience in graduate school she was bitten by a mouse and urinated on by a rabbit; all in the course of learning how to immunize these animals. Times had certainly changed.

"Celeste," she heard a man's voice say, "are you there?"

She focused in front of her. It was Ben Duncan, the other junior faculty member in the Department of Microbiology.

"Hi, Ben," she said. "Just lost to brilliant thoughts." She smiled. It wasn't difficult to like this earnest and attractive colleague whose passion in life was cataloguing bacteria of the gut that cause ulcers. Celeste completely understood why, in contrast to Ben, the senior faculty perceived her as prickly and defiant. "I guess you're headed for the same entertainment."

"No kidding," said Ben. "It sounds like the department's in real trouble." He was only starting his second year as a faculty member, though he had been a medical fellow in the chairman's laboratory for several years. He still took everything that the administration said at face value.

"Oh, they've been complaining about the budget since before I came," said Celeste from the hardened experience of a fifth year assistant professor. "Dr. Rosenthal told me that nothing has really changed since we left the state system. It's just that we no longer have the state legislature to blame."

"I heard that they're going to put pressure on every-one with industrial connections to solicit funds for a spe-cial departmental endowment," said Ben. "I wish I could help, but so far I haven't made any connections independent of Dr. Rosenthal.

"It's always dangerous to make wishes," said Ce-leste. "I don't think it's going to be very pleasant for those who do have connections."

Twenty minutes later, sitting around the conference table with twelve senior men and one other woman, Ce-leste saw her prophecy realized. It was Dr. Butler who singled out Celeste. "I would imagine that your heroics or heroine-oics for Fukuda last year must have made them pretty grateful." There was some snickering at his joky pretense to be politically correct.

"I've never heard the term 'heroic' applied to solving a case *after* two guys are murdered," said Celeste. "Anyway, you all know that my consultancy agreement with Fukuda was in exchange for a donation to our post-doctoral fellowship fund. I don't know that I can ask for more than that."

To his credit, Dr. Rosenthal came to Celeste's rescue. He would be retiring as chairman within the year, but he wasn't going to let things get out of hand yet. Be-sides, Dr. Toshimi Matsumoto, the vice president for research at Fukuda, Osaka, was a longtime colleague of his. Rosenthal knew how much Toshimi respected Ce-leste, and Rosenthal valued that connection with the BAU microbiology department. He didn't want Celeste to be forced into abusing that trust.

Celeste barely heard Dr. Rosenthal's defense of her, though she realized that it was sufficient to get Butler off her back. Instead, her thoughts were hijacked to thinking of Kazuko and her mysterious E-mail message. Kazuko was now director of Fukuda's virology research division in Sapporo. The appointment had been pushed by Toshimi, at the Osaka headquarters, after the murder of Kazuko's husband and her boss, the former director. All involved were cognizant of the irony that advancement of a capable woman in Japan could occur only under such extreme circumstances. Celeste, who had been consulting for Fukuda during this ordeal, admired Kazuko enormously and they had become good friends. Celeste hoped that Kazuko wasn't in trouble.

"Celeste," said Ben, "the meeting's over. Are you all right?"

"Yeah, yeah, fine," said Celeste, a little embarassed. "You'll start becoming absentminded too, in a couple of years. It comes with the territory."

When Celeste returned to the laboratory the door to the corridor was unlocked. Judging from the jackets and backpacks that had appeared at several of the benches, the work of the day was getting under way. Still, there was no one present at the benches just outside of Celeste's office. Her lab personnel were probably already in the tissue culture room or in the darkroom that housed the microscope or, more likely, getting a cup of coffee.

Celeste's office was at the back of the laboratory, which had evolved into a maze of standing equipment obscuring the regular placement of benches. There was a clear, narrow path that dodged through the maze to Celeste's office door, hidden between a refrigerated cabinet and a centrifuge. Celeste made her way through the lab, noting by the personal debris who had come in. She also noticed that someone had dripped red stain on the floor, more or less delineating the path to her office. Eric had used the conventional blue stain for his gel, so it was probably somebody else.

But when Celeste reached her office door, she realized that it wasn't stain at all. She stood frozen, staring at the strange and macabre sight in front of her. The full length of the door was defaced with two long smears of what was unmistakably fresh blood. The smears met at an angle at the bottom, forming a V that dribbled to a gory point.

Celeste tested the doorknob, her heart pounding. It was still locked, as she had left it. Gingerly she turned the key in the lock, trying to avoid touching the blood. She opened the door slowly, not knowing what to expect. As she pushed the door away from her a few drops of blood dripped onto the wall-to-wall carpet at the office entrance.

Celeste let out a huge sigh. Nothing had been disturbed inside the office, which had apparently not been entered. The horror that had gripped her was replaced first by disgust, and then by anger.

In the laboratory and clinically, blood was an invaluable fluid. Out of context, it was gruesome. Her first thought was that if this was Eric's idea of a political statement, things were getting out of hand. In spite of the fact that the work he had begun was useful, she would have to consider asking him to leave the laboratory given that his responsibilities conflicted so strongly with his *beliefs*.

But Celeste wasn't completely sure that it was Eric who had defiled her door. She supposed she should report it to the campus police in case it was harassment from one of the animal liberation groups. But, if it did turn out to be Eric, a report to the police would only stimulate the tension between them. After a few moments of consideration, Celeste realized that the perpetrator's object could only be to draw attention to his or her cause, so she decided that probably the best reaction to the incident would be to ignore the incident.

There was still nobody working at the benches immediately outside the door to her office. And, with momentary irony, Celeste observed that for once she could be grateful for the scarcity of her personnel. She went into the dishwashing room and collected a clean lab coat and a bottle of diluted bleach, used for disinfection. She then returned to the laboratory and, from the bench outside her office, picked up a pair of disposable latex gloves and a wad of paper towels and set to work. Fifteen minutes later the only sign that anything out of the ordinary had occurred was that Celeste deposited a taped-up bag of biohazard waste in the bin and a soiled lab coat in the laundry basket. The sight of Celeste with lab paraphernalia raised a few eyebrows since she spent most of her time in the office these days, but given her seniority, no one made any comments.

When she returned to the laboratory, Celeste looked over the chaos on Eric's bench. She found no sign that he had been dealing with blood and instead saw a perfect gel floating in the destain solution in the tupperware container. He had been right about his ability to run a reliable gel analysis. And his preparations of virus proteins looked sufficiently pure that they should be effective for immunization. Maybe there was hope after all.

Feeling temporarily relieved about Eric, Celeste had to consider the alternative that someone else, possibly from the outside, had violated the privacy of the laboratory. Her only recourse was to write a memo to the lab personnel reminding them to lock up when they weren't in the laboratory, even if they just stepped out for a coffee break. Without mentioning the bloody mess she had just cleaned up, Celeste cited animal liberation week as the need for increased vigilance and an excuse for the security reminder. After printing, copying, and distributing the memo, Celeste had the illusion that she had done something constructive about the attempted intimidation. She took refuge in her office to face the next mystery of the day, which was to phone Kazuko.

The call was answered after two rings. *"Moshi-moshi,"* said a female voice.

"Kazuko, it's Celeste calling."

"Oh, Celeste. I am so glad you call. Are you well?"

"Yes, I'm fine," said Celeste, a little impatiently. "And you?"

"Fine," said Kazuko, and paused. "I think there is something you should know. It is private, so I don't send E-mail."

"What is it?"

"Yesterday, Japanese police come by my office at Fukuda. They ask a lot of questions. They want to know about your work with Fukuda and how you connect to murder cases. They say that they need to finalize some police records."

Celeste realized how painful it must have been for Kazuko to review the incidents, which had occurred only slightly more than a year earlier. "I would have thought they had tied up all the information long ago," she said, puzzled.

"I think so, too. Most of what they ask is about you," said Kazuko. "They want to know how long I live with you in San Francisco and what kind of things you do outside of the lab." She giggled. "I tell them you do nothing outside of lab. I think they really want to know more what kind of person you are."

"Too bad what you said is true," said Celeste.

"Then," continued Kazuko, "it just so happens that Toshimi is visiting the Sapporo lab and he arrives just as the police are leaving. He, of course, wants to know what is going on. When I tell him police are asking for some old information about Celeste and her work with us, he says he suspects it was not just police. I ask him why and he says that car was not marked and he saw a non-Japanese sitting in car. We discuss it and think you should know about this."

Celeste was perplexed. "Well, thanks for telling me. I'm not sure what's going on. But it's a relief to know you guys are looking out for me."

"You must be careful, Celeste," said Kazuko. Toshimi and I both worry about you. We will call again soon."

"Okay," said Celeste, "I'll keep in touch. Take care."

"You also," said Kazuko.

Perhaps the fact that Celeste had been awake since early that morning exacerbated her rising paranoia, but she was succumbing to the distinct impression that she was being pursued.

5

Miami Vice

"We don't want you renting a car. No unnecessary records." Jack Minot had said to Celeste. It was the week after Celeste had spoken to Kazuko, and Celeste was in the Miami area ostensibly to visit her great-aunt. Thus, Celeste landed at the exclusive West Palm Beach Airport instead of Miami International. Minot had not been explicit about why he wanted Celeste to come to Miami. But he had made it clear who he was and that it was urgent. Celeste wondered why he wanted to meet her in his home territory and didn't fly to San Francisco to talk to her, but she supposed it would all be revealed in due course. They were meeting for lunch at a restaurant in a mall near where Celeste's great-aunt lived. Again, Celeste would have been curious to see the FBI headquarters, but Minot must have had a reason for meeting her off-site.

Celeste followed the signs to ground transportation, then down the escalator to the baggage claim area. She was confronted by a crowd of limo drivers holding signs, waiting for their passengers to appear. The drivers were uniformly wearing short-sleeved shirts and light trousers, advertising that the business of the area was to cater to

holiday makers who had left their jackets and ties behind. Some of those holiday makers pushed aggressively
past Celeste as she stood at the bottom of the escalator,
haranguing one another in nasal New York tones and
jostling to be first to pick up their baggage.

Traveling only with hand luggage allowed Celeste to
escape the crush into the thick Florida heat to find the
taxi rank. Celeste could easily differentiate which coast
she was on from the feel of the heat alone. She took a
seat in the back of Lorrie's Taxi, the first in the queue.

The driver was a large, balding man whom Celeste
judged to be in his late sixties. He was quite tanned and
looked like he spent his time out of doors when he
wasn't driving a taxi. Celeste asked him if he knew the
Pavilion Restaurant in Boca Raton.

"Sure, lady. I take the locals to that mall all the
time."

"Great," said Celeste. "Let's go."

They pulled out of the airport parking lot, sealed off
from the atmosphere in chilly isolation, and rode along
in silence while the driver navigated the wide boulevards
to Route 95.

Once they were cruising south toward their destination in Boca, Celeste said, "You don't look like your
name is Lorrie."

"Lorrie's my wife," he explained. "I drive on Tues-
days and Fridays to help out. It's her business, and she
wouldn't take any time off if I didn't stand in for her.
I'm on call for coastal patrol the other days. You know,
the volunteer coast guard."

"No, I don't know. What's the volunteer coast
guard?"

"Well, it's a pretty good deal for small craft. See,
lot's of 'em get in trouble while they're out fishin' and
stuff. They call in an SOS to the coast guard, who just
can't handle all the trouble themselves. The coast guard

then sends out a pickup bulletin on an open wavelength. If the boat in trouble gets picked up by the commercial tow boats, it costs 'em a fortune. So we help out the coast guard by answering SOS calls before the commercial boats get 'em. We try to keep the rip-off factor down.''

"Who's we?" asked Celeste.

"Oh, a bunch of us retired guys who got our own small craft. We get free maintenance of our boats for being volunteers, and it's pretty interesting. Like last week, we were called out to tow in an unmanned boat that was reported, and it had a dead body in it. Mafia killing for sure. Corpse had its guts cut out in a V. No drugs on board, though. But when the police showed up, the narc dogs went crazy sniffing around the boat. It's like the drugs were saved, and the man was garbage.''

Celeste felt queasy. "What do you mean a V?"

"Everybody round here knows that. V for Valentino, the big Mafia boss from South Miami Beach. It's his signature.''

"You don't say." Celeste lapsed back into silence, no longer feeling very conversational.

About fifteen minutes later, which seemed much longer to Celeste, the taxi pulled off the highway and stopped at a traffic light at the intersection of two broad boulevards. Celeste could see the windowless edifices of several large department stores forming the edge of a shopping mall diagonally across from them. Projecting above the stores, a gravity-defying sign indicated that the Pavilion Restaurant, evidently Chinese, was located in the complex. By now Celeste was extremely anxious about confronting Mr. Minot with what she had just learned from the driver. Or maybe that was why Minot was waiting in the Pavilion, to confront her.

The taxi driver was oblivious to the impact of his earlier remark, however. "Hey, that's pretty smart," he said. "See that license plate in front of us? TA2 U. It's for a permanent cosmetic outfit. You know, where they tattoo your eyebrows and stuff. The wife would get a kick out of that. I gotta remember to tell her." Roused from her preoccupation by this bizarre comment, Celeste had to acknowledge that Florida and California did have some idiosyncracies in common, even if the nature of the heat was different.

The interior of the Pavilion was cool and dark, with the tables sequestered between gold-filigreed screens placed strategically for privacy. Nonetheless, Celeste could have found Jack Minot without the help of the headwaiter. Minot was the only male patron in the entire restaurant, and the only patron who didn't look like he had just spent several hundred dollars browsing in the shopping mall. He was probably a good ten years younger than the taxi driver who had just dropped off Celeste, but he looked a good deal more careworn. He was well on his way to becoming as bald and as paunchy as the driver, and had a strong, stocky stance. He treated Celeste to a no-nonsense handshake and a very brief, open smile that gave Celeste immediate confidence in him.

They exchanged small talk about Celeste's trip and ordered lunch before Minot got down to business. When the waiter left them alone, he began. "Dr. Braun, I sure appreciate you coming out here. We got ourselves in a situation where we need some expertise like yours. You were the obvious person to ask for help because you're kinda' indirectly involved in the case already."

"I assume this has something to do with my discovery in El Morro."

Minot looked puzzled.

"The fort in San Juan."

"You could say that," he said.

"Does it have anything to do with the Mafia?" asked Celeste. Might as well be direct.

"Why do you say that?" Minot sounded alarmed.

"According to my taxi driver, it's common knowledge around here that the Valentino family marks their victims with a V. Only it's common knowledge that I acquired about twenty minutes ago."

"You told him about the body?" Minot sounded horrified.

Celeste chuckled, shaking her head, and Minot looked even more horrified. She realized she had to explain herself. "I guess you guys have to start by assuming that everyone you talk to is a complete idiot, unless proven otherwise. I guess I do too, for that matter," she reflected. "No. I did not tell him about the body I found. He told me about one he found in the course of his volunteer coast guard duties, and I realized it had the same signature as mine."

"Oh, yeah," said Minot, a little chagrined. "The Spanish Bay body that turned up last week. That was one of the reasons I was inspired to call you."

They paused while the waiter delivered a steaming bowl of Seafood Delight soup for them to share, along with the other specialities of the house; cold, sesame noodles and jellyfish with pickled vegetables. Minot had looked suspicious when Celeste ordered these dishes, but their fragrant aroma suggested she would be vindicated.

"Before I get into the details, I better just make sure that I'm making the right assumption here. As we agreed on the phone, your work for us is more than secret. It doesn't even exist. Right?" asked Minot.

"Well, it certainly doesn't exist as of this moment. I've kept my mouth shut since I was asked to in March. And I don't plan on opening it either."

"Fine," said Minot. "It seems we understand each other." He slurped a mouthful of soup, deciding where to begin, and raised his eyebrows in surprised approval.

"I have spent the last three years knowing that the most successful drug distribution ring in Miami is operated by the Valentino family. I'm not boasting when I say that I know everything about the operation except how they manage to keep one step ahead of us. The drugs always appear on the streets before we can intercept them, so we can never actually connect them to the Mafia. Every time we get close, the body that's been helping us shows up with its guts slashed in a V. No matter how hard we try, we just can't nail these guys."

"Sounds like I ran into one of your bodies," interupted Celeste.

"Yeah, he was an FBI plant, too." replied Minot bitterly.

"That doesn't bode very well for your next agent." Celeste's voice expressed her serious concern.

Minot looked at her. Jeez, what kind of spook ever used the word *bode,* he thought worriedly. But he carried on. "A couple months ago, I got a lead on how the distribution orders are being issued. It was a lucky break from talking to a buddy in the Los Angeles bureau. They uncovered a distribution ring for similar high quality junk in LA. It was the quality of the junk that made him call me, more like what comes out of South America than Asia. They traced the original shipment to Taipei and, through a courier they arrested, tracked the distribution order to a medical clinic there. It was called . . . lemme see," Minot consulted a small, spiral notebook that he drew out of his pocket. "The Sinica Institute of Herbal Remedy. Ever hear of it?"

Celeste shook her head negatively.

"What's interesting is that our man, the one you found, had tracked a Miami distribution order to the clinic where you attended the conference last March."

"The Instituto de Medicina Botánica?"

"Yeah, that one. So the common thread, besides the

qualilty of the junk, is that distribution orders are coming from medical clinics.''

''Well the Instituto is a *bona fide* clinic,'' said Celeste.

''A what? Remember, you're not talking to a fellow doc.'' Minot thought she had thrown some fancy scientific term at him, and then realizing his erroneous assumption, reddened as she responded.

''Sorry,'' said Celeste. ''It's Latin for genuine.''

''Yeah, we know it's genuine,'' said Minot. ''That's the clever part, and that's why we need you. We've had a round-the-clock watch on both clinics for a while, just keeping track of who goes in and out. The only pattern we could see was that drugs usually hit the streets in Miami or LA within a week of a non-native patient showing up at either clinic. But, up to the time the orders arrive, no one knows when and where the distribution operation will take place. This way the drug couriers never have any information about what's going down until right before it goes down, if you see what I mean. However, we predicted a distribution order from the San Juan clinic based on the admission of a non-Hispanic patient. The Spanish Bay body wasn't one of ours, but a drug runner in our pay. Just before he was found, he confirmed that a distribution order had gone out.''

''So why don't you arrest the patients if they're working for the Mafia?'' asked Celeste.

''We don't have any grounds. Their connection to the drug distribution is strictly circumstantial. And, they could be being used to transmit messages without even knowing it.''

''How could that be?''

''That's what we need you to find out. We've gotta have someone on the inside to get some idea of what these patients are up to or what's being done to them or even where they're coming from. The confidentiality agreements associated with medical treatment are a pain in the butt when it comes to getting this kind of information. We don't even have a clue about how the Valentinos are linked to the clinics. That's something we're still working on from the outside, but if you happened to see a connection while you're poking around the inside, it would sure help.''

"Two questions," said Celeste.

"Shoot."

"I found the corpse with the Valentino's signature in a tunnel of the catacombs that are supposed to connect up to the clinic in the old city. If the San Juan police could confirm that the connecting tunnels are clear, wouldn't that provide some evidence of a link?''

"Not exactly," said Minot. "To start with, these PR guys are pretty sensitive about interference from the mainland and are not the most cooperative bunch. I think you met the chief over there, Raul de Leon, so you know what I'm talking about. Kinda' snooty. Anyway, Raul did confirm that the tunnels connect all the way. But what does that prove? You got in through the museum so the body could've been dumped by the same route. We have no evidence to show that it came in from the clinic side.'' Minot took a breath. "What's your second question?''

"How do you expect me to go back to the clinic and just start 'poking around,' as you described it. I'll need some kind of professional excuse.''

"I could make a suggestion. . . .''

"Feel free," said Celeste. It seemed he had a plan already worked out.

"Because the PR guys are so touchy, and you're likely to be recognized over there, we think it would be better for you to investigate the clinic in Taipei. We understand that you're a buddy of the woman who's the boss at Fukuda Pharmaceuticals in Sapporo. Uh, Kazuko

Hagai," he said, again checking his pocket notebook to get the name right. "It would make sense for Fukuda to be planning a therapy trial at the Taipei clinic. After all, it's in their neck of the woods. Many of their drugs are based on Chinese herbal medicines so they wouldn't need to get the equivalent of FDA approval for their trials. We thought it would be convenient if Fukuda appointed you as a consultant. We know you've worked as a consultant for them in the past."

These guys had obviously done their homework. Had they already done their groundwork, wondered Celeste. Maybe they had already spoken to Kazuko and intimidated her in some way. Had Kazuko been totally straightforward with Celeste when she'd called the other day?

Celeste's worry must have shown on her face. Minot reassured her. "You should be getting a call from Dr. Hagai when you get back from this trip. She has a lunch date on Monday with my man in Japan. Do you think she'll help?"

Celeste was partially relieved. "I'm sure she'll help as long as 'your man' demonstrates that you trust her. Which you can, absolutely."

"Gotcha'," said Minot, understanding completely. "I'll make sure he does. And if she agrees to our proposal, she'll contact you, and you'll proceed from there."

"Is there a chance that your associates were already over at Fukuda last week?"

"Maybe," said Minot. "Why?"

Celeste didn't want to make Kazuko seem unreliable, so she slightly edited Kazuko's report. "Kazuko mentioned that the Japanese police had been around asking questions."

"We do work with the local police," said Minot.

"Well I must have an FBI file a mile long at this

point,'' said Celeste, not sure what to make of Minot's response.

"That's about it," said Minot with finality. "But, at least·we're still trusting you."

"I should hope so." Their transaction apparently completed, Celeste rose from the table. "Thanks for lunch. I can take a taxi to my great-aunt's from here."

"Thanks a lot for coming," said Minot, standing and holding out his hand. "I've got a feeling we'll be able to do business just fine. But don't forget what I told you when I first called, about how to get in touch. Just deal with me directly through the number I gave you. Don't go through headquarters. We've gotta be extra secure communicating with an outside recruit like you. It's for your own safety."

"Don't worry, I'll be circumspect," said Celeste as she shook the proffered hand.

Another fancy word, thought Minot. It must come with the territory. It looked like he'd have to brush up· on his vocabulary for this operation.

Celeste sat back in the taxi and shifted gears to being a visiting grandniece. It didn't take much shifting since Audrey was hardly the conventional great-auntie. Audrey was born Ada Cohen, youngest sister of Celeste's maternal grandfather. She'd never finished high school since her employment was perceived as much more valuable to the family, and she eventually attained the position of buyer for the main department store in Providence, Rhode Island. Along with many women of her generation, Ada was liberated by the Second World War. When ready-to-wear clothing became scarce, she went on a buying expedition to Chicago where she outbargained the representative from Saks Fifth Avenue for a whole shipment of women's suits. He was so impressed that he offered her a job on the spot. Ada never looked back and spent close to twenty happy years as a career woman in New York City, living in a penthouse suite in the Mayfair hotel.

At the age of forty, three years before her grandniece Celeste was born, Ada married Nate Rubenstein, a Harvard-educated lawyer with a lucrative practice in Newark, New Jersey. She quit work and became the consummate golf playing, country club hostess. Celeste had two memories of Aunt Ada during this period. One was visits with her little brother to swim with Ada at "the club," where luncheons consisted of crustless, turkey sandwiches and milky, iced coffee. And where the pool held the terrifying opportunity to jump off the high dive. The other was being taken shopping in New York for her eleventh birthday, and Ada buying Celeste her first pair of nylon stockings.

Ada became Audrey after Nate retired and they moved to Florida. While he took his turn at country club life, she opened a boutique clothing shop, Audrey Ruben's "for the Rubenesque." It was this Audrey whom Celeste had got to know as an adult, and whom she had hosted for a visit to San Francisco after Nate had passed away three years earlier.

The taxi turned off Yamato Road into the extensive private domain that occupied the heart of Boca Raton, "rat's mouth" in Spanish. A rather ironic name, thought Celeste, for a community of exclusive country clubs and condominiums. Appropriate however, she reminded herself, for the commitment she had just made to Minot. Celeste did not understand her own desire for danger and, even more puzzling, her enjoyment of deception. Her friend Harry would probably say that if she was getting laid more often she wouldn't have these cravings.

The taxi dropped Celeste off at the locked door of Audrey's condominium building, one of at least ten clones that extended along the private drive. The buildings were beige low-rises of cement-block construction. All the condominiums had front doors opening onto balcony walkways overlooking the large cars in the front parking lot. They also all had screened porches overlooking the extensive golf course at the back. This layout appeared to be designed to remind the inhabitants of the amenities that their retirement had bought them. Celeste dialed the code for Audrey's apartment and was buzzed in. She took the elevator up to the second floor, as there were no stairs in sight, and stepped out into Audrey's enthusiastic embrace.

"Celeste, darling. Why don't you come to see me more often?" complained Audrey in her deep, rasping voice. She'd been a pack-a-day smoker during her fashion career. Celeste could just about remember when Audrey had quit in the late sixties.

"Oh, Audrey, you always say that," said Celeste. "You know you'd get bored with me if I were around all the time. Or worse than that, we'd probably argue."

"I could never argue with you, baby," said Audrey, pinching Celeste's cheek affectionately.

Celeste looked her great-aunt up and down. "You look like you've lost weight. Have you been on some new Florida fad diet?" Indeed, Audrey was uncharacteristically trim in elegant pale yellow trousers and a white cotton knit top; loaded down, as usual, with heavy gold jewelry. Celeste used to joke with her brother that Audrey could be mistaken for a man in drag. But today, Audrey felt surprisingly slight when Celeste hugged her.

"Yeah," said Audrey dismissively, "I have lost some weight. Wasn't even trying. Must be shrinking with old age. Now, what about you, bubbula? What brings you here?"

They had entered Audrey's cool apartment and Celeste was struck, as always, by the sudden transformation from Florida kitsch outside to New York chic inside. "Oh, just some science business," she said in answer to Audrey's question, which was pro forma anyway. "It's over now and we have the whole weekend to fool around."

"Good," said Audrey. "I managed to get you an extra ticket for Robert Goulet in *Man of La Mancha* at the West Palm Beach Theater tomorrow afternoon. The girls and I have been going to matinees lately since it's easier to drive in the daytime. Then there's the Saturday night lobster special at the Fishwife. We'll all go out for an early supper, if it's okay with you."

"Fine," said Celeste. "Sounds great." She had walked to the back of the apartment and was standing on the screened-in porch, looking at the golf course. It was covered with white birds with comical, curved beaks, pecking in the short grass. Celeste fished out her pair of Leica 10 X 25 binoculars from her shoulder bag and focused them. "Yes, definitely, white ibis," she said with satisfaction.

"What are you looking at, dear?" asked Audrey, puzzled by Celeste's distraction.

"Those birds on the golf course. Are they always there?"

"I suppose so," said Audrey. "I never really looked."

The white ibis reminded Celeste that Florida was a well-known birder's paradise. Having spent the first afternoon with Audrey exhaustively exploring the art galleries of Boca Raton, Celeste felt the need for a break from the elaborate and man made. That evening she consulted a faded map from Audrey's glove compartment and noticed the Loxahatchee National Wildlife Refuge appeared to be just the other side of the Florida Turnpike from Boca Raton. It took some convincing, but Audrey finally agreed to lend Celeste her car to indulge in some prebreakfast bird-watching the following morning. Celeste had to promise to be back in time to be able to go clothes shopping before lunch, before the matinee, before the lobster dinner. Celeste felt like a teenager again.

It took Celeste a lot longer to get to the refuge than she had expected from looking at the map. She crawled through the stop-and-go traffic of Saturday morning errands on the local strip, a relentless string of mini-malls. Finally, after Celeste crossed the turnpike, the suburban density was replaced by swampy farmland and the occasional mobile home. Then she had the road more or less to herself. In her rearview mirror she could see only one car about a quarter of a mile behind her.

Celeste soon reached a T junction, where the Loxahatchee National Wildlife Refuge was signposted to the right. A half mile after the right turn, she slowed down to turn left into the refuge entrance and noticed that the car, a black sedan, was still behind her. During the few seconds that Celeste was making the turn, she wondered if she were being followed. It was pretty deserted out there in the swamp, and she was certainly unprotected. Of course, there might be other birdwatchers wanting to take advantage of the early morning activity. Celeste stopped at the unmanned sentry post about fifty yards down the drive and got out of the car to check Audrey's license plate number so she could write it on the fee envelope. To her relief, the car behind her sped by the turn-off to the refuge. She smiled to herself. She would have to keep this FBI recruitment from going to her head. Celeste did not consider the possibility that, just after the refuge driveway, the passing car would slow down to make a U-turn.

Celeste parked Audrey's Oldsmobile Cutlass in front of the refuge headquarters and walked up a boardwalk to the front door. The boardwalk traversed a wooden bridge from which Celeste could see a huge alligator warming itself in the morning sun. It was 8:30 A.M. and, according to the sign on the door, the refuge headquarters didn't open until nine. A posted trail map indicated that the boardwalk continued on a half-mile circuit through the mangrove swamp behind the headquarters. Celeste figured that she just about had time to make the circuit before she would have to head back to the impatient Audrey.

About halfway around the boardwalk trail, Celeste added two new species to her bird list. A green-backed heron landed less than five yards in front of her, completely oblivious to her presence. She only disturbed it when she was startled by the raucous cry of a red-bellied woodpecker that obligingly displayed its orangy-red hood as it flitted from trunk to trunk. Celeste had done very little bird-watching outside of California and was enjoying the early stage of the hobby in which every new environment offered new species to be identified. Feeling that the excursion had been worthwhile, Celeste rounded the bend in the boardwalk, heading back to the refuge headquarters. Suddenly, to her right, the black water of the mangrove swamp started churning violently. Celeste jumped and her heart began to race.

With ferocious splashing, three sleek dark heads protruded above the surface of the water and then dove into silence. Celeste stood for a moment, calming herself down, and then laughed out loud. Three otters had managed to achieve a greater physical effect on her than the threat of the mob.

Celeste was still a little trembly, however, when she got back to the headquarters, which had opened a few minutes earlier. She stopped to use the bathrooom and then reported her otter sighting to the elderly man, wearing a park volunteer uniform, who was setting out brochures on the reception counter. He was wearing a large white circular badge that read, in red letters, "Hi, I'm Mel. Ask me about the local wildlife."

"Lucky you," he said in response to Celeste's report. "I've been trying to spot the otters for months, and you just stumbled across them. No fair."

"Nature isn't always fair," said Celeste.

"Here," said Mel, pushing a large guest register towards Celeste. "You should make your sighting official."

Celeste picked up the ballpoint pen attached to the register and was just about to sign her name when she caught herself. Instead she wrote the date followed by, "Ada Cohen, Boca Raton, FL. Three otters sighted off the boardwalk, 8:55 a.m." Minot had explicitly stated that there should be no written records of her visit to Florida.

As she left the refuge headquarters, Celeste noted that Audrey's car had been joined by three others in the parking lot. One had a ranger's insignia, and one was a classic boat, similar to Audrey's, that presumably belonged to Mel. The third car pulled out just as Celeste reached the end of the boardwalk, where it met the parking lot. It was a black sedan. She was nervously reminded of the car that had been trailing her en route to the refuge.

Curious and a bit uncomfortable, Celeste quickly got into Audrey's car and started the engine to try to catch up with the sedan. When she reached the end of the parking lot turn-off, Celeste saw that the sedan had turned right and was heading further into the refuge, towards the bayous she had seen marked on the map. Celeste stopped Audrey's car at the intersection and lowered the electric window on the passenger side. Using her binoculars, which still hung around her neck, Celeste could just make out the sedan's rear license plate. It appeared to be a U.S. government plate. Celeste observed, for the third time that morning, that her paranoia was getting out of hand. This was a national wildlife refuge, after all, and wasn't she now working for the FBI? Either friendly surveillance or refuge business were perfectly reasonable explanations for the presence of a car with federal plates.

For Mel, the morning continued to spiral downhill after Celeste left. A second tourist also reported an otter sighting, and Mel had just overcome the disappointment of missing the otters once again, when a much more unpleasant incident occurred.

Mel hadn't realized that being a volunteer at a national wildlife refuge meant that he would be subject to intimidation by any federal agent who happened to be passing through. The "agent" had no uniform and never removed his sunglasses, but his identification card looked real enough. Mel hadn't shown him anything that wasn't public information anyway. Whoever he was, he only demanded to see the register, and after a quick look, asked Mel if it accurately represented the day's visitors so far. Mel answered that he had been there the whole morning and that everyone he saw come through had signed the book. The guy then grunted, as though he didn't believe Mel, and said, "If we find that you haven't been keeping accurate records, there'll be hell to pay." He then left, seemingly frustrated. Mel was just glad there had been no tourists in the headquarters at the time whose visit might have been tainted by this sinister behavior.

6

Candid Camera

Celeste was all too familiar with the song "To Dream the Impossible Dream." However, she had never seen *Man of La Mancha*, so hadn't appreciated that it was a song of political idealism, reflecting the spirit of the sixties when the show was written. Celeste was totally captivated by Robert Goulet's performance as Cervantes and Don Quixote, his imaginary knight errant fighting socio-political corruption. The theme of the show and some of the issues seemed quite radical for the neo-conservative nineties. Celeste was curious how Audrey and her friends would respond to the dramatically choreographed rape scene.

They discussed the show in the car, on the way to dinner. "I thought Goulet was as good as ever," said Julie, the snowbird from Chicago.

"Yes, but I was a little disappointed in the rape scene," said Grace, the youngest of the three, having just turned seventy. "I've seen the show at least three times. It was Bernie's favorite. I thought the choreography in this version diminished the impact. We saw it when it first came out on Broadway. In that production, they just did it, kind of violently, on stage. It was much more effective.'' So much for Celeste's concern about their delicacy.

The four women arrived at the Fishwife Restaurant at 6 P.M., only to be reminded that this was peak dining time for the population of Boca Raton. The place was mobbed because of the bargain price advertised for the boiled lobster dinner. The fact that they had a reservation and had been regular patrons on countless Saturdays didn't cut any ice with the harassed hostess. Just about every customer there could have made claim to the same loyalty. They had fifteen minutes to wait for the tables ahead of them to clear, and Grace made a big deal about whether Audrey could sit down while they were waiting.

''Stop fussing over me,'' said Audrey, annoyed.

''You know I'm worried about your cough,'' said Grace. ''You shouldn't get tired out.''

''I told you,'' said Audrey, ''the tests were negative.''

''What tests?'' asked Celeste.

''Oh, Dr. Kirshner gave me a complete lung workup a couple of weeks ago. He was concerned by this bronchitis I have that won't go away.'' Celeste had heard Audrey coughing in the middle of the night, and it had worried her enough to ask Audrey about it at breakfast. Audrey had dismissed it as the residue from a bad cold.

''Why didn't you tell me it was chronic when I asked you about it this morning?'' said Celeste with alarm.

''Honey, if Dr. Kirshner says I'm fine, I'm fine. It wasn't worth going into. I'd rather talk about more fun things than my health.''

''Oh, Audrey,'' said Grace with some exasperation. They had obviously been through this before. Grace then turned to Celeste and said, ''What are you working on now, dear? Are we any closer to a cure for the big C?'' Celeste hated questions like this. She was about to launch into her usual explanation that not all researchers in biology studied cancer directly. She would add the caveat, of course, that the knowledge they all gained was relevant in the long run.

"Grace!" said Audrey, sharply. "I said I didn't want to talk about it." Fortunately at that moment the hostess, looking like she was ready to blow the place up, came over to seat them.

Celeste and Audrey were back in the apartment by 8:30 P.M. and were changing into their dressing gowns in preparation for watching the evening news, with a nightcap. Celeste was across the hall from Audrey's bedroom, in the study, which doubled as a guest bedroom. She heard the phone ring and Audrey answered it. "Celeste, its for you," called Audrey across the hall. "You can get it in my bedroom."

Celeste walked around to the opposite side of the queen-size bed, where Audrey stood holding the phone out to her. Audrey mouthed the words, "It's a man."

"Hello?" said Celeste.

"Hi, Celeste? This is Stash calling. Stash Romanicz, your friendly host from Virginia."

"Hi Stash," said Celeste, surprised. "How did you find me here?"

"It certainly wasn't easy," he said. "I thought you told me you didn't have any trips planned. Anyway, I finally managed to track down a direct number for your laboratory, and they told me you were away, and gave me the administrator's number. It took some convincing, but she gave me this number."

Celeste had reluctantly left Audrey's number with the department administrator, who was annoyed that Celeste had cancelled attendance at a finance committee meeting in order to make this trip. The adminstrator had been under strict instructions not to give out the number and Celeste wondered what Stash had said to "convince"

her. He was probably well-trained in persuasive techniques. In any case, Celeste was glad to hear from him,
and the fact that he'd bothered to track her down was
encouraging for her social life, if not her life as a secret
agent. She would stick to the cover story for her visit,
so there was really no harm done.

"I had a last minute call from my aunt to come see
her, uh, about her medical condition." Celeste registered
Audrey's look of surprise. "But I'm glad to say it was
a false alarm, and I've had a nice weekend here. And
now, what can I do for you?"

"Well, I found out my plans for San Francisco. The
hotel management seminar starts Wednesday and ends
Friday evening. It looks like I won't have to get home
until Sunday, so I was thinking about going up to Point
Reyes on Saturday. But if you're out of town . . ."

"Oh, no, I'm coming back tomorrow night. I've got
to teach on Monday," said Celeste quickly. "I'd be
happy to take you up there."

"Excellent," said Stash. "I'll give you a call when
I arrive, and we can figure out the details. I look forward
to it."

"Me, too," said Celeste. It was remarkable how
pleasant his simple statement made her feel. She had a
sense they were on the same wavelength. The momentary silence was companionable. "Talk to you next
week, then."

" 'Til next week."

"Bye."

"Bye."

Celeste put down the receiver. For the second time
that day, she felt like a teenager. She couldn't remember
the last time she was so reluctant to hang up the phone.

Celeste was smiling to herself, and Audrey gave her
an encouraging look, anticipating some good gossip. But
it wasn't immediately forthcoming. Celeste stood staring

at Audrey's bedside table which was spilling over with bottles of medicine, an inhaler contraption, and a vaporizer. The medical debris appeared to validate Celeste's supposedly fictional cover story for her visit. The signs were that Audrey was considerably more ill than she let on. In the face of Audrey's attitude, Celeste would have to probe carefully to find out what the real state of Audrey's health was, and frankly, she feared the worst given Audrey's smoking history. But first Celeste would have to face Audrey's interrogation about her mysterious caller.

On Sunday morning, while Celeste was enjoying a send-off brunch of lox, bagels, and low-fat cream cheese at Audrey's country club, her laboratory was once again the scene of Eric's ill-timed diligence. Even though it was three hours earlier on the West coast, Eric was in a hurry. The bike race that had stimulated his confrontation with Celeste about the California Serum Company had qualified him to be among the starters of today's ride down Route 1 to Half Moon Bay. The race began at noon, so Eric needed to get an incubation going within the next hour to be at the starting line in time.

He wouldn't be able to face Celeste on Monday if he hadn't at least tried this experiment, and somehow yesterday had just slipped away. Just before Celeste left for her sudden trip they'd had another altercation. This one focused on the hazardous waste being generated by the laboratory. Celeste was pushing Eric to use chemically synthesized pieces of protein, called synthetic peptides, to analyze some antibody samples he was working with. He pointed out to Celeste that the methods used to make these peptides generated unnecessary chemical waste. He was convinced that the analysis could be done just as well with material produced by biological means—introducing recombinant DNA into bacteria. He was determined to prove his point using the results of the experiment he was in the process of setting up.

Eric concentrated on measuring twenty-five microliters reproducibly into the twenty bullet-shaped plastic test tubes in front of him. When he looked up he was startled to see a blond man in a khaki physical plant uniform. It looked like he was trying to get into Celeste's office. Eric realized he must have left the door to the laboratory unlocked.

"Can I help you?" asked Eric. "She's not in."

Usually, the *she* raised eyebrows since people generally expected the occupant of the office to be a man. The intruder didn't seem at all surprised, though Eric couldn't recall having seen him before.

"Boy, I can't believe I was that dumb," said the man, rattling a ring of keys. "Wouldn't you know it, I left my office master for this floor over at physical plant. I'm off this shift in twenty minutes, and I was supposed to complete the six-month checkup on the Internet wiring job this morning. They wanted it done on the weekend when the server downtime isn't such a problem. But it's gonna' take me more than twenty minutes just to get back to my locker." Indeed, physical plant was halfway up the hill, in the eucalyptus grove behind the lab towers. Eric had been there once to solder a fitting that had fallen off his bicycle. He sympathized with the guy, who was kind of in the same boat he was in, trying to deal with the demands of his boss.

"I can let you in," said Eric. "We have the office key hidden in the lab in case there's some emergency." He walked over to the drawer next to the techician's desk and untaped the key from the inside front panel.

"I won't be a minute," said the electrician. "D'ya want me to put the key back?"

"No, just give it to me," said Eric. He was suddenly uncomfortable that the visitor had seen the hiding place and irrationally did not want to reinforce his blunder.

Five minutes later, the electrician emerged from Celeste's office, locked it behind him, and handed Eric the key.

"Thanks, pal," he said inspecting Eric, who was wearing an open lab coat over his skintight biking gear. "That your mountain bike out there in the hall?"

"Yeah," said Eric. "I'm starting in the Half Moon Bay race today."

"Hey, good luck! That's a pretty tough course."

"I'm ready for it," said Eric with confidence.

"Well, I'm sure glad it's not me riding up and down all those hills," said the electrician.

Three hours later Eric made a sharp turn at Devil's Slide, feeling good. However, his front wheel made a decision of its own: It popped off to take a break with a loud metallic snap. The instantaneous loss of momentum flipped Eric head over handlebars. Luckily for him he landed out of range of the onrushing bicycles behind him. But as he impacted hard with the gravelly shoulder and skidded several yards through the rough dust, leaving pieces of skin behind him and collecting bits of rubble in the open abrasions, he didn't feel so fortunate. Just before Eric lost consciousness he incongruously remembered that he had left Celeste's office key in the pocket of his lab coat.

When Eric awoke in the hospital bed he had forgotten all about the incident that had led him to pocketing the key, as well as the experiment he had set up earlier that morning. Instead, once he did an inventory of which limbs were in traction and asked the nurse what had happened, he became obsessed with thinking about the maintenance routine he had performed on his bike the previous evening. He knew that he had checked and double-checked that both wheels were securely locked in place precisely to avoid this kind of accident. Mountain bikers were cool in Eric's eyes. It was inconceivable that one of his fellow bikers could have been so uncool as to sabotage his bike just for the sake of competition.

Celeste was extremely upset when she came in Monday morning and heard that Eric was in traction. But when she heard the reason, she was furious. Eric was already behind in his work, and she felt the pressure of the March grant deadline acutely. She was annoyed with herself for putting someone so unreliable in the position of producing material that other members of the lab needed. But at the time, his was the only pair of free hands to get the project off the ground. It wasn't like she was tenured and had the luxury of being able to miss a grant renewal deadline. She wondered if and how the necessary work would get done to make the grant application as strong as it needed to be.

Being the principal investigator of a laboratory has certain responsibilities that seem almost parental in nature. Perhaps that's why it took Celeste a whole day to simmer down sufficiently before she could entertain the idea of paying Eric a civil visit. What finally pushed her into the realm of tolerance was a rather disturbing realization. Before her trip to Florida, Celeste still harbored a suspicion that Eric might have been responsible for smearing blood on her office door. But, in confronting why she was so irritated with him Celeste became aware that there were other more likely culprits, ones who signed their handiwork with the letter V. The defacement could have been a warning or even a threat. But why had this intimidation occurred even before she was summoned by Minot? Had someone else been aware of her impending recruitment?

Thoughts of Minot got Celeste fretting further, worrying about the outcome of the meeting between Kazuko and "the man in Japan." She hoped that Kazuko had been treated with the courtesy and the respect she deserved. Celeste then got to wondering about whether the FBI's problem was possible to solve and whether they were on the right track about the patients. Even if she was able to visit the Taiwanese clinic as a supposed consultant for Fukuda, would she be able to find out enough about patient treatment protocols to determine whether they were being used to transmit messages in some way? Celeste couldn't imagine that such a treatment could be performed without the patient's knowledge. A patient would notice if something had been implanted and needed to be removed, or at least would ask about it. She recalled a grisly story about a street person in India who woke up in the hospital to discover he had been drugged and that one of his kidneys had been removed for illegal organ transplantation. These thoughts were not particularly productive.

By noon on Tuesday, however, Celeste had calmed down. She had visited Eric first thing in the morning. When she saw him strung up in the white hospital bed, looking doubly vulnerable with his shaven head uncovered, she realized that he was just a kid away from his real parents and should be considered as such. Letting him annoy her was a waste of energy. Tuesday morning Celeste also received a formal fax from Fukuda Pharmaceuticals asking her to renew her consultancy agreement. They needed some advice on a product they were testing in Taipei. If she was agreeable, they would send her tickets to join them at the testing clinic the following week. Celeste had faxed back that she was agreeable.

So by Wednesday morning, when Stash phoned, Celeste was beginning to feel that for the first time in months, her personal life had something going for it. Being a scientist made it easy to be unsociable because running a lab was so energy intensive. Even though Celeste hardly worked at the bench herself these days, she spent a lot of time supervising the research projects of her graduate students and postdoctoral fellows. That is, when she wasn't writing grant proposals or teaching classes. These pursuits were sufficiently varied that Celeste was never bored. But her professional life had taken on a relentless quality such that, whenever one task was finished, several more materialized to co-opt her attention. A personal life would have provided some perspective. It used to be that attending a conference was a welcome break from the academic routine. But lately even conferences had been empty experiences for Celeste. Thus the prospect of a weekend date, on top of seeing Kazuko again, and the FBI recruitment, gave Celeste's spirits a badly needed boost. Celeste arranged to pick up Stash at his hotel first thing Saturday morning and said she would pack a picnic lunch. Stash agreed but only if she promised to let him treat her to dinner in Point Reyes Station at the end of the day. He seemed to be looking forward to the encounter as much as she.

Stash stood waiting for Celeste at the hotel entrance with a canvas bag bulging with photography equipment. His slicked-back hair was hidden under a corduroy visored cap. A few curly strands protruded from the cap at the back, giving him an almost boyish look. Celeste noticed that he had a pleasant smile when he was relaxed, and he certainly looked relaxed. When Celeste pulled up, his smile turned into a big grin.

"How did I guess you would drive a convertible?" he asked with evident delight. "Good thing I brought my leather jacket." He swung his canvas bag into the little space behind the two seats and put on the jacket that he was holding. He opened the passenger door to get in beside Celeste but hesitated a moment. Celeste was wearing dark glasses and a black wool beret over her hair, which was compacted into a French braid turned under at the back. Her gold-colored suede jacket complemented the British racing green of the MGB.

"I just can't resist," said Stash. "The colors are too good." He fished around in the canvas bag and pulled out his camera. With all the moves of a professional fashion photographer, he backed up and took a few angled shots of Celeste sitting in her car, calling out to her to tilt her head a little this way and that. The effect on Celeste was extraordinary. Normally she hated being photographed but his appreciation of the image as a whole was so enthusiastic that she forgot to be self-conscious. Besides, she loved her little car and was well-disposed toward anyone who also responded to it.

"Great start," said Stash as he tucked the camera back in the bag and got in the car. "This looks like it must have been one of the last MGB's, about when, late seventies?"

"Nineteen-seventy-eight," said Celeste. "I call it the wombat. Used to be owned by an Australian friend, and it does sort of snuffle along the ground."

Stash nodded in appreciation as they set off through the looming, cool shadows of the deserted high rises in the financial district. Out on the Embarcadero the Saturday morning tourist trade was just getting under way. The wombat sailed past the lines forming at the ticket window for tour boats to Alcatraz, past the converted brick factories of Ghiradelli Square, and down Lombard Street through Cow Hollow to the Golden Gate Bridge. The bridge was defiantly red against the clear blue sky. The red color had originally been meant as an undercoat but was then retained for the top coat as well when the engineers saw the effect at sunset. This made Celeste think of the bridge as boldly exposing its underwear, a suitable icon for San Francisco.

Celeste and Stash ambled up Route 1 towards the Point Reyes National Park. The tide was out, revealing heaps of harbor seals and flocks of waterfowl in the wetlands north of Stinson Beach. Stash was in his element, photographing herons and curlews through a telescopic camera lense, which he mounted on a tripod whenever they stopped. Celeste was just as happy taking a census of the different species through her binoculars. There was such change throughout the year that it was always a treat to see what was around. They shared the voyeuristic experience of spying on nature and the fleeting sense of acquisition derived from capturing things on film or in binoculars.

Stash and Celeste spoke very little as they continued up the coast, each sensing in the other a temporary soul mate. After picking up a trail map in the national park headquarters, they decided on a short walk that led to rocky outcroppings hanging over the sea. Stash thought that the formations would provide some of the atmosphere he was looking for to produce the "perfect portrait" of Celeste.

"I don't know about this," said Celeste. "I'm not very photogenic because I don't like posing."

"The last thing I want is a posed portrait," said Stash. "I brought some wine for the picnic. That should help. You did bring a picnic, didn't you?"

"I said I would," said Celeste.

"Good, because I made a reservation for dinner."

Indeed, a half bottle of light, dry Pinot Noir along with the paté, cheese, and crusty French bread that Celeste had brought had a very soothing effect. They ate their picnic on one of the larger outcroppings and lay out comfortably in the sun afterwards on the smooth, warm rock surface. The rocks were completely sheltered from the view of hikers on the path above, but even if they had been visible, Celeste and Stash had encountered no other hikers progressing in either direction. It was a private and beautiful spot.

"Okay. You can take your clothes off now," said Stash, very matter of factly.

Celeste opened her eyes and saw that he was sitting up, holding his camera and inspecting her quite seriously. Somehow prissiness didn't seem appropriate in this situation, which appeared to be an aesthetic one. Celeste was also a little bit drunk, which gave her the courage not to think about it.

"All right," she said. She reached up under the back of her sweater and unhooked her bra. Then in one move she drew her sweater, long-sleeved T-shirt, and bra over her head. Before she had time to free her hands, Stash said, "Don't move," and he clicked several shots. "Now, toss me the tops and lean back a little onto the rock." Click, click. "Now get on your knees and face the ocean, unzip your jeans and slip them down around your knees. Now look over your shoulder back at me." More rapid clicking. He continued to issue instructions quite quickly, not giving Celeste time to think about posing. When she was completely nude, he had her sit in profile leaning with her elbows on her upright knees looking out to sea.

"Brilliant," said Stash. "Absolutely beautiful." He handed Celeste her clothes. "Now put these back on before you catch cold." She looked at him quizzically, surprised and somewhat disappointed that this situation was not going to develop further. She had felt caressed by his photography and quite aroused.

While she put on her clothes, Stash packed away the remains of the picnic lunch and his camera. He stood and held out his hand to help Celeste up. She took it, feeling a charge from his touch.

"Shall we walk out to the lighthouse to see the sun set?" asked Stash.

"Mmm," agreed Celeste. She was happy to stretch the day out as long as possible.

Later they sat opposite each other at a table in the bar section of the Point Reyes Station Café, drinking slightly sweet beer from the local microbrewery. The old-fashioned saloon was hopping with locals, who greeted one another loudly and caught up on gossip. The restaurant was clearly the center of this prospering agricultural community and, although it had a reputation among San Francisco restaurant goers, there was no friendly encouragement of outside patronage. Stash and Celeste were oblivious to this attitude however and appreciated being indoors, out of the buffeting wind that had left their cheeks tingling.

Celeste was curious to know what Stash was up to. It had been a magical day. They were so comfortable together, it seemed they had known each other for years. Celeste felt that Stash felt it, too. Celeste wanted more, but in some ways she didn't want it to start so she wouldn't be disappointed in the end. "Tell me more about your wife," she said in an effort to protect herself.

Stash smiled. "It's kind of a long story, but I don't mind boring you with it if you really want to hear it," he said. Celeste nodded encouragement so he continued. "Being in the business is sort of like having family obligations. After I got my doctorate, I signed on full time instead of doing a postdoctoral fellowship. I didn't let myself get involved with anyone during college and graduate school, partly because I didn't want to be tied down and partly because I was already working for the company in my spare time. Then it was too late to settle down with someone because they kept me moving around. Almost everything I did was under cover so I never had a chance to be any one person for long. I think I would have lost my sense of self entirely if I hadn't had my photography to keep me sane during that period. That personal blackout lasted for almost fifteen years. Then, as the cold war wound down, my job slowed and they settled me in the D.C. area.''

So far, Stash hadn't told Celeste much more than she knew or could guess already from their conversation in Virginia. She must have looked a little impatient because he said, ''Are you sure you want to hear this? How 'bout a glass of wine instead?''

''How about a bottle of wine and some of their famous oyster stew, along with the rest of the story?'' suggested Celeste. Maybe Stash would loosen up like she had earlier that afternoon and do the equivalent of taking off his clothes.

''Sounds good to me,'' said Stash. He waved over the waiter and ordered a bottle of the local chardonnay recommended on the blackboard over the bar and two bowls of stew. Then he carried on. ''Stuck in D.C., I went through a serious crisis. I was forty and had no companion to share things with and had lost the excitement of my job, which had been everything to me. What stabilized me was meeting Jill, who was more of a lost soul than I was. She was the 'bad girl' of the D.C. society set. The only way I can think to describe her is that she seemed to be the female incarnation of the Stranger, from the book by Camus. Have you read it?''

Celeste was amazed that Stash should mention this. ''Not only have I read it, but that book has been haunting me lately,'' said Celeste. This was surely another sign that they were on the same wavelength. ''The Stranger disturbed me a lot when I first read the book in high school French class,'' she told Stash. ''Until recently though, I never found the character very believable. I just couldn't understand his amorality and disinterest in the events of his life. But recently it occurred to me that the Stranger could be a stereotype for the students in Generation X. They want to be engaged but can't make themselves see the point. So they can't make a commitment to anything. They'll do what's expected, but there's no internal drive there."

It was Stash's turn to feel Celeste was uncannily tuned to his thoughts. "You know exactly what I'm talking about," he said with complete sympathy. "So this young woman, ten years younger than I am, starts talking to me at some boring fund-raiser and, I think to shock me, she tells me she's pregnant from an affair she'd had with a married man, which broke up. She also tells me that she can't see the point of getting an abortion, though that's what all the matrons are counseling her to do. It's not because she thinks it's wrong, it's just that she can't be bothered to resist what life has thrown in her path. As you might expect, she made a huge impression on me. The end result was that I took her under my wing, which may have been my way of finding a new purpose for my life. Anyway, it was a wonderful thing for both of us. We became almost like a normal couple expecting their first baby and decided to get married."

Stash drained his last gulp of beer, before continuing. He looked distressed. "Then, in the final two months of her pregnancy, Jill shut me out. It was like the baby had taken my place. She refused to come to my house at the conference center anymore and took the house in Georgetown off the market."

Celeste was touched that Stash had been such an innocent about his wife, and she felt sorry for him. "Once she gets used to the baby she'll come round," said Celeste. "It's a pretty classic behavior pattern."

"That's what I'm told," said Stash. "But it's made

me feel so alone. Now, I'm not sure I ever really connected with Jill. I look such a fool to myself.''

Celeste was moved to put her hand on his, lying on the table. Stash turned his hand over and clasped hers in return.

They were interrupted by the arrival of the wine and their oyster stew, which turned out to deserve every bit of its reputation. As they ate, they returned to discussing existentialist attitudes. Stash seemed particularly interested in the Generation X students that Celeste had mentioned. Then she told him the story of Eric and his knee-jerk morality, which was almost worse than being amoral.

''The annoying thing is that the one student who apparently has principles has completely misplaced priorities. For him, mountain biking unquestionably takes precedence over lab work.'' Then she added, ''Poor kid. Once he's spent the next few months in traction maybe that will change.''

''So what happened to him? Biking accident?'' asked Stash. Celeste was a little taken aback by the sarcastic tone in Stash's question, even though she presumed he was trying to be sympathetic to her case.

''No kidding. He would have been run over and killed if he'd landed any closer to the rest of the bike pack.''

''Oh, that's a shame,'' said Stash, as he poured more chardonnay into their glasses. ''But, enough about students. Where do professors stand on conventional morality? For example, what would you say if I told you I had reserved a hotel room nearby?''

The next morning Celeste was awakened by the sun streaming onto the pillow of the four-poster bed, which was constructed from rough-hewn logs. It was a cosy, woodsy room. The pillows were covered in checkered flannel, making Celeste feel like she had slept in a pile of lumberjack's clothes. Stash was still naked and squatting by the fire place, trying to ignite a morning fire.

She tiptoed quietly behind him, heading for the bathroom. Without looking around, he said, "Oh, well, I was hoping to have this blazing before you woke up."

"Never mind," said Celeste. "I'll be right back and you can pretend I just woke up." In the bathroom she saw a new tootbrush laid out for her. Was there anything this guy hadn't planned?

She stopped thinking about it though when she came back out into the room and Stash, still prodding the fire, turned around and caught her on her way back to bed. He drew her down next to him by the fire.

There was a simultaneous sense of respect and desperation in Stash's lovemaking that astonished Celeste. He seemed to know her body well, wanting and waiting for her to respond, enjoying her pleasure. But when he came, he lost himself completely and cried out in an almost anguished wail of relief, such that Celeste felt her heart pierced along with her body at the loneliness in his cry. Afterwards they lay in front of the fire, separated, breathing hard. Stash then touched Celeste's arm, almost politely like he was waking up a stranger who had been sleeping next to him on a train. "We should probably get moving," he said.

In the dining room over breakfast, they reverted to a formal interaction that was curiously detached from the passion of the bedroom. Any overt acknowledgment of their recent closeness seemed inappropriate, but Celeste could feel it smoldering.

"I'd like to see you again," said Stash. "And, of course," he said eagerly, "you'll want to see the photographs. I can't wait to see them myself. I should finish the developing and printing by the middle of next week and could even bring them myself to show you next weekend.''

Without thinking Celeste said, "I'll be in Taiwan next weekend.''

"Oh?'' said Stash.

Celeste was instantly annoyed with herself. At least Stash was someone who would respect her privacy, but she would have to make an effort to be more careful about revealing her plans. She had fantasized that he might be a useful confidante, though she should be more reserved until they knew each other better. "I've resumed some consultancy duties with my colleagues in the Japanese pharmaceutical industry. They have a project they want me to check out in Taipei.''

"When do you leave?'' asked Stash.

"On Monday,'' said Celeste.

"Maybe I could come out again when you get back?''

Celeste figured out the dates. "I'll probably return through Japan, and that brings us to the second weekend of October. I've got a friend from back East visiting that weekend. He's coming with a new girlfriend he wants me to meet.'' She paused, thinking also that she needed some time to decide whether pursuing this thing with Stash was a good idea. The intense power of it seemed to ask for trouble, but she didn't see how she would be able to resist. "I'll give you a call when I get back from Japan and we can take it from there.''

"Fine. You do that,'' he said, rising. "Well, it's time to get back to the city. I've got a plane to catch.''

7

Chinese Coiffeur

In the heart of Taipei, in the private dining room of the Hong family restaurant, Sunny Hong dropped a salted, dried plum into a ceremonial glass of rice wine and handed it to his distinguished visitor. His two henchmen did likewise and handed glasses to their counterparts. The six men had just finished the last course of their banquet, birds' nest soup. The three guests were trying hard not to think about the fact that they had been consuming reconstituted bird saliva. Mentally, they tried to cleanse their palates by imagining the flavor of some favorite Siciliano specialty like "horse's head" cheese, which had the reputation of being able to walk about on its own.

The climate for the Chinese underworld had never been better, and Sunny made a special toast to his special guests. He wanted them to know that he foresaw a long and fruitful collaboration between their respective families. Then, superstitiously, Sunny toasted the struggling Taiwanese president. After all, if their leader hadn't been so anxious to protect his fragile position as Taiwan's first democratically-elected president, he would be more assiduous about enforcing law and order. And that was the last thing the Hong family and their colleagues wanted. The government was willing only to issue formal apologies for the multitude of unsolved crimes that were being cited as evidence of their powerlessness. While this remained the case, the Hong family had free rein.

Sunny's distinguished guest signaled to his younger companions and they helped him rise to reply to the toast. He too was gratified that their business connection had been so successful and thanked Sunny for hosting this visit. He expected that his errand here in Taipei would be peaceful. But he hoped that if it wasn't he could call on Sunny for help. Sunny assured him that all the resources of the Hong family were at his disposal. The Italians left shortly thereafter, anxious to make contact with the fourth member of their family who was due to arrive momentarily at the Grand Hotel.

The Grand Hotel was part of the legacy of Madame Chiang Kai-shek to the people of Taiwan. Its sheer size was extravagant, but its opulence on top of that made it a monument to her self-indulgence. As the taxi approached the city from the airport, Sandra Lovett could see the hotel in its red and green splendor, situated majestically at the foot of the hills that constituted the wealthy residential neighborhoods of the city of Taipei. She pointed it out to Buffy.

"Wow," said Buffy. "It looks like a palace. Do we get to stay there?"

"You'll stay there tonight and then, of course, you'll be in the clinic for the next few days. The rooms aren't quite as luxurious as the exterior promises. It was built more as a showpiece than to provide comfortable accommodation. You know, one of the projects of Madame Chiang Kai-shek, to demonstrate her power."

Buffy didn't know, since she had never heard of Madame Chiang Kai-shek.

It was about 5 P.M. when they checked in and Sandra instructed Buffy to have a two-hour nap, no shorter, no longer. It was important for the treatments to get her diurnal schedule adjusted as soon as possible. Sandra had arranged for them to take a driving tour of the city in the early evening and to have supper near the night market where, afterwards, they could see the infamous skinning of live snakes, in ''reptile row.''

Sandra didn't normally accompany her patients to the Taipei clinic, but she had been unable to refuse the command to attend an ad hoc family reunion. At least the trip provided a good opportunity to confirm arrangements at the clinic. She checked into her own room and was welcomed by an elaborate basket of fruit sitting on the dresser. The card read, ''With compliments from your uncle. Room 853.'' Sandra sat down on the bed and asked the switchboard to connect her.

When the phone in room 853 was picked up, she said, ''Thanks for the fruit.''

''Alessandra,'' hissed her uncle. ''What a pleasure. Shall we have tea?''

''Isn't that a bit risky?'' asked Sandra.

''Don't be silly, *cara mia*. You will be our guest in the suite,'' he said.

The decor of the suite contradicted what Sandra had told Buffy about the lack of luxury in the rooms. Sandra's cousins were each seated on the edges of low, stuffed footstools upholstered in green and gold brocade. The bluish pallor of their faces from chronic five o'clock shadow and the steely fabric of their suits clashed with the rich, yellow-ochre hues of the room. The awkward semi-squat into which they were forced by their seats made them look like flies that had landed on pieces of overripe fruit. Sandra's uncle was holding court from a divan littered with silken pillows. He was not looking well. A formerly handsome man, he had shrunken into a caricature of a Mafia don, with sunken grey cheeks and thick glasses with grey-tinted lenses and heavy black frames. It amused Sandra to see how out of place three stiffly-suited Italian thugs looked in the midst of oriental splendor, making it easier to tolerate her servitude and take up her expected role pouring the tea.

"Now," said Sandra's uncle, "you have a little problem with your clinic. It would not be nice if it got worse."

"What problem is that?" asked Sandra defensively. Were they going to tell her off for double-dipping?

"You seem to have attracted some interest, but we need to be sure. So we take it one step at a time. There is another American lady doctor, traveling with a Japanese businesswoman. They are visiting the clinic here that you are using. We think you will recognize the American."

"Ah," said Sandra. "This must be the Dr. Braun whom Luigi warned me about. The one who was in Puerto Rico and found your calling card, so to speak."

"Bravo, *cara,*" said her uncle, with heavy sarcasm. "Your information is excellent. I must remind you, however, that we had to leave that card because the clinic security was not what it should have been. We do not want this to happen again. We need to know why this Dr. Braun is now here. It is too much of a coincidence."

"I'll keep my ears open," said Sandra. "But you know it's not my clinic. I just rent beds there and get the same treatment as their other clients, privacy but no privilege."

"We know, *cara.* But we have confidence in your discretion." These last words were hissed so emphatically in his strong Italian accent that Sandra suspected her uncle of choosing words just for the sound effect. No doubt she would get vicarious satisfaction out of seeing the snakes skinned alive that evening.

"If this is just surveillance, what is the cleanup crew doing here?" asked Sandra, gesturing towards her thuggish cousins.

"Just enough to discourage Dr. Braun from further visits," said the serpent.

"I'll be in touch," said Sandra and let herself out.

"La Principessa di Ghiaccio," said one of the cousins, and made a shivering sound.

"Hey! You show respect to your cousin."

"Sorry, boss."

"Now boys," said Sandra's uncle. "I trusted you on this because you said the source was good, someone with an interest in Alessandra's business. But if I find we are wasting our time . . ."

"You won't boss."

The following morning Kazuko arrived at Taipei International Airport on the early flight from Osaka, where she had been visiting Fukuda's national headquarters. She took a taxi to the clinic. Celeste decided to walk to the clinic from the Grand Hotel, where she had gone to bed immediately after arriving in the early evening from San Francisco. She had, of course, then awakened very early from jet lag so the long walk was a way of filling in the time before their appointment at the clinic.

Celeste's progress through the streets of Taipei was slow. There had been no royal decree specifying the layout as she had so conveniently encountered in San Juan, Puerto Rico. Celeste had to check the map they had given her at the hotel desk at almost every corner. However, Celeste noted that her progress was not any slower than that of the vehicles caught up in traffic. The streets were clogged with bumper to bumper cars in every direction. It was more like a mobile parking lot than a transportation system.

The clinic was on the opposite side of a park, presided over by the National Museum of Taiwan, from where Celeste now stood. The sandstone museum was on a hill in the center of the park, proudly elevated above the crawling, hooting traffic; a casket housing the most precious objects of Chinese civilization. The building glowed like the Holy Grail and held a treasure that would someday be restored to its rightful place on the mainland. But, Celeste was well aware that if the Nationalist Chinese hadn't absconded with these treasures, almost no relics of Chinese civilization would have survived the so-called cultural revolution. The building was a testimony to greed, but also to some of the finest works of art of human civilization and to the cultural sensibilities of the Chinese Nationalists. Celeste was very much looking forward to seeing the collection when her business was completed.

Celeste's contemplation of the building was broken by a taxi honking wildly behind her and then hearing her name called out. She turned to see Kazuko waving at her through the taxi window. Kazuko opened the door and jumped out. The two women embraced warmly.

"I know this place," said Kazuko. "We can walk through the park garden and find the clinic on the other side. I will send the taxi to the Grand Hotel with my bag."

The serenity that Celeste had found in Japan and which was embodied in Kazuko accompanied them through the splendid Chinese garden below the museum. They made an unusual pair, talking, laughing, and exchanging news as they headed toward the clinic. Celeste was tall and lanky and looking like Virginia Woolf in her white T-shirt, striped vest, and long, narrow, navy-blue linen skirt. Her companion was delicate and diminutive in a perfect, cream, silk, Japanese businesswoman's suit. The morning was still cool and pleasant though the sun, already high in the sky, warned of the inevitable heat of day.

They did not speak directly about why they were really there. Kazuko filled Celeste in on some details about the Fukuda product that would be tested in the clinic. She also filled her in on the background of the clinic director, Dr. Nan Shin. Women in Taiwanese science constituted an extremely powerful and tight network and played a dominant role, in strong contrast with the situation in Japan and, to a lesser degree, with that in America. This was largely due to the fact that the scientific careers of Taiwanese men were interupted by military service, while the women in science could train abroad sooner and progress more rapidly upon returning home.

When Kazuko introduced Celeste to Nan Shin, Celeste noted the differences between the two cultures immediately. In fact, Nan Shin's no-nonsense, nonapologetic manner was something that Celeste rarely saw in American professional women either, probably because the majority of their colleagues were still men. Nan Shin had trained in the seventies, at the Dana Farber Cancer Institute in Boston with one of the leading specialists in treatment of lung cancer. It was a significant cause of death all over Asia, where anti-smoking campaigns had never managed to get off the ground. Half of Nan Shin's clinic in Taipei was devoted to testing new treatments for this particularly insidious form of cancer. When Celeste learned this, she immediately thought of her great-aunt Audrey and wondered if there was anything going on in Taipei that might be relevant to her illness. Celeste was convinced that her condition must be least precancerous, if not full blown malignant. Not surprisingly, she had been unable to extract any further information from Audrey regarding her doctor's report, and Celeste was worrying on speculation, but fairly reliable speculation.

As soon as they arrived, Nan Shin led her guests to her office to discuss their business. She mentioned that she was expecting another visiting American later in the morning and that she had arranged for them all to have lunch together at a restaurant down by the lake in the park near the museum. Nan Shin promised Celeste a tour of the whole clinic facility before lunch.

Nan Shin's office was like that of any senior physician in the U.S. The bookshelves were lined with medical texts and journals and a large wooden desk dominated one end of the room. The only unusual feature was a ferocious-looking curved dagger in an opulent scabbard mounted on the wall behind Nan Shin's desk. When Celeste admired the dagger, Nan Shin said with a laugh, "In Taiwan, there is no such thing as sexual harassment."

Kazuko and Nan Shin discussed the possibility of arranging a trial for one of Fukuda's anti-cancer products that was under development. Celeste was impressed that Kazuko had cooked up this legitimate and even potentially useful collaborative venture between Fukuda and Nan Shin's clinic, providing a perfect cover for their visit. In Japan, Fukuda had only been able to test their new drug on patients whose condition had already progressed beyond the point of cure, and the treatment clearly delayed the onset of terminal illness. In Taipei, they hoped to test a population of patients with a more recent diagnosis and hopefully less progression of illness to see if it could cause remission. The Fukuda product that was being tested at the clinic was a cell growth inhibitor. It was developed from an extract produced from sea cucumbers that was used topically in Chinese herbal medicine to stop cancerous skin growths. The Fukuda chemists had figured out how to make the active compound synthetically, and it was being tested for its effect on growth of cancerous cells in the lung when delivered by inhalation. There was some discussion about whether it might also be useful as an anti-viral agent to inhibit growth and spread of certain types of virus. This is where Celeste's advice was ostensibly needed. They discussed what tests might be done to investigate this possibility.

"We have very sophisticated blood analysis labs here," said Nan Shin. "We could easily analyze infected patients for the level of different antibodies against virus to see if the drug affects the immune response to the virus. We could also measure the virus load in the blood by polymerase chain reaction." Nan Shin's clinic clearly boasted techniques that were state of the art. "The blood lab is used heavily by some of our other contract work, but I'm pretty sure it's not at capacity at the moment," Nan Shin added.

"What other contract work do you do?" asked Celeste.

"Well, half of our work here is contract work, either clinical trials or just renting out beds and use of the lab facility. And like the work for Fukuda, we keep the nature of the contracts confidential. In fact, we don't even know all of what goes on here. For example, Dr. Lovett, the woman you'll meet at lunch, hires a local freelance medical technician to do all the treatment and analysis here using our facilities. Apparently at home, she doesn't have access to some of the medications that we use here on a routine basis."

"The name Lovett sounds familiar," said Celeste quite honestly. Indeed it rang a bell, but she couldn't place it. "Doesn't she have connections with a clinic in Puerto Rico?" Worth a try, thought Celeste.

"Yes," said Nan Shin thinking for a moment. "I believe you're right. Apparently some of her patients come from Puerto Rico for their second treatment or go there for the third one. The staff at her office in Washington sometimes calls to make bookings. They get confused about where they're calling and what time it is here. It happens I've answered a few of those calls myself very early in the morning, or late at night depending on how you consider it.'' Nan Shin rose. ''Are you ready for the grand tour?''

The clinic facilities were impressive and well-equipped. There was obviously no shortage of funds. The clinic building had an internal atrium with a large skylight. The physicians' offices and administration were on the ground floor, the patients' private bedrooms and treatment rooms were on the second floor, and the laboratories were on the third floor. Corridors on the second and third floors ran around the inside of the atrium. On the second floor the corridor was open around the atrium and hanging plants trailed over the balcony railings, giving the atrium a pleasant, gardenlike aspect. A grand, pink-marble staircase extended from the center of the atrium up to the second floor balcony. Nan Shin told them that the marble came from the jade mining region near HuaLien, on the east coast of Taiwan. The corridor on the third floor was closed off from the atrium by a one-way mirror. The bright mirrored glass reflected some of the light from the skylight, making the atrium seem more open than it was.

They finished their tour with an inspection of the laboratories. The blood analysis lab made Celeste's lab at BAU look like a dumping ground for old equipment. As they came out into the third floor corridor, Nan Shin, Kazuko, and Celeste looked down through the one-way mirror into the atrium, where a receptionist was completing the paperwork to check in Buffy. Sandra Lovett stood by Buffy's side and Celeste recognized her immediately. They had even had a conversation at one of the conference cocktail parties in Puerto Rico, so Celeste knew that she too would be recognized. Her heart rate doubled. Lovett could be the connection between Puerto Rico and Taipei that the FBI were looking for.

Celeste knew she would have to get out of there unseen by Dr. Lovett, and she certainly couldn't participate in the planned luncheon. She barely heard the rest of what Nan Shin was saying about the clinic as she watched the receptionist hit the bell on her desk. An orderly in whites came down the staircase from the second floor to escort Lovett and presumably her patient upstairs. While the patient was being settled in her accommodation, Celeste would have an opportunity to escape. She doubled over and groaned as though struck by a stomach cramp.

"Celeste, what is it?" asked Kazuko.

"I don't know," Celeste said with as much alarm as she could muster. "I feel really weird. It must have been something I ate on the flight over. I'm gonna have to lie down."

"I'm sure there must be a free patient bed on the second floor," said Nan Shin and walked over to a phone hanging on the wall to call downstairs. Celeste held her breath as she saw the receptionist pick up. A second later the receptionist shook her head in response to Nan Shin's request. The clinic beds were completely full, she had just assigned the last one. Celeste breathed again.

"I'll have the clinic ambulance drive you back to the Grand Hotel," said Nan Shin. "One of our physicians can look you over on the way."

"I'm sure I'll be fine," said Celeste, hoping that her bluff wouldn't be called. "It's probably mostly jet lag anyway."

"Okay," said Nan Shin. "Whatever you please. Too

bad you'll miss lunch at the Swan Lodge. But I would rather you rested today to be well for the museum tomorrow.''

''Me, too,'' said Celeste. She would have to get Kazuko to find out whether Dr. Lovett was going to be included in the museum tour and discourage it if necessary.

Nan Shin called for an orderly to accompany Celeste down to the ambulance dock, and Kazuko went with her to see her off safely and to have a quick private word with her. The orderly took them via the freight elevator, and they stepped out to face a stack of yellow-painted metal barrels with Chinese characters and the English word DANGER! written on them in red. Celeste recognized the international symbol for organic chemical waste pasted on the barrels. Something about it struck her as odd, but she had to shelve her thoughts on this while trying to discreetly communicate her concerns about Lovett to Kazuko. Having seen Celeste strapped into the back of the ambulance, Kazuko returned with the orderly to Nan Shin's office. She would attend the luncheon and find out what she could about Lovett's plans.

Celeste then had the fastest ride through the streets of Taipei that she would undoubtedly ever experience. Lying in the ambulance, Celeste mulled over what she had learned at the clinic. She had confirmed that patients were trafficked between San Juan and Taipei in both directions. The link appeared to be through Lovett and her clinic, which was located in Washington. On site, Lovett made use of the clinic laboratory and local technicians. If her patients were carrying information, it could easily be funneled out of the clinic.

But the mystery remained as to how the information could be carried by patients. Celeste hadn't learned much about patient treatment except that Lovett's technician made extensive use of the blood analysis laboratory. The laboratories were exceedingly well-appointed, reminiscent of the finest research laboratories in the U.S. Celeste then considered the waste barrels on the ambulance dock. They held a kind of waste that was the byproduct of research activities involving chemical synthesis, as opposed to clinical treatment. Celeste's recent argument with her student Eric about the necessity of generating organic chemical waste in the course of their work had heightened her sensitivity to this issue. But Nan Shin hadn't mentioned an active research program at the clinic, which suggested to Celeste that some of the treatment protocols might require on-the-spot chemical synthesis. Maybe patients were being injected with chemicals that could then be found in their blood or secretions as some kind of message. But this sounded biologically impossible to Celeste since such compounds would likely be toxic if injected in doses that could be detected by standard analytical methods.

Somehow, she would have to learn what Lovett's treatments involved and what kinds of tests were done. Apparently the clinic in Taipei had no records of that, only of the hours of bed time and lab time rented. Celeste was disappointed in herself. It didn't seem like she'd made much progress, considering the investment the FBI had made in her trip.

Kazuko joined Celeste in her room about four P.M. that afternoon. The lunch had ended over an hour earlier, and Nan Shin insisted on driving Sandra Lovett and Kazuko back to the hotel. The traffic was relentless. Nan Shin was planning to telephone around seven to see if Celeste was feeling any better and whether they wanted to have dinner and go to the night market. She had invited Sandra Lovett as well, but Lovett said she had taken her patient to the market the previous evening. She preferred to have a quiet evening at the hotel since she was leaving first thing in the morning. She did, however, recommend a restaurant near the night market where she and Buffy had eaten an excellent meal. Nan Shin had heard about it and was enthusiastic about trying it. It was believed to be owned by the notorious Hong family, and the food was supposed to be superb.

"Sounds like I should be feeling well enough to go out this evening, then," said Celeste in response to Kazuko's report.

As Kazuko was reporting to Celeste, the phone in the eighth-floor suite rang. "Yes," hissed the occupant.

"I had lunch with the Japanese woman but the American was suffering from jet lag and went back to the hotel so I didn't get to speak to her directly. All I could find out was that they are both here working for Fukuda Pharmaceuticals, starting a drug trial," reported Sandra.

"This is not very satisfactory," said her uncle.

"Give me a chance to finish," said Sandra, annoyed. "They're planning to go out tonight, to see the night market, and I recommended Hong's place. I passed on Hong's card, which I picked up last night. I would think you might be able to get some more information from Hong's private dining room." The one-way mirror business had always thrived in the Far East and was now equaled by the wide availability of surveillance devices.

"*Cara mia*, I will make a reservation for our little family reunion."

Celeste, Kazuko, and Nan Shin continued their discussion of the Fukuda trials over dinner and then moved on to cultural issues. They soon discovered that none of them had any desire to see the skinning of the snakes. Nan Shin said that there was a recent, widely-supported campaign to ban the practice as inhumane. Drinking the

fresh snake blood was traditionally meant to impart vi-
rility and, of course, no one believed that any more. The
main argument for continuing the trade on reptile row
was to pander to bloodthirsty tourists. However, the
night market itself was another matter. It was still very
much a part of Taiwanese life, Nan Shin said, and very
much worth seeing. These markets thrived because it
was so unbearably hot during the day for most of the
year. The business of selling fresh vegetables and fruit
and bargaining over merchandise was tolerable only after the sun went down and the city had time to cool off.
Nan Shin loved the market and loved to show it off. As
they stood up to leave for an exploration of the night
markets, sans snakes, they discussed their plans to visit
the National Museum in the morning. In addition, they
all enthusiastically agreed that Dr. Lovett's recommendation of restaurants had been excellent.

Dr. Lovett's family also agreed. Though they had no
further evidence that the clinic visitors were anything
but legitimate, they decided to pursue prophylactic
measures. And the cousins had managed to get a good
look at their prey through the mirror in the adjacent
dining room, so why waste an opportunity? There was
an unusually warm familial feeling between Sandra
and her relatives at the end of the evening.

The night market impressed both Celeste and Kazuko
with its novelty. It was, in fact, no different from a daytime market with stall after stall of fresh fish and vegetables, and stall after stall of household goods, touristy
junk, and cheap plastic toys. However, because the market was taking place in the dark, it had a magical, car-
nival air created by the strings of colored lights hanging
from the poles between stands as well as the eery, bluish,
fluorescent lights emanating from the more permanent

fish and meat vendors. Kazuko was particularly taken with the atmosphere's dramatic contrast to the sterility of a typical Japanese market. Celeste, though fascinated, felt she was biding her time until her anticipated Taipei highlight, the visit to the National Museum.

Celeste was not disappointed by the museum. Not only was it like walking through a treasure chest, but it was well-explicated by the information cards available in several languages at the entrance to each room. The treasures that Celeste particularly loved were not the elaborate, intricately carved jade and ivory ornaments, though they were unquestionably impressive. She preferred the pure, simple forms of the colored ceramic vases whose experimental glazes would never be reproduced. They were like the original genetic stock from which all decorated porcelain would arise. Kazuko and Celeste arrived at the museum at the ten A.M. opening time and within the three-and-a-half hours before they were to meet Nan Shin for lunch, Celeste visited the porcelain room four times. In between, she lingered at the centuries of paintings, in which ferocious battles, kinky sexual practices, the serenity of nature, and philosophical ideas were all equally well-rendered with stylized brush strokes that communicated them perfectly. Celeste noted one illustration of an ancient poem praising ''the fisherman trying to catch a fish, not a reputation.'' These wry sentiments were as apt to twentieth-century science as they were to politics in sixteenth-century China. Celeste could have happily spent another week, or at least the rest of the day, soaking up what the museum had to offer.

With considerable reluctance, she accompanied Kazuko down the huge staircase of the National Museum, past the garden to the busy street in front of Nan Shin's clinic. They waited in a large crowd for the pedestrian light to change since there would never be any letup in the surge of traffic. Celeste was centuries away in aesthetic pleasure and in a cloud of her own thoughts as she was drawn along in the crowd crossing the street.

She was startled out of this reverie by a sudden squeal of rubber tires. She looked up just in time to see a dark blue Mercedes with tinted windows pull out from the rank of cars parked in front of the clinic. It was charging toward the crowd of pedestrians in which Celeste and Kazuko were caught up. At that moment Nan Shin emerged from the door of the clinic and saw the huge car aiming straight for Celeste and Kazuko. Pedestrians were scattering in all directions but it looked to her like those two were the intended target. Nan Shin dashed toward them and pulled them into a tiny alley between the clinic and the next building. The Mercedes stopped at the alley opening, where it could go no farther. Two Chinese men in dark suits and dark wraparound glasses jumped out, one from the passenger door in the front and one from the back seat. They had momentarily lost sight of Celeste and Kazuko in the scattering crowd.

While the men were looking about frantically, Nan Shin shoved Kazuko and Celeste through a glass door in the wall of the building adjacent to the clinic and hustled them to a room in the back. She pulled a curtain behind her to close off the room just as the lights went out. Celeste had barely registered the black basins lining the walls of the room that they had run through, but she could smell the characteristic smell of cut hair and re-alized that they were in a hairdressing salon. Nan Shin had shouted something in Chinese as they had rushed toward the back and immediately all taps had turned off and everyone inside fell quiet.

A loud banging on the glass door followed and no-body in the salon moved. The shouting and banging persisted. Then Celeste heard the door being unbolted and a frail female voice said something crossly in Chinese. She was answered by loud shouting in Chinese, which sounded like cursing. But the sound of the shouting diminished, followed shortly by another squeal of tires. Five minutes later the lights went on and the salon was filled with soft, buzzing conversation.

Celeste and Kazuko stood petrified in the back room and realized that they were holding hands. Nan Shin looked at them and said, "We are safe. Please sit down." They let go of each other and collapsed onto nearby chairs, hearts racing furiously. "I do not want to know," said Nan Shin. "But I did not think your visit was just consulting. However, you have stumbled into another Taiwanese custom. I think we should get our hair washed. After all, we owe Madame Chen some business."

Madame Chen was miniscule and bent almost double. Celeste guessed that she was long past celebration of her eightieth birthday. This tiny, concentrated woman stood looking at Nan Shin and shaking her head. Then she said something in Chinese and smiled, exposing some serious toothless gaps and looking very pleased with herself.

Nan Shin translated. "She says she might change her early closing day to Thursday. It seems to be convenient."

Celeste and Kazuko both smiled gratefully, if a little weakly, at Madame Chen, and she beckoned them out into the salon. Two beauty operators were back at work on two customers as though nothing had happened. One was cutting hair and the other was smearing pearly, steel-colored paste onto her client's head, which Celeste assumed must be a black coloring to cover grey. Three other hairdressers were grouped around one of the basins, talking in low tones and giggling.

"Getting your hair washed is a common way to get refreshed during the hot day here in Taipei," Nan Shin explained. "I have an American shampoo I leave here because I don't like what they usually use. I stock up when I go to conferences in the U.S. You are welcome to use it."

Celeste and Kazuko simultaneously nodded. "Thank you," they said in unison. Nan Shin barked out her instructions in Chinese.

Bidden by one of the giggling hairdressers, Celeste sat down with her back to the basin and leaned back, unpinning her hair from its French braid and dangling it into the sink. She could feel the cold ceramic rim at the base of her neck and the chill penetrated her whole body, which was still in considerable shock. Then she was treated to the most incredible hair-washing experience it was possible to imagine. The hair washing was just an excuse for an intensive scalp, neck, and shoulder massage that penetrated to the core of Celeste's tense body. She could feel the operator attacking the knots that existed in a semipermanent state between her shoulder blades. As her neck relaxed, so did her mind.

This threatening incident was presumably not a coincidence. It appeared that the intent was to scare her off. But on whose toes had she tread? Celeste figured it was likely that Lovett had something to do with it. Even though they had not met directly, Lovett might have recognized her name. That pretty much eliminated her usefulness to the FBI unless she could go undercover somehow. The ideal thing would have been to register as a patient in Lovett's clinic to learn first hand what they were up to, something that Celeste had been toying with in the back of her mind. Given the present circumstances, that would now be impossible.

She heard her beauty operator say something to the room at large. She then heard Nan Shin say, "Celeste, she wants to know if you want your hair blow-dried or to let it dry naturally."

"She might as well dry it," answered Celeste. It was not a remark she would have expected to be exchanging with Taiwan's leading lung cancer specialist, although the circumstances were unusual. At that thought, Celeste's mind turned to Audrey and her secret hoard of medications. If only she could get an expert like Nan Shin to have a look at Audrey. But maybe she could.

Celeste could ask Audrey to go to the clinic as a favor. Audrey would probably only go if she knew the real nature of Celeste's business there and was enlisted as an accomplice. But then if Nan Shin took her on as a patient, she might get some expert help, and Celeste could find out the truth about her condition. In turn, Audrey could find out firsthand about patient treatment at the clinic. No one would suspect a seventy-nine-year-old woman of anything worse than hypochondria. Celeste would have to check out her plan with Jack Minot first, but she had a feeling he would like it.

Laughter in the salon brought Celeste's attention back to her surroundings. She was sitting up now and the hairdresser, giggling, was vigorously grabbing strands of hair with a round brush and holding them out straight in front of the blow-dryer.

Nan Shin was laughing too. "Celeste," she said, "your girl wants to know if you cut your hair yourself."

Celeste saw what was so funny, but was not sure her hairdresser in San Francisco would if she told her about it. The free form cut, which made the best of Celeste's wavy hair, looked to the Chinese beauty operator like a hack job. The young woman was desperately trying to get Celeste's hair to lie as straight and smooth as Nan Shin's and Kazuko's. Celeste hardly recognized herself in the mirror.

8

Southern Belles

Alessandro Valentino was well aware that the coded drug distribution was the key to continued success of his operation. The Taipei–LA connection was too lucrative to abandon completely, so he would have to step up security. In principle, he did not like having to share his niece's services with other clients. Particularly when she thought she was getting away with cheating on the family. On the other hand, at the moment the situation seemed to be mutually beneficial. According to his nephews, another client of hers was also keeping an eye on Sandra's clinical activities to make sure they were not infiltrated. As his nephews snoozed during the flight home from Taipei, amply filling their first-class seats, Sandra's uncle continued to scheme.

It would be sensible to give the LA drug route a short rest while the Taipei site cooled down a little. Valentino didn't want to overstep his welcome with the Hong family, and he certainly didn't want them to start insisting on a piece of the action. The current distribution order, delivered by Sandra's latest patient, should be the last until the new year. Business had been so good that they

could afford a brief suspension of activity, and he knew
that Sandra would use the same route to service another
client. This way, he could double check the security situation at the clinic while his own enterprise was not at
risk. Valentino congratulated himself on his prudent
strategy.

The following week, top-quality South American heroin
was once again showing up on the streets of LA. When
Jack Minot heard the news from his counterpart in the
LA bureau, his heart leapt. He anticipated that maybe
this time he would have a connection and impatiently
awaited Dr. Braun's report.

Celeste was proofreading the report back in her office
at BAU, when the telephone rang. She listened to the
caller's message. As she expected, it was similar to the
three previous messages, which had made her decide
to screen her calls. "Hi, this is Stash calling. I was
hoping you'd be back by now and that everything is
all right."

    As soon as she'd heard his voice Celeste knew that
she wanted to see him again, badly. That in itself was a
problem. And she had too many other problems on her
mind to deal with it rationally. Her date with Stash was
the first time in a long time that she'd fully enjoyed a
man's company. His marital status wouldn't have bothered her so much if their encounter had been a fling, but
it seemed to Celeste that her feelings could be stronger
than those appropriate to a fling.

    She had long since outgrown a fleeting fancy for
country music, but lately she had a regressive desire to
listen to its songs that bemoaned the irony of wanting
someone who was already spoken for. If Celeste were
going to see Stash again, she needed to define the terms
as much for herself as for him.

Celeste also wondered, in passing, what Stash meant when he asked whether everything was all right. There was nothing overtly dangerous about her trip as she had described it to him. Perhaps he had seen too many dangers in the Far East during his CIA days to think of it as a safe place. Or maybe she had conveyed some of her apprehension about the trip to him without being aware that she was doing so. Possibly he was asking whether things were all right between them. As this latter issue was still a matter of debate with her, she concluded that the easiest course of action was to avoid talking with him until some of her other anxieties were sorted out.

Although Celeste was physically all right, the narrow escape in Taipei had made its mark emotionally and acutely sensitized her to the reality of the Mafia. Celeste knew she had been warned off by a threat that, with only the slightest effort on their part, could have become a fait accompli. Now as she finalized her report to Minot, Celeste knew what she wanted to do about the FBI assignment. But it had taken a few days in Japan with Kazuko to make up her mind.

After they had left Taipei, she and Kazuko booked into a spa in Hakone, where Toshimi and his wife joined them for the weekend. It was a peaceful, beautiful spot, and the autumn colors were at their peak with the brilliant reds of the Japanese maples spread like small fires throughout the hillsides. The four of them toured around, enjoying the scenery and consuming autumnal delicacies like gingko tree nuts. Sitting in the fragrant, deep wooden baths at the Hakone spa gave Celeste the opportunity to contemplate her situation. It was there that she made her strategic decisions. First, there was no way she was going to quit the case now, in spite of the efforts to discourage her. But to proceed, she would have to

convince Minot to recruit Audrey and have her attend
Lovett's clinic as a patient.

Celeste did not, however, propose this plan in her
written report. She thought it would be better explained
by telephone after Minot had digested the information
she had picked up on her visit and had come to terms
with the fact that Celeste's cover was apparently blown.
She sealed the report in a Federal Express envelope and
posted it to Minot by the circuitous route that they had
worked out. She knew she would hear from him in a
couple of days.

Once Celeste had dispatched her report she tried to
reach Audrey. It would be useful to make some plans to
get together. But she was informed by Audrey's answering machine that she would be away until Monday
evening. In a follow-up call to Grace, Celeste discovered
that Audrey had gone off on a merchandise buying trip
with the woman who had taken over Audrey's clothing
shop when she'd retired. This left Celeste sitting at her
desk with her future plans unresolved, facing her weekend visit from Harry and his new flame.

Ten minutes late for their rendezvous, Celeste walked
into the lobby of the huge hotel where Harry and
Cammy were staying, near the Moscone Convention
Center. Hotel guests were milling about the fountain in
the middle of the enormous lobby, giving the place the
feel of a shopping mall rather than a hotel. But Celeste
was sure that even in this crowd she should be able to
spot Harry's burly form and bushy red beard. And
though his body was now otherwise engaged, she was
still looking forward to seeing him. What mattered
most was their friendship of almost fifteen years. It
had begun the first day Celeste had joined the laboratory where she'd carried out her doctoral research.
Their occasional bed sharing they considered a con-

venient extension of their intimacy, but not a necessary one.

A slender, clean-shaven man wearing fashionable, wire-rimmed glasses with oval lenses stood in front of Celeste while she scanned the lobby beyond him. Finally, he spoke her name.

"Harry?" she said, focusing on the man in front of her.

"None other," said Harry. At least his bear hug hadn't changed, though he felt less substantial to Celeste's embrace.

"Wow," said Celeste, looking him up and down. He was clean shaven and tidily dressed in a blue blazer and pressed khaki trousers. Underneath his jacket was a teal polo shirt. He must have opened an account at Brooks Brothers.

"All it took was losing fifteen pounds and falling in love and voilà, a new me," said Harry proudly, beckoning to a blond woman lurking shyly by his side. "And this is Dr. Camilla Polson, Cammy to her friends, of which you are automatically one of course. M-theory expert to her colleagues."

Celeste held out her hand and shook Cammy's limp one. Celeste had no idea what M-theory actually was, but she knew that it was the latest mathematical attempt to solve the incompatibility between quantum mechanics and Einstein's theory of relativity.[1]

"Hi," said Cammy softly, extending the word over three syllables. "I'm so pleased to meet you." Her

[1] The mathematician Witten, the guru of the previous theory, called string theory, is quoted as saying, "*M* stands for Magic, Mystery or Membrane, according to taste." From Michael J. Duff. "The Theory Formerly Known as Strings." *Scientific American*, February 1998, pg. 64.

Southern accent was as sweet as Harry had promised.

"The pleasure's mine," said Celeste. "You've got a great guy there."

Cammy blushed prettily and she and Harry exchanged gooey looks. Celeste was embarrassed and wondered if she would be able to stand a whole weekend with them. Luckily they weren't staying with her or she'd spend most of the night picturing, pretty vividly, what they were doing. After all, she knew all of Harry's bedroom moves.

"Cammy's arranged for us to join one of her mathematician friends for dinner tonight at a local restaurant. There'll also be some other guys from the conference who live here. Cammy's friend Jim is based in Indiana, so they don't get much chance to see each other besides these meetings."

"Where are we going?" asked Celeste.

"A place called Bubba's," said Cammy.

"Oh, yeah, I've heard of it." Bubba's was a funky, white-trash themed restaurant in the Castro that served mayonnaise sandwich appetizers, chicken-fried steak, and grits. Celeste doubted that this was the southern cuisine that Cammy had grown up with. But maybe her friends were more down home.

Down-home was not exactly the word to describe the Queer Homeboys' Mathematician Project, or QHMP as they called themselves for short. Celeste, Cammy, and Harry arrived at Bubba's by taxi and found Jim, the math professor from Indiana, already settled with the two local members of QHMP, Roger and Dan. They were drinking large, sweating mugs of Shiner Bock dark beer. Jim looked like the classic image of an engineer with black-framed spectacles, a short-sleeved, white button-down shirt, and rumpled, high-water trousers. Roger was clean-cut and collegiate, and Dan was a bulging, tanned muscle man with a crew cut. He was wearing a black T-shirt with the sleeves ripped off, and stretched across his well-defined chest was an inscription in white letters "dx/dt=0."

After introductions were made, the table fell awkwardly silent. Cammy then said to Harry, "Do y'all know what Dan's shirt means?" And without waiting for an answer, she said, "The rate of change over time equals zero. What is it that you don't want to change?" asked Cammy of Dan.

Celeste, who had sufficient knowledge of calculus and of San Francisco, had already figured it out and wondered how Cammy would react.

"My partner's positive," grunted Dan. "And we don't want him to progress."

"It's the logo for a money-raising campaign we've had for the AIDS hospice," explained Roger, more graciously. "I've got it on my license plate."

"Oh," said Cammy, her eyes round.

"How's the campaign going?" asked Celeste. "I know that one of our faculty, a guy named Brad Firestone, has been really involved in it. The hospice is the one place through which he can legitimately order the alternative medication he's been prescribing."

"Hey, you know Brad?" asked Dan, breaking his macho-man cool. "Good man, good man."

"Yeah, he's a clinical affiliate of the micro department at BAU. He started a really productive project with the HIV research lab. Brad provides new virus isolates and they track the virus variation."

"So what's the latest on HIV vaccine development?" asked Jim.

"Well, it's still a major hurdle," replied Celeste. "The degree of virus variation is so rapid that there's no way to immunize to protect against all the potential variants. It's different from the flu vaccine problem where the variation rate is slow. With flu, as long as the yearly variant is identified, an effective vaccine for that year's epidemic can be produced. But with HIV, variants arise even in one infected individual, so an individual's immune system can't keep up. However, a new strategy looks like it might come out of studying patterns of variation that the virus undergoes in response to combinations of drugs—when it tries to escape from the effects of the drugs. If those patterns are sufficiently predictable, then you could force certain drug-resistant variants to appear by giving the drugs. The immune system might then have a chance to eliminate the variants if you were already immunized with some crippled form of those variants.''

''Immunization is when you give some incapacitated form of virus that won't cause disease in order to boost the immune system, isn't that right?'' asked Cammy in her sweet accent. Celeste wondered if Cammy was trying to compete with her.

''Exactly,'' said Celeste. ''The primary exposure to any microbe, like a bacterium or virus, stimulates an increase in white blood cells that specifically recognize that microbe. This immune system boost will occur even if the bug is inactivated so it can't cause disease. The white blood cells can either make antibodies or kill virus-infected cells. If there's secondary exposure to the real microbe, then the response is quicker and more specific.''

''That's interesting—what you just said about predicting patterns of virus variation,'' said Dan to Celeste. ''Roger's and my mathematical expertise is in simplifying complex patterns. It's the kind of mathematics that Turing developed when he was working on code breaking during the war. It sounds like we should have a crack at predicting HIV variation. I could talk to Brad Firestone about it.'' He then added, with enthusiasm, ''Before you explained about the variation, I never realized

I might be able to help scientifically. I'm really psyched about this.''

"I can also give you the name of my virology colleague who's been analyzing Brad's isolates, if you want to contact him directly,'' Celeste replied. "I'd be happy for you to use my name as an introduction. In fact, I'll mention it to him on Monday if you like.''

"That'd be great,'' said Dan. "Thanks a lot.''

Harry joined in. "I saw that play about Turing, with Derek Jacobi in it, what was it called?''

"Breaking the Code,'' said Dan and Roger, simultaneously.

"Fantastic piece and performance,'' said Harry. "Unbelievable how repressive post-war British society was. That someone could be imprisoned for being gay. Especially someone who had cracked the German code, which everyone knows was the turning point for stopping the air raids on Britain.''

"It's not so different here in the U.S.'' said Jim. "Turing's been kind of an inspiration for us gay mathematicians. The first reunion of the three of us was at this same conference, when it was in New York. We went together to see the play. It was a watershed event when we ran into each other again since Dan, Roger, and I had gone to the same high school in Kentucky. We had this incredible teacher, Guy, who was responsible for all of us getting hooked on math. Later, when Roger and Dan independently wound up in San Francisco, they found more soul mates who had gravitated here. Now there are eight members of the QHMP. It's easy to qualify. You just have to be queer, from the South, and into math.''

"I guess two out of three makes me ineligible,'' said Cammy lamely, feeling unexpectedly out of place. She could relate to Alan Turing, since he was a famous mathematician. But she was having a hard time

relating to much else that was being discussed. To
make matters worse, the restaurant served only beer or
bourbon, neither of which she would touch. She could
have used a glass of white wine. It was what proper
young ladies from Atlanta were taught to drink, if
drink they must.

Celeste noticed Cammy's discomfort and started to
ask her about herself, a sure way to make someone feel
better. But she was interrupted by the arrival of a drag
queen with entourage, temporarily distracting the restaurant clientele with their outrageous behavior. After that,
their meal arrived and Cammy became preoccupied with
picking the deep fry coating off the shrimp she had ordered.

While Celeste chatted comfortably with the founding
members of the QHMP, she wondered whether
Cammy really was the answer to Harry's matrimonial
desires. Harry was someone who could get along in
any situation, mostly because he was always himself
and never really fit in anywhere. Cammy didn't appear
to be as easygoing. But Harry was clearly head over
heels about the woman, and when Cammy said she
wasn't feeling well, he insisted on taking her back to
the hotel. They made arrangements to meet Celeste the
following morning for a quick tour of the new Museum of Modern Art, followed by a drive up to Napa
Valley for wine tasting and a picnic. Celeste stayed for
two more mugs of Shiner Bock and, after a beery
exchange of addresses and phone numbers, headed
contentedly home, leaving her companions to the de-
lights of the Castro.

Deeper in the South than the homeland of the QHMP
it was warm, unusually hot for mid-October. The tall
palm trees in front of the U.S. federal government offices in Miami cast scrawny late-afternoon shadows

under which Jack Minot parked his vehicle. He hauled himself up the steps and into the marginally cooler lobby. Its temperature was maintained more by the ambitious stone pillars spanning the huge expanse of the classical, vaulted entryway than by the decrepit air-conditioning system. The building had been constructed in the days when government was proud and dimensions were powerful.

"Aftahnoon, Mr. Minot," said the receptionist, smiling from her seat behind a battered wooden desk to the left of the front doors. They were the only human beings in the great expanse of space that had, earlier in the day, been teeming with would-be legal immigrants inquiring in broken English as to the locations of various offices they needed to visit for the privilege of becoming a different kind of alien.

This building housed the Department of Immigration as well as the Federal Bureau of Investigation, as well as Marjorie to oversee the comings and goings.

Marge had started working for the FBI in her fifties, when her daughter's no-good husband had left the two women with three kids to support. She had been cleaning on the night shift and she and Jack Minot had bonded over late-night coffee. When the kids were old enough for both Marge and her daughter to work during the day, Minot took Marge on to do less strenuous jobs around the office. Luckily, when the bureau's office budget was cut, the building receptionist job had just opened up and Minot was able to pull a few strings. Marge was forever grateful to Minot for getting her off her feet. She was probably the most loyal field-worker the bureau in Miami would ever have.

"Got your package right here, Mr. Minot," said Marge. "Just came in this morning like I said in my phone message."

"Thanks, Marge. You're a peach as usual," said Minot, taking the Federal Express envelope from her. No one would raise an eyebrow at a mailing from Dr. Braun to Dr. Marjorie Crawford, U.S. Department of Health, Education, and Welfare at this address.

"Kind of a large, brown peach, Mr. Minot," said Marge, and laughed. Indeed, that was probably a suitable description of her ample backside.

Minot decided to take the package home to his place. It would be cooler than going back to the office. Since his wife had died two years earlier, the place had become an extension of his office anyway, but at least an extension where he could sit and look out at the bayou and have a drink if he needed it. And after reading Celeste's report, he needed it.

Celeste's information, combined with the recent flood of drugs in LA, confirmed what Minot had pieced together. Most importantly, Celeste had added the Lovett clinic as a missing link in the chain providing the patients whose appointments were linked to drug distribution orders. Minot still needed evidence of a Lovett–Valentino connection. He was also disappointed that Celeste hadn't made any headway in learning about the patients' treatments.

But it was, of course, the renegade Mercedes that worried Minot the most. They'd been damn quick about fingering Celeste. Too damn quick for comfort.

To Minot, this proved the existence of the mole he had suspected. Not only that, but he hadn't managed to outsmart this mole in spite of his secrecy in dealing with Celeste and Kazuko. Minot thought, with some irony, that he wasn't even sure if his boss knew the details of what he was up to. In fact, the only person outside of his immediate command who knew that Celeste was being considered for recruitment was Raul de Leon, the police chief in San Juan. But it was hard to figure Raul as the mole for two reasons. First, Minot had never told

Raul that he did finally take Celeste onboard. In fact, he'd tried to give the opposite impression. Second, the mole had probably been the cause of the assassination of the FBI's courier in the San Juan fort, and evidently Raul hadn't known the guy was a courier until they called Minot about the V-signature on the body. Still, Minot couldn't help feeling there was something untrustworthy about Raul's lack of sympathy for the FBI operations in San Juan.

If someone else from inside was squealing, Minot was clueless as to whom it might be. Anyway, it was obvious that Dr. Braun wasn't going to be of much further use, and even more obvious to Minot that he would have to make his next plans considerably more carefully.

Minot lit up a cigar to go with his two fingers of bourbon. As he sat down to do some serious thinking, the telephone rang.

"Minot, it's Navarro. We need to talk pronto. Can you meet me at the usual place in an hour?" The urgent voice was low and gravelly.

Minot looked at his watch. 5:30 P.M. It would be nice to have a shower before resuming his work day. Did the feds have no concept of business hours? He knew the answer to that one. "Make it seven P.M.," he said. "Lucky I don't have a date tonight."

"See you at seven then, lover boy," growled Navarro.

Minot put his glass of bourbon in the refrigerator. He was sure he would want a nightcap after his date with George Navarro. Navarro was nominally his boss at the bureau, but was so involved in administration that he never interfered with Minot's casework. Well, hardly ever. When he did, it was inevitably some political issue where he was worried that Minot would step on some greasy toes. Minot figured he was anticipating a big infraction since their rendezvous was not at headquarters.

After showering, Minot got in his car and re-lit the cigar that he had only just ignited when Navarro had called. The forty minute drive to Boca could at least be in a thought-provoking haze of the best Honduran tobacco and some light Caribbean jazz to go with it. But by the time Minot turned off Route 95 towards the Pavilion Restaurant, he hadn't made any progress in second-guessing who was sabotaging his operation.

Navarro spoke the same language as the political bosses in Miami and made sure that FBI business was unobstrusive. He had tremendous respect for Jack Minot, who kept his branch of the bureau one of the most productive in the country. Thus he was not happy about what he had to say to Minot and did not look very friendly as he sat nursing a glass of iced tea, waiting for Minot to show up.

"George," nodded Minot, taking a seat at the table.

"Jack," responded Navarro, holding out his hand in solemn greeting. "Hungry?"

"Not really," said Minot. "But we oughta order something."

"Yeah," agreed Navarro. He waved to the waiter and asked for spare ribs and potstickers.

"OK, Jack, I'll be straight," he said when the waiter was gone. "Got a call from headquarters. Orders. You're to back off on the Valentino case."

"Says who?"

"Higher ups."

"Any clue as to why?"

Navarro thought for a minute. He had been told to keep quiet about it, but he owed Minot the same explanation he himself had demanded. After all, he wasn't about to interfere with Minot without a damn good reason. "They say it's a special request from the CIA."

"Fuck them," said Minot. "They've been outa' control since they were conceived. You know the history as well as any of us. It's in their fucking charter that they're not even supposed to tell the president what they're up to. Now that their Red watch has been called off they have nothing better to do than to interfere with our business. I've been working on this case for nearly three and a half years and I'm finally seeing my way to cracking it."

"Cool it, Jack," said Navarro. "Apparently, this does have something to do with their international operations." He sighed. "But I couldn't get anything more out of Washington than that, except . . ." He hesitated.

"Except what?" said Minot.

"Washington specifically said to tell to you retire the latest recruit. She and her Japanese partner are in deep shit if you don't."

"How did they even know?" asked Minot, suddenly looking around the restaurant for signs that he was under surveillance. But the early-bird special crowd of blue hairs looked quite harmless.

"I don't know. I didn't even know who they were talking about. But it sure looks like it made sense to you, so I'm ordering you to back off."

"The whole fucking case?"

"The whole thing."

"Man, just when I'm starting to put the pieces together. What a waste."

"Maybe this is a good time to take a break. Go on a Club Med or something. You gotta stop grieving sometime."

"No, I don't," said Minot. He rose. "I got some calls to make before it gets too late."

The waiter laid the two steaming dishes on the table in front of Navarro as they both watched Minot's angry retreating back leave the restaurant. "You want to wrap for take out, sir."

"Yes, please," said Navarro. He was thinking he would have to come up with some new project for Minot PDQ.

The first call that Minot made didn't get him any closer to figuring out who the squealer might be. He had hoped that Raul might let something slip, but it was a long shot. Minot speculated that for all he knew, the Mercedes that had tried to frighten off Celeste and Kazuko in Taipei was the CIA trying to be clever. Shit, their interference made things confusing.

The second call was more difficult to make. Minot used a local cellular phone he kept just for this purpose, having learned from a drug dealer he picked up that certain local cellular phone companies were untraceable. He punched out Celeste's home phone number. Speaking to her at home, he would have to be, what was that word she used? Yeah, circumspect. Her line could very well be bugged.

Celeste had just returned home from a send-off drink with Harry and Cammy as they left to catch the early evening flight back to New York. She kicked off her shoes and headed straight for the phone to try to reach Audrey, who she figured would be back from her buying trip and not yet in bed. As she reached for the receiver, it rang.

"Hello," she said, following the FBI instructions not to identify herself.

"Uh, yeah," said a man's voice. "I'm calling about the Federal Express package you sent to Audrey Ruben in Boca Raton, Florida. It needs a phone number for us to be able to deliver it."

After a moment of confusion in which she couldn't

remember sending Audrey a package, Celeste recognized the signal. She said, "I'll just go get her number. Hold on please." Then she checked her list of local pay phones and picked one that she could get to by five minutes past the next hour.

Celeste was slowly sipping a beer in the bar down the street when the pay phone next to her bar stool rang.

"Hello," she said.

"Hi, I got your report. Thanks a lot."

"You're welcome. I hope it was useful."

"It definitely was. But I have a question for you. Did you get a look at the men in the car?"

"I didn't see them, but we heard them and got a description from Madame Chen. She said they were the Chinese version of rough trade in suits. I suppose the equivalent of your Valentino family."

"Hmmm," said Minot. It didn't sound like CIA. "Well, thanks. I guess that about wraps it up then."

"What do you mean? You don't want me to do more? I only just got started. I know it's a problem that I've been recognized, but I had a really good idea about how to proceed."

"We work in piecemeal these days, so that's really all we need from you."

"Don't you even want to hear my idea?"

"Babe, if it were up to me, I'd be all ears. But what I'm trying to say is that there are some things happening that we can't control, and I don't want you involved any more."

"Well, glad I could be of service," said Celeste with heavy sarcasm.

"You were more than you think, and believe me, I really 'preciate it. Now take care of yourself."

"OK," said Celeste. "Whatever you guys want."

They both hung up, completely dissatisfied.

Celeste went gloomily back to her beer. Minot wasn't even going to give her a chance to save the situation. Thoroughly disheartened, Celeste was suddenly overwhelmed by loneliness, feeling sorry for herself that she had no one with whom she could share her frustration. Harry was blissfully attached. Calling Stash was absolutely out of the question. Kazuko had her own life in Japan. Only Audrey was left.

Celeste signaled to the bartender to bring another beer. She'd call Audrey anyway and maybe plan to go out there for Thanksgiving. When she was intending to recruit Audrey, Celeste had considered suggesting a trip to Puerto Rico to see the sights she'd missed on her last trip. This would have had the added benefit of doing a little snooping around, perhaps seeing if she could get into the tunnels again. Maybe they should do the trip anyway. After all, she didn't promise to check in with the police, and she had a right to go there as a tourist. She could skip the snooping around and try to enjoy herself like a normal person.

While Celeste moped, Minot looked out at the bayou and sucked on his cigar. Out of long habit, cultivated in him by his late wife, he carefully eased his growing ash into an ashtray. The overflowing receptacle was sitting on top of the pile of clippings about drug traffic in LA that he had looked over the previous evening, wondering what would be in Celeste's report. This order to back off wasn't just a waste, it was damn criminal. He was definitely closing in on the case, and now he was grounded for no good reason.

Dr. Braun was no fool. He should have asked her to at least tell him her idea. It might be worth something. Maybe she would still be at that phone number. If she was, it wouldn't hurt just to ask. And, there was always the bonus of expanding his vocabulary.

Celeste picked up the phone after the second ring.

"All right. What's your idea?"

Celeste smiled at the bartender, who assumed she must have reached her date.

9

Tunnel Vision

Thanksgiving was perfect timing for Audrey's recruitment as far as Minot was concerned. His activity on the Valentino case would visibly cease, and Navarro would be satisfied that he had moved on to other work. No one, including the mole, would know that Minot planned to continue business as usual. Celeste's visit to her great aunt for Thanksgiving wouldn't cause any concern, particularly since the aunt was unwell. And Celeste assured him that, given her academic commitments, she wouldn't be going anywhere until that trip so there would be no reason for anyone to suspect that she was still working with him.

Minot intentionally left the details of the travel and the method of recruitment to Celeste. It would certainly be too risky for them to meet in Miami, and he instructed Celeste to contact him only when she returned to San Francisco after seeing Audrey. Celeste, therefore, did not mention that she intended to meet Audrey in Puerto Rico for their Thanksgiving holiday. Seeing as she was still on the case, Celeste saw no reason to alter her original plan and harbored a secret hope that she could come up with further information that might be useful to Minot.

As November gathered speed toward the end of the first quarter of the academic year, Celeste barely had time to think about plans for her trip. Audrey was happy to make the hotel reservations, with the help of one of her friends who still ran a travel agency part time. Celeste became so busy that she even ceased worrying about the fact that Stash had stopped trying to call her. Though she was initially disappointed, she told herself she should be relieved. She was now convinced that the urgency to see him had passed, and she even didn't think about him for several days on end. If he did happen to call, she felt she could handle it, but how she would handle it she still wasn't sure.

When Celeste had a break from the parade of whining medical students bargaining for extra exam points, she made her weekly visit to Eric's hospital bedside. He was recovering slowly from his bike accident, and Celeste noticed that on his bedside table, *Biking High* magazine had gradually been obscured by scientific journals. Eric's hair was now about a quarter of an inch long and he looked like a collegiate anachronism from the 1950s.

He greeted Celeste with a genuine smile and enthusiastically informed her that he had just heard he would be out of traction by Monday and be walking on crutches by Thanksgiving.

"I could be back at the bench after Christmas. Can't wait," he said.

"I'm so pleased," said Celeste. At least the near fatal accident had had a good outcome with respect to Eric's priorities. "We'll get your lab coat ready for you."

"Oh, shit," said Eric. "Uh, sorry Celeste. You just made me remember something I blanked on after the accident. Something that happened right before." He paused and collected his thoughts. "I was working early in the lab that morning, trying to finish something before the race, and a guy came in to check the Internet wiring in your office. I let him in with the extra key we have in the lab, which I left in the pocket of my lab coat. I bet it's still there. Do you think you could put it back in the drawer for me?''

"What guy?"

"A physical plant guy. Didn't recognize him, but there's a lot of them. I think he had blond hair."

"Physical plant didn't do the Internet wiring," said Celeste. "It was an outside company, contracted by the university." She was getting that strange paranoid feeling that had become familiar recently. "Didn't you question him at all?"

"Well, not really, he seemed totally legit. He was a nice guy. Asked me about the bike race."

"Oh, my God," said Celeste. What if someone had searched her office or tapped her phone or something like that? Then they might have tried to get rid of Eric so he wouldn't tell. Was there a chance that she was indirectly responsible for Eric's accident?

"Man, Celeste," said Eric, responding to the stricken expression on her face. "I didn't think you would get so bent out of shape about it. It's only a misplaced key, and I guess no one's been looking for it or you would have known it was missing. No harm's been done, right?"

"I hope so," said Celeste. Then realizing that Eric must think she was totally overreacting, she said, "Don't worry about it. You're right, it's not a problem since no one's been looking for it."

She was anxious to get back to her office and figure out if there was some way she could tell if her phone was bugged. "Look I've gotta get back to the lab and check on something. And I'll take care of replacing the lab key in the drawer before I forget so, really, don't worry about it. I'm very glad to hear the news about your release. Now, rest up and don't jeopardize it," she said, and laid an uncharacteristically motherly hand on the nearest part of his arm that was not in a cast.

Back in the lab, Celeste found Eric's lab coat hanging on the hook behind the door and, sure enough, the key to her office was in the pocket. Under the circumstances, Celeste decided to hang on to the key rather than return it to the official hiding place. Then she went into her office and shut the door. She stood staring at her telephone as though it might explode and thought hard about the many espionage movies she had seen in which people swept for bugs. Finally, she walked over to the phone and, with deliberation, picked it up off the desk and looked at the underside. There was nothing there except the smooth metal casing with the wire protruding from a hole at the back end.

Celeste felt foolish. It was all in her mind. The phantom physical plant man could easily have been a university electrician following up the contract work. Now with the confidence of responding to a false alarm, Celeste unscrewed the mouthpiece from the receiver. But sitting inside, she saw a little round metal object that certainly looked like it didn't belong there. She carefully removed it and laid it on her desk. Then she walked out to the lab, filled a small beaker with tap water and brought it back into the office, setting it on her desk. With no hesitation she dropped the transmitter into a silencing bath.

She watched as it beeped once, bubbled a little, and then sank. Well, here was a use for her retired CIA lover, if he ever did call again. Maybe he could give her a positive ID on the object.

Coincidentally Stash phoned Celeste that evening at her home number, catching her completely off guard. She was sitting on the sofa, reading, and picked up the receiver right away, no longer in the habit of screening her calls.

"Hello, Celeste," he said. "It's Stash calling." As if she might not recognize his voice. "I thought I might have more luck in getting through if I tried you at home."

"Yeah, well," she hesitated awkwardly. "I guess I don't always return my phone calls, I'm so used to E-mail. But I'm glad to hear from you, really. I've been thinking about you."

"And I've been thinking about you," he replied. "I've got photographs to remind me." She could hear him breathe heavily. "It would be nice to show them to you in person."

Celeste found herself taking a deep breath in response. This was not the cool encounter she had anticipated at all. "Well, I'm not so anxious to see the photos . . ." She still blushed with embarrassment and disbelief at her own lack of inhibition when she thought of that photography session.

"But you wouldn't object to seeing me, would you?" asked Stash.

He sounded so eager for affection. Celeste felt herself melting. This was precisely what she had been trying to avoid.

"How about Thanksgiving?" asked Stash. "You must get some kind of break."

Celeste was almost relieved to have a legitimate excuse. "I'm sorry," she said. "I promised to spend a few days at a resort with my Aunt Audrey. She's not getting any younger and hasn't been too well lately. I thought it would cheer her up."

"I still need cheering up, too," said Stash, plaintively.

"Hasn't Jill come around yet?" asked Celeste, trying to act like a friend. "I thought she might have got used to the baby by now."

"Nothing's changed," replied Stash. His voice revealed his disappointment. After a pause in which Celeste could hear him take a breath, he said, as though taking a plunge, "Look, Celeste, I won't bother you anymore if you don't want me to. I just felt that something clicked between us and it's hard to turn away from something that seems so compatible. I'll leave it up to you. If you want to see me, you know how to reach me. I'll be there." He hung up the phone before Celeste had a chance to respond. Stash's little speech had come out in a rush. It didn't sound rehearsed but it did sound as though he had thought for a while about what he planned to say. Celeste was totally disconcerted.

She sat for a minute and looked at the phone. Then she got up, wandered into the kitchen and opened the refrigerator. She looked at the shelves wondering what she wanted. She let the door fall shut and went to the liquor cupboard. Malt whiskey might take the edge off her hunger.

With a generous shot of Aberlour and a little water, Celeste went back into the living room. She settled herself on the overstuffed couch, trying to think clearly. Now the ball was in her court if she wanted to see Stash again. Her sense of self-preservation told her she should let it go. But she hadn't been very mindful of her self-preservation these days. And apart from her imprudent desire for Stash, he might be useful as a resource for her current work for the FBI. Or was she just kidding herself as an excuse to see him again?

Then Celeste realized that she had completely forgotten to ask Stash about bugging devices. He certainly wouldn't be useful if she allowed herself to be so distracted by him. However, there hadn't really been an opening to introduce this topic casually into their conversation. She'd have to spend some relaxed time with him if she wanted to take advantage of his expertise without being explicit. If only she could be sure that, if she saw him again, she could confine her emotions to the moment and not develop an unrealistic attachment.

The Normandy hotel in San Juan was a fantasy gift from a multi-millionaire to his wife. It was built to replicate the S.S. Normandy on which they had first met. The outside of the building was white with black trim and ship-shaped and the decor was a perfect reproduction of a ship's interior. The hotel was located in the exclusive resort area near the yacht harbor of San Juan, just below the walls of the old city. Due to a delayed connection at O'Hare airport, Celeste arrived late on Tuesday evening and didn't have a chance to appreciate the setting until she'd met Audrey for breakfast Wednesday morning.

Audrey was waiting for Celeste at an outdoor table under a striped umbrella. The patio on which they met was designed to look like an open deck. As if afloat, they were looking out onto a deep green-blue sea flecked with white caps meeting a cloudless blue sky. The clarity of the sun and the intensity of the color was unmistakably Caribbean.

Audrey thought of emeralds and blue topaz as she gazed on the scene. Celeste focused on the frigate birds soaring fantastically high, their M-shape reminiscent of their teradactyl ancestors.

Audrey was wearing large sunglasses above her bright orange-red lips and a white floppy hat with a large brim. From the apparent structure under her gauzy white beach cover, Celeste could see that Audrey had her bathing suit on. Audrey's perfectly pedicured toenails, matching her lipstick, projected from gold mules which complimented the gold jewelry dangling from her ears, wrists, and neck. After they greeted each other, Audrey looked critically at Celeste, who was wearing her bathing suit under the black and white AIDS hospice T-shirt that read "dx/dt=0." Celeste's version of the shirt still had its sleeves and was tucked into baggy khaki shorts. Her polish-free toes peered out from black suede Birkenstock sandals.

"Darling, you could really use some resort wear. Let's see your bathing suit."

Celeste lifted up the T-shirt to reveal a red Speedo tank suit.

"You have no boobs!" exclaimed Audrey who, with considerable engineering, supported a veritable shelf of flesh on her chest. "That will never do."

Celeste reminded herself to tolerate Audrey's customary critical appraisal of her appearance and tried to swallow her annoyance. "Well, there's not a lot I can do about it. Anyway this kind of bathing suit sort of presses you flat."

"Precisely," said Audrey. "You need a Wonderbra design. You'll be amazed at what a little prodding and a little padding here and there can do for you. I'll take you shopping after lunch. There are some good resort wear boutiques up in the old city."

They spent a lovely, breezy morning down by the ocean lounging on deck chairs put out for them by a handsome young man in a white, shipboard uniform. His aristocratic face reminded Celeste of Señor Raul de Leon, the chief of police. She certainly wouldn't be getting in touch with him on this trip. Audrey would have preferred to sit by the hotel swimming pool on the so-called top deck to people watch. But Celeste wanted to swim in the sea. The compromise was that Celeste agreed to go to the pool later in the afternoon to show off the new wardrobe they planned to acquire. That way Audrey didn't have to be ashamed of her niece's appearance.

Celeste's offending tank suit was perfect for swimming in the ocean, partly because of its smoothing effect. She felt like some kind of sleek sea creature bobbing in the leisurely waves. But what Celeste loved most about swimming in the sea was the slightly stinging feeling of her skin when she got out of the water and the tight feeling after it dried in the sun, as though it had shrunk one size. Sitting on the beach, absorbing the sun, Celeste's mind baked too, and she enjoyed the hypnotic pleasure of not thinking about anything at all. Audrey was pleasantly silent. And when Celeste looked over at her great aunt, she saw that she was dozing.

A superb lunch of local fish on the deck overlooking the sea, followed by siestas, left both women energized for their expedition into the old city that afternoon. The street with the high-fashion boutiques was in the center of the grid formed by the old city streets. As the taxi navigated through the one-way streets from the dock area, they passed Señor de Leon's police station and turned right, in the direction of the fort. Then they doubled back and cruised down the main shopping street, and Celeste recognized the side street where the Instituto de Medicina Botánica was located. She noted that it was slightly more than one block from the boutique where they finally wound up. Celeste was at the heart of where she wanted to be to establish whether the clinic could be accessed through the catacombs. She was anxious to get into the tunnel system to have a look around.

La Playa was the name of the boutique that Audrey chose to patronize. From the window display it was apparent that both men and women could be fashionably outfitted there. The shop was dark, presumably to keep it cool, and as Audrey pushed the door open a buzzer rang to alert the shopkeeper of customers. Celeste thought that the buzzer must drive the shopkeeper crazy on busy days, but when she looked at the prices of the merchandise she realized they probably never had any really busy days. The shopkeeper, a fading Spanish beauty, immediately recognized that her customers knew what they wanted. Audrey began with great efficiency to collect bathing suits and matching cover-ups for Celeste to try on, and the shopkeeper hung back, letting Audrey take over her store. She knew that it was a matter of which they would buy and not whether. While Audrey combed the racks, she chatted with the shopkeeper about the business and they became fast friends.

In the curtained dressing room in the back of the shop, Celeste felt like a doll being played with by these two women. The shopkeeper said her figure was better than most who came into the shop and wanted to see what some of the designer bathing suits looked like on her. Audrey said, "Yes, her figure's good. But we have this little problem." She took ahold of Celeste, who was wearing an Oscar de la Renta bathing suit that gaped at her front, and pressed Celeste's breasts up and closer together from each side to fill the gap.

"Ah, I understand," said the shopkeeper and went back out into the shop, presumably in search of some bust-enhancing models. Waiting in the dressing room, Celeste and Audrey heard the buzzer signal the arrival of another customer, a man who spoke rapidly in Spanish to the shopkeeper. While he was being served and shown to the curtained dressing room next to theirs, Celeste looked down at the floor and noticed that there was a square cut in the wall-to-wall carpet.

The shopkeeper returned shortly with another armload of swimsuits. As she stripped off the one she was wearing, Celeste asked, "Does your shop connect to the catacombs?"

"*Si, Señorita,*" said the shopkeeper. "Almost every shop in the old district connects to the tunnels. We use gunpowder storing space for some of our, how do you say it?"

"Stock," said Audrey.

"*Si, si* that is it."

"I'm a history student," fibbed Celeste with a warning look at Audrey, "studying the history of San Juan. I'd love to see the tunnels. I've read about them, of course."

"The public is not permitted to go into the tunnels. I could not let you go down while someone might come into the shop."

"Is there an early closing day when I could go down? Then I could let myself out, after the shop was closed."

"Well, you are a good customer," said the shop-keeper, not wanting to jeopardize the hefty sale she was anticipating. "We could try on Friday. Come at two o'clock, we close after that."

"*Muchas gracias, Señora,*" said Celeste. "I am very grateful." Having achieved her goal unexpectedly, Celeste gave herself over completely to the two women. It took ten more bathing suits and five cover-ups to select the perfect outfit for Celeste. During this time Celeste was being continually prodded, stroked, and fitted by Audrey, who was in her element. It suddenly occurred to Celeste why Audrey had married so late. Neither Audrey nor Nate were physically attractive and, of course, Audrey had had her career, but Celeste suspected it was more than that. Celeste thought about the deep affection between Audrey and Nate, but there had been no passion. This revelation of Celeste's endeared Audrey to her even more, convinced that Audrey had made an inadmissable sacrifice in her life: giving up her attraction to other women.

Finally, everyone was satisfied with the transaction. Audrey and Celeste said good-bye to the shopkeeper after

Celeste reconfirmed her appointment on Friday, and the door buzzed them out into the warm early evening. The shopkeeper waved farewell and then returned to her desk to tidy up the paperwork before re-hanging all the garments that Celeste had modelled. A few moments later, she was startled to look up and see her male customer standing before her. She had completely forgotten about him.

He did not look Puerto Rican, Spanish, or Mexican, and indeed his fluent Spanish was accented with an American inflection, which might have been expected from his fair hair. In spite of the fact that he was not speaking his native language, he made himself extremely clear.

"*Señora*, I do not think that the police would be very happy if they knew you were planning to open the catacombs to a tourist," he said unpleasantly.

The shopkeeper understood that he had heard everything. "Please don't report me," she said, in a panic. "It was just good business to agree."

"I will not report you if you do what I say. On Friday, you must let me into the shop after the American woman goes into the tunnel. Then you will leave, as planned."

The shopkeeper knew she had no choice since she could not report this threat to the police under the circumstances. She knew that the man standing before her also knew this. "*Si señor.*" She sighed. "I will do as you say."

"*Muchas gracias, señora,*" he said. "Until Friday, then." The door buzzed as he left.

Celeste and Audrey were deep in conversation as soon as they left the shop. "What was that all about?" Audrey asked. "Since when have you been studying the history of Puerto Rico?"

Celeste told Audrey the whole story as they walked

down the street leading to the fortifications around the old city. She started with the body in the fort, told her about the FBI recruitment and her visit to Taipei. Along the way Celeste pointed out the regular grid pattern of the streets that was supposedly reflected by the tunnels forming the catacombs. She also pointed out where the Instituto of Medicina Botánica was located and the direction of the fort. During this discourse Audrey was silent and attentive. Celeste found that being taken seriously by Audrey was slightly unnerving.

"You must be frustrated, dear. If these Valentino people know you're working with the FBI, you can't do much good any more," said Audrey, when Celeste finished her story.

"No kidding," said Celeste. "The FBI tried to dismiss me because of that. But I had an idea that gave me a reprieve." She looked at Audrey, who looked back at her as though she knew what Celeste was about to say and was ready for it.

"No one would recognize me," said Audrey. "And I'm in need of a good clinic anyway. Didn't you say that the doctor in Taipei was a lung expert?"

"Audrey, you're serious aren't you?"

"Never more," said Audrey. "Now, let's see how long it takes to walk from the boutique to the institute. You'll need to have some idea when you're under ground."

"Are you sure you're up for it?"

"Do you mean walking a few blocks or traveling to Taipei?"

"I meant walking to the institute since your cough doesn't seem any better. But either, since you asked."

"Well, I can't think of a better way to go, as long as it's exciting," said Audrey.

Their excursion began slowly. Celeste figured she would have to go over the distance herself on Friday morning, but she didn't want to spoil Audrey's fun. However, they never made it.

When they reached the end of the second block Audrey succumbed to a severe coughing fit. Fortunately she had an inhaler, which Celeste found in her purse. After a few tokes, the spasms subsided but Audrey's breathing remained shallow and Celeste was afraid to let her walk any further.

Celeste needn't have worried however. A young police officer had observed Audrey's distress and had rushed to his car, expecting that he would need to drive her to the hospital. Instead, when he pulled up in front of the two ladies, the older one seemed to have recovered and they asked if he would take them back to their hotel.

After a quiet Thanksgiving hanging around the resort, Celeste was eager to get down into the catacombs the following afternoon. She spent Friday morning counting blocks between the buildings she recognized in the grid. She also counted the number of steps it took to cover a block. Once again she noted the proximity of the police station to the boutique and was grateful that the Thanksgiving holiday had prevented any report of Audrey's police rescue that might have come across the desk of Señor Raul de Leon.

Celeste also bought a cheap, nylon backpack, an industrial strength flashlight, and chose the most tolerable tourist's sweatshirt she could find. The sweatshirt was the only one without glitter or felt appliqué and simply read "Puerto Rico!" in turquoise letters on a white background. Back at the hotel, Celeste added some money and her Swiss army knife to the backpack and, after a civilized lunch with Audrey, she changed into lightweight jeans, a T-shirt, and sneakers and headed back into the old city, with her equipment.

The beginning of Celeste's excursion was heralded by
the buzzer connected to the door of the La Playa boutique. The shopkeeper looked distressed. "I hoped that
you were not going to come," she said. "It really is
forbidden to go into the tunnels. It could be dangerous."
She had labored over the Spanish–English dictionary the
previous evening to try to find the most discouraging
words possible. The shopkeeper had not liked the look
of the man who planned to follow Celeste down below.

"I promise I won't do any damage," said Celeste.
"Or tell anyone that I've been down there. It would just
help me so much for my work to be able to see the
tunnels."

The shopkeeper saw that she was not going to be able
to dissuade Celeste. She also feared that the man might
turn her in anyway, if he saw Celeste come out of the
shop. So she didn't say anything further in protest. She
just showed Celeste how to let herself out of the shop
and described how to switch on the light in the storeroom. She then opened the trapdoor in the dressing room
and watched Celeste climb down the ladder into the
darkness.

Celeste had been so intent on getting into the tunnels
that she hadn't thought about the reality of it. She
reached the bottom of the ladder and felt above her for
the string dangling from the overhead light. The naked
bulb in the ceiling above revealed that Celeste was sur-
rounded by racks of clothes hanging like limp human
carcasses. The watery light barely illuminated the far
walls so Celeste reached in the small backpack, withdrew her new flashlight, and switched it on. The plastic
bags that covered the hanging garments refracted its
beam with an eery glint as Celeste explored the storeroom with the light. Then she saw the door at the far
side of the small storeroom, presumably the access to
the rest of the catacombs' tunnels. She walked between

the clothes racks to get to it. The racks were so close together that she rustled the garments as she passed through and the flimsy plastic bags clung to her, letting go reluctantly in her wake. It was hard not to feel that they were trying to hold her back.

The door to the catacombs had a metal skeleton key in the lock, which turned easily. Celeste could hear the rusty release of the bolt. However the door did not immediately yield to Celeste's cautious pressure. She pushed with a bit more conviction and, when the door gave way, it swung out into the corridor with a creak, almost pulling Celeste with it. As she regained her balance, she felt the cool, musty air of the catacombs waft into the storeroom. Simultaneously she became aware of the scratchy scampering of small feet fleeing down the corridor. She was tempted to flee back up the ladder herself.

Instead, she tried to mobilize her self-control with the practical gesture of putting on the sweatshirt, a kind of protective armor. Then she heard the faint sound of the door buzzer in the shop above her. It must have been the owner on her way out. This small sound, providing contact with the world above, broke her indecision and gave Celeste the courage to step fully into the corridor of the catacombs. The corridor jogged right and, about ten yards from the storeroom door, she reached the connection to the main tunnel network. Celeste turned left and began counting steps in the direction of the tunnel that should connect to the clinic.

Celeste had her flashlight trained on the compacted dirt floor of the tunnel, from which a damp chill rose. She shivered and was glad she had decided to wear jeans. She had taken forty-five steps when she intersected with the main tunnel. Turning to her right should lead her in the direction of the clinic. Turning to her left and left again would have led her to the police station.

Old San Juan City Streets

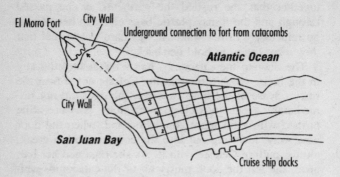

1-hotel   2-police station   3-Institute clinic   4-boutique

Celeste turned right and faced a delicate network of cobwebs reflecting off her flashlight beam. Again the distant scampering of feet could be heard just beyond where the beam penetrated. It occurred to Celeste that such an elaborate network of cobwebs could only have been constructed over several days. Clearly this region of the catacombs was not heavily used.

She remembered she had run into a similar network right before she discovered the corpse in the tunnel last spring. Not wanting to repeat the experience, she removed her backpack and swung it through the network to clear an opening. As she did, she realized the significance of the cobweb wall. The fact that the web had not been disturbed for many days would also have been true for the web between the fort museum and the corpse. Therefore her corpse had to have been delivered to its resting place from inside the catacombs. Here was the missing evidence in support of Minot's hunch that the corpse originated in the clinic.

CATACOMB TUNNELS

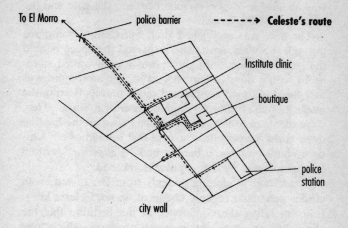

This moment of revelation energized Celeste and she felt an increased sense of purpose rising, which gave her the will to proceed. She set off, almost jauntily, down the tunnel to her right and initially forgot to start counting her steps. She had to turn back to the tunnel intersection to begin again.

Celeste counted the number of steps that should cover a street block and reached the cross tunnel running underneath the street on which the Instituto de Medicina Botánica was located. She turned right, in the direction of the clinic, into the pitch black tunnel. If there was an opening into the tunnel from the clinic, it was certainly not illuminated. Celeste moved along, cautiously counting steps and periodically stopping to scan the walls ahead with her flashlight. After about half a block's worth of steps Celeste detected a depression in the mud wall ahead. When she got closer, she saw that there was a recessed metal gate filling the opening in the wall, approximately ten feet wide and eight feet tall. There was about a foot of clearance between the gate and the mud wall of the tunnel.

The gate was padlocked shut, but Celeste could see through the wire mesh. She inspected the space behind the gate with her flashlight. It was a mud-walled storeroom with a door at the back of it. The storeroom was half-filled with yellow-painted metal barrels bearing the international symbol for organic chemical waste. They were identical to the barrels she had seen on the loading dock at the Taipei clinic, except that instead of red Chinese characters, these barrels had *"Peligroso"* written on them in red. Celeste's pulse quickened.

In addition to sharing patients from Dr. Lovett, both clinics generated organic chemical waste. Celeste knew from attending the conference at the Instituto that the clinic had an associated research program, which may have explained the waste. Thus, if she had not seen similar waste at the primarily medical clinic in Taipei, she would not have made much of this find in San Juan. But she had a feeling that it could be related to the clinical activities she was investigating.

Celeste quietly pressed on the gate to see if it was really shut as tight as it looked. Finding that it was, she knew she had seen everything there was to see so decided to return to the main tunnel, which should lead to the fort. When she reached it, she hesitated a moment before turning right. Left would take her back to the cross tunnel leading to the boutique. The other direction promised a long, dark, rat-infested corridor.

Celeste decided to be sensible. She would walk for thirty minutes, which should be long enough to reach the fort. However, when thirty minutes was up, she would allow herself to turn around. She wasn't sure that there was anything to be gained by this exploration, but having come this far, she might as well check it out.

Twenty minutes into her walk, Celeste's progress was halted by a blockade of wooden sawhorses festooned with police tape. It looked like it was the residue of the police investigation of the corpse she had found almost half a year earlier. Celeste realized belatedly that the catacombs were probably accessible from the police station and decided it wasn't worth scaling the barrier if the police had already combed the area. She checked the time and started on her way back to the boutique.

According to her watch, Celeste was just about to reach the clinic tunnel when she heard a noise. It sounded like the creaking of the door she had come through from the boutique's storeroom. She had left the door slightly ajar, but not wide enough for a person to pass through. She stopped and held her breath, listening intently. If someone had followed her into the tunnel they would have to walk ten yards to connect to the cross tunnel, leading to the main tunnel where she stood. She picked up her pace, turned left into the clinic tunnel and switched off her flashlight. Celeste waited, her heart pounding.

Then she heard the breathing. It was rapid, panting breath, like that of a dog. Whatever it was, it was approaching the main tunnel.

10

Dog's Dinner

After their lunch, when Celeste set off for the catacombs, Audrey returned to her room to change for an afternoon by the swimming pool. She sat down heavily on the bed. It was these moments of being alone that she dreaded. Her sense of self was sound when reflected off the company of other people, or even when she was just watching other people. In her own company she felt lost, a sensation that she had fought her entire seventy-nine years and that had only intensified since Nate's death. As though it were related to this feeling, her cough rarely surfaced in company. Yesterday's fit was an aberration, probably brought on by the excitement of Celeste's proposition or maybe they had just set off on their walk a little too vigorously. Audrey's cough was more frequently the product of wakeful periods in the middle of the night, when there was no visual or social distraction and the possibility of morning was hopelessly remote. Its origin was deep in the lungs and its ferocity commanded her whole body.

Audrey contemplated the contents of her traveling medicine chest. They were spread out on the bedside table: five bottles of prescribed pills, the small inhaler, the battery-operated vaporizer, the two bottles of drops to add to the water in the vaporizer, and the mentholated chest rub. She knew she would never be without these things and was gripped by the feeling that these aids to life would multiply to such an extent that she would be immobilized from the sheer impossibility of being able to transport them. A deep sense of fatigue washed over her, and she decided to lie down for a few minutes before battling the latex of her bathing suit.

Two hours later, Audrey was still fitfully asleep and began to dream that she was in a hospital room with a visitor knocking on the door. She wanted to open the door and admit the visitor but she couldn't because she was strapped to the bed. The dream evolved into a nightmare of frustration and Audrey woke with a start and a sudden intake of breath that set off a cascade of hoarse coughing. She reached out for the inhaler nearby and, after sitting up for a few minutes, managed to get control of the spasms in her chest. Once she was breathing more calmly, Audrey realized that the knocking on her door had been real. She eased herself off the bed, registering with annoyance that she had fallen asleep in her Celine slacks, which now bore unsightly creases, and went to the door.

She opened it to confront a large and tasteful arrangement of tropical fruit in a basket with a card in a white envelope. As she bent down to pick it up she noticed a bouquet of white roses sitting on the threshold of Celeste's hotel room door across the corridor. The card in Audrey's basket was an old-fashioned calling card with RAUL DE LEON engraved on the front. On the reverse side, it read, "I hope that you are feeling better. With compliments from the Chief of Police, San Juan." Audrey had left her room key on the dresser or she would have satisfied her curiosity and crossed the corrridor to read Celeste's card as well. As it was she would have locked herself out, which forced her to exercise some self-control.

The fruit basket raised Audrey's spirits. Thinking of the gallantry of the sender, she washed up, changed into a fresh outfit, and stepped out to enjoy the late afternoon crowd by the pool.

It was only when people started to leave the poolside to change for sundowners at the terrace bar that Audrey began to wonder when Celeste would be back. Celeste had planned to be at the boutique by two and should easily have finished her exploration by four and been back at five, and that was generous. Now it was almost six. Audrey convinced herself that Celeste must have come back and, perhaps, finding that Audrey was not in her room, decided to shower and get ready for the evening. But when Audrey went back to her own room she saw that the roses were still sitting outside Celeste's door.

Audrey was in the midst of her afternoon nap when Celeste became aware that she had company in the tunnel. Celeste could hear the rapid breathing coming down the main corridor that intersected with the tunnel to the clinic in which she was standing. It was unmistakably the panting of a restrained dog. It sounded large. A dog would be able to sniff her out even if she found a hiding place in the tunnel. She needed to get the hell out of there. But how?

The only exit she knew was the route by which she had come. The dog, and presumably whomever was restraining it, was blocking her escape. She could hear the breathing coming closer. It was momentarily amplified by a strange echo, which then faded. Celeste guessed they had reached the main tunnel and turned into it. The dog was most likely following her tracks.

Celeste was stuck in the clinic tunnel, where her tracks already led. Her tracks also led down the main tunnel in the direction of the fort. She had no choice but to hide and hope that the dog would pursue the tracks to the fort. Keeping her flashlight off, Celeste crept up close to the tunnel wall and felt her way toward the clinic gate. It had just enough clearance for her to squeeze against it so that she would not be visible from the main corridor. The panting was growing louder, approaching the clinic corridor. Celeste felt the break in the wall just in time. She shrugged off her backpack and shoved it with her foot up against the gate. She then pressed herself against it, facing outward into the corridor and grasping the bars to flatten herself against the gate. Holding herself still and flat in this posture and trying to control her own breathing was like a bizarre yoga exercise. If she ever got home she'd have her yoga teacher to thank for the fact that this kind of body discipline was not unfamiliar.

She started drawing deep breaths so that she could hold her breath when the dog and its handler passed, if they passed. Now Celeste could hear the scrabbling of the dog's toenails on the dirt floor of the main corridor and the rapid, dull footsteps of someone being dragged behind the dog. She stopped breathing. A beam of light flashed into the corridor, but Celeste was tucked out of sight. The beam was suddenly jerked away. The dog had evidently picked up the scent to the fort. Celeste allowed herself a relieved expulsion of breath, which helped her think more clearly. She would give the dog ten minutes to progress towards the fort and then make her way back to the boutique entrance. Celeste was glad she had counted her steps on the way to the clinic so she wouldn't have to use her flashlight.

It was a long ten minutes of waiting and finally Celeste edged her way back to the main corridor and turned left, staying close to the tunnel wall, counting her steps. It took her less time to get to the cross tunnel leading to the boutique than she expected. She turned left into it and then right into the short passageway to the boutique storeroom. She approached the storeroom door and tugged vigorously on the handle, remembering how resistant it had been when she first opened it into the corridor. She tugged again. The door did not yield. Celeste shone her flashlight into the keyhole where she had left the skeleton key. It was completely clear. The door was locked and the key was undoubtedly with her pursuers.

The boutique was in a dead-end corridor relative to the tunnels of the catacombs. And when Celeste returned to the first cross-tunnel, her flashlight revealed that it terminated just to the right of the passageway to the boutique. To find another exit Celeste realized she would have to go back to the main tunnel from which she had just come. She felt her way out to the main tunnel in the dark and peered around the corner to see where the dog and its partner were. She could see a flashlight beam dancing erratically in the distance. It gave the disturbing impression that the dog was in control of the situation.

Celeste hesitated at the junction with the main corridor. She knew that the dog would stop searching at the police barrier before the fort, and she figured that when her scent was lost, the handler would be able to start a more methodical search of the cross corridors on the way back. Ultimately, however, they would return down the main tunnel and the dog would pick up her scent again, first to the clinic gate and then to the boutique. If she was going to escape, her only option was to go left, in the opposite direction from the fort. Celeste knew she didn't have much time before they turned around, and she would need to make a break in her tracks.

So, first, Celeste turned right into the main corridor and walked about twenty yards toward the fort. Then she turned around, switched on her flashlight, and sprinted away from the fort, following her earlier tracks in the dust. When she came to the cross corridor leading to the boutique, Celeste tensed all her muscles and leapt across it, aiming to land as close to the wall as possible on the other side, so footprints wouldn't be visible. With any luck, this would create a hiatus in the scent as well as the footprint trail, which the dog would hopefully follow back to the boutique. Perhaps they would assume that Celeste had been able to get out of the catacombs by that route. They may not have known that she didn't have another key.

Celeste switched off her flashlight and strained to see what was happening at the end of the tunnel while she caught her breath. She could not make out whether her pursuers had already turned around. She began to creep along the wall of the main corridor, away from the fort, to find a hiding place to wait for them to give up on her. She felt a break in the tunnel wall and briefly flashed her light, illuminating a cross tunnel to the right. She turned right and felt her way along, looking for a turn-off or a recessed hiding place. In less than ten yards she came to a break in the wall, a bit deeper than the area in front of the clinic gate, with a padlocked door in the recessed wall. Here Celeste settled, for what seemed an interminable period of waiting, during which she considered her situation.

It was at least half an hour later when Celeste heard panting again that it occurred to her that she might be able to get out of the catacombs through the police station. The station probably wasn't that far from where she was hiding and in the opposite direction of the fort. She wished she had thought of this earlier. The panting sound became more audible but then faded, as though the dog were searching a cross corridor. When she heard the animal again, Celeste crept back to the edge of the main tunnel. Peering around the corner, she saw the dog bounding in and out of a flashlight beam and a shadowy figure, dressed in dark clothes and a dark cap, behind it. The dog was approaching the cross corridor leading back to the boutique. Celeste plastered herself against the wall of the cross tunnel, holding her breath and praying that they would head back to the boutique access point. She heard the panting fade again and decided to make her move.

Celeste switched on her flashlight and ran faster than she had imagined was physically possible in the direction of the police station. She tried to concentrate on counting the number of steps she was taking, knowing that the station was on the street parallel to the boutique two blocks away. Then she heard a low growl behind her. They had not found her at the boutique storeroom door and evidently they knew they had the only key.

Celeste heard the dog jumping about, straining against its lead, and she heard the handler struggling to control it. It was going to be a race without a finish line. A race that Celeste couldn't possibly win.

Suddenly Celeste saw a beam of light dance into the corridor ahead of her. She was being closed in on from both sides. She stopped dead in her tracks in panic.

The beam ahead of her was shortly followed by the appearance of a bearded man in white shirtsleeves and green military trousers. "Celeste!" shouted the man. "It's Raul. The station is this way."

She ran toward him. The dog was now barking sharply behind her. Raul held out his left hand as though passing a baton in a relay race. As soon as Celeste reached him, he grabbed her hand and, almost dragging her with him, turned and ran along the short corridor. He then sidestepped abruptly into the tunnel entrance to the police station, pulling Celeste with him. The change in momentum and sudden stop flung Celeste against

Raul and he caught her, holding her up with his left arm behind her back. With his free hand, Raul slammed the barred door behind them, shutting off access from the corridor. The menacing bark behind them stopped abruptly.

The silence left behind was ominous. Celeste and Raul were breathing too hard to speak and Celeste became aware that two uniformed police officers were staring at them. Raul looked at the police officers and flicked his head toward the gate. They both nodded, pulled their guns out of shoulder holsters and let themselves quietly out of the gate, gently clicking it shut behind them. Raul kept his hold on Celeste but as soon as the officers left, she could feel him stiffen with formality.

"Okay?" he asked.

"Yeah, okay," she said. "You can let go now. I'm all right."

Raul let her go with the manner of setting down a fragile object that he should not have been holding and replacing it on a curio shelf. They looked at each other, still breathless. It was a breathlessness born of tension gone quiet, like the aftermath of having made love. In the glance they exchanged, they recognized their mutual awareness of this strange intimacy, but this was not the moment to pursue it.

"How did you know I was down here?" demanded Celeste.

"Fortunately for you, your aunt was impatient for her dinner companion."

"But how . . . ?"

"I read about your escort back to the hotel on Wednesday, going through the beat reports after Thanksgiving. I sent a little get-well greeting to your aunt with my card. It looks like it arrived just in time. She phoned me, when you hadn't shown up for sundowners."

"Thank goodness for Audrey," sighed Celeste.

"Any idea who was chasing you?"

"No, I haven't a clue. I doubt the woman who let me into the tunnel would have told anyone." Celeste paused, and then said anxiously, "It was my fault. I pushed her into it. Please don't give her trouble."

"I'm sure you can be very persuasive," said Raul with a chilly smile. "We'll consider taking that into account." Then, sounding more authoritative, he said, "Now, perhaps you should tell me what you were doing down there, as if I couldn't guess."

"It's a pretty long story. Do you think we could phone Audrey first and let her know I'm okay?"

"*Si, si.* You're absolutely right. I do apologize. My police duty was getting the better of me. Come upstairs and we'll do that immediately. We have plenty of time to discuss things. The men will take care of any further, uh, business in the tunnel."

Raul gestured for Celeste to go ahead of him and directed her with a polite, but controlling touch in the small of her back. They made their way up a flight of stairs, down a corridor flanked by small offices with names lettered in gold leaf on the doors, and into the main foyer of the police station. From her previous visit, Celeste remembered the grand dimensions of the entry hall, appropriate to the old-city architecture of the building. This time she was spared the stark investigation room and found herself in Raul's office. The office was not extravagantly furnished, but the carved mahogany desk and leather-covered chairs and settee bespoke power, and the heavily framed Impressionism paintings of Puerto Rican scenes bespoke class.

Raul walked directly to his desk, picked up the telephone receiver and spoke rapidly in Spanish, evidently asking the receptionist to connect him to the Normandy hotel. He stood silently while the connection was being made and then asked for Señora Ruben. He handed the receiver to Celeste.

She heard one ring and then Audrey's voice croaked, "Hello?"

"Audrey, it's Celeste. I'm fine. Raul found me and everything's okay."

"Baby," said Audrey. "I've been so worried. I've been lying here in bed, waiting. Did something happen to you down there?" Audrey sounded as exhausted as Celeste was suddenly feeling.

"Well, it wasn't as easy to explore as I had expected," said Celeste, "And I got kind of trapped."

"How do you mean trapped?"

"Well . . ." Celeste was reluctant to tell Audrey what had happened. But if Audrey was going to help her, she needed to be informed about the dangers. "Actually, somebody was chasing me around down there."

"Darling!" exclaimed Audrey. And then in a tone that implied no one should get away with frightening her baby, she said, "I hope your police chief friend is on the case."

Celeste had to smile. She looked at Raul, who of course had no idea what was being said and didn't smile back. "I think the whole force is on it," said Celeste.

"Darling, I'm so glad," said Audrey, with a sigh. "You know, I'm just beat from worrying. Now that I know you're okay, all I want to do is order room service and call it an early night. Are you coming back soon?"

Celeste looked again at Raul standing next to his desk. Though he was not in full uniform and his white shirt was open at the neck, he looked to her more like a prison guard than a saviour. "We still have some things I have to clear up here," said Celeste with a questioning glance to Raul, who nodded assertively. "I think it's an excellent idea for you to have an early night. Raul will make sure I get back safely. You definitely don't have to worry anymore.''

"That's wonderful, dear," said Audrey. "But, should I do something about the roses?"

"What roses?" asked Celeste.

"There's a big bouquet of white roses sitting outside the door of your room. Pretty fancy. I think they came from your, uh, friend."

"Do you think or know?"

"I know."

"Then why don't you ask the room service waiter to bring them into your room and you can enjoy them for the evening."

"Thanks, I will. Have a good night, honey."

"Good night to you too. Sweet dreams," said Celeste, and put down the receiver. "White roses?" she asked Raul, raising her eyebrows.

"Well, at least the fruit basket to your aunt was useful."

"Who knows," said Celeste. "Maybe the roses will be useful, too." She smiled tentatively at him. A wave of fatigue washed over her, compelling her to give herself over to this man, to answer his inevitable questions and be protected, to hand over her quest to authority. But there was something in his manner that warned her not to succumb completely. She couldn't read him at all. The formal attitude did not match the mutual awareness of physical intimacy she had felt. And what did white roses mean? Were they a courtesy? Were they a bribe? Were they a flirtation? Raul and Celeste stared at each other, not giving anything away. Celeste braced herself for interrogation.

Raul surprised her by saying, "You must be tired. Perhaps you would like to clean up. There is a shower and fresh clothes in the bathroom. The weather here in San Juan means I have to change at least once a day."

Celeste looked at Raul's body. He was not a large man, and given his slender Latin shape, his clothes might come close to a loose fit. A hot shower would also refresh her mind. The offer was irresistible and she accepted.

As soon as Raul heard water running he dialed Miami and waited for the characteristic, minimal identification.

"Minot," said Jack Minot as he picked up the phone.

"It's Raul de Leon, calling from San Juan. We've had a surprise visit from Dr. Braun. I see that my advice was well taken."

"What?" said Minot. "What's she doing there?"

"She appears to be here on holiday with her aunt."

"Jeez," was all Minot could say while he collected his thoughts. He felt simultaneously sheepish that Raul had caught him ignoring his advice and embarrassed that the advice had been correct in that Dr. Braun was not behaving like a sensible spook. "All I can say is that she wasn't supposed to be there, but I guess it's my fault that I didn't make that clear. I'm sorry, bud. I hope she hasn't been causing trouble."

"She's been sneaking around in our tunnels," said Raul, not particularly mollified. "We try to keep them inaccessible to the public. Not only did she find her way in, but she was followed. She could have been in a lot of trouble if we hadn't stepped in."

Minot shook his head, not registering that the gesture was invisible to his caller. "Did you get a take on who followed her?"

"Not yet, but my men are still down there."

"I owe you big time, buddy, but I'd appreciate it if you could let me know if you find anything. Sorry for the hassle." He paused, thinking of the last time he spoke to Raul. "I guess it's our specialty."

Raul sighed. "I'm not too happy about having to keep cleaning up your messes," he said. "Next time you should consider my advice a little more seriously.''

"I hear you," said Minot and hung up, fuming. What was Dr. Braun thinking of when she decided to go to San Juan? Surely she could have recruited her aunt in the pleasant surroundings of Boca Raton. Now whoever was in pursuit of Celeste might be aware of the aunt's existence. The whole situation was getting too damn risky. And if Raul complained to anyone besides him, Minot's own butt would be on the line. The doc had a lot of explaining to do to make it worth Minot's while to continue with her plan.

Twenty minutes later Celeste emerged from the police chief's private bathroom to find Raul sitting at his desk, sifting through papers. He removed a pair of half-moon reading glasses and gestured for Celeste to sit in an armchair on the other side of the desk.

"Feeling better?" His smile of slight amusement gave the impression of humoring a child who had dressed up in his clothes.

Celeste was not going to be condescended to by this man, and she bristled internally. "Much better, thanks. Now I can think clearly about what happened," she said. And only tell you what I want you to know, she thought.

"Well," said Raul. "You were trespassing on government property. The catacombs are officially not in the public domain. I can only assume that you were investigating something about the murder you witnessed last spring."

Celeste wondered how much he knew and tested the water. "My curiosity got the better of me, I guess. I've been wondering ever since I found that corpse where it might have originated, and wanted to see the rest of the famous catacombs."

"I may be Puerto Rican, but I'm not a fool, and I'm a chief of police" said Raul haughtily. "It doesn't look like you wandered down there from mere personal curiosity.'' He gestured to the pile of Celeste's practical clothes on top of the nylon backpack. ''You should know that we cooperate closely with the FBI here. I understand that you also, have been working with them.''

Okay, thought Celeste. But she still didn't trust him. When he had finally agreed to Audrey's recruitment, Minot had hinted that he was concerned about internal leaks regarding Celeste's activities, and urged her to be discreet. She couldn't be too careful. ''I was just trying to jog my memory, as long as I was back here. If I found anything, I would have let you know.''

''And did you?''

''Cobwebs,'' said Celeste. ''I had forgotten about the cobwebs. The body had to have been delivered from the catacombs and not the museum, since I walked through a huge cobweb network before I found it.''

''Interesting,'' said Raul. ''We were quite convinced of that. But I suppose your observation confirms it. It is unfortunate that you did not remember the cobwebs last spring.''

''Well, it should be helpful now,'' said Celeste, feeling defensive.

''What about your aunt? Where does she fit in?'' asked Raul, apparently dismissing the topic of Celeste's new find.

''My great aunt,'' said Celeste. ''My grandfather's sister. What about her? I asked her to spend Thanksgiving with me over here to cheer her up. She's not well.'' She hoped Audrey hadn't said anything about Celeste's proposition when she called Raul for help.

''She seemed to be aware that you could be in danger.''

''It's only natural that she would worry when I didn't show up.''

''Hmph,'' said Raul, clearly indicating he was not

thoroughly satisfied with Celeste's explanation. He looked like he was about to say something, but was interupted by the shrill pierce of the telephone, which he picked up. *"Si?"*

Celeste watched him while he listened and responded, periodically saying, *"Si."* His imperious manner had not helped to soften his handsome features in her eyes. The neat beard and mustache hid too much for her taste. She couldn't tell if he was just being protective or was pressing her for information.

When he hung up, Raul looked across the desk at Celeste and sat quiet for a minute. "They found the dog. Shot dead. Apparently gave its companion a nasty bite. There was a blood trail back through the boutique. You're lucky it wasn't you."

"I am," said Celeste. "And I am grateful," she added genuinely, looking at Raul.

"I am, too," he said, rising from his seat. He walked around to where Celeste was sitting opposite him and, standing in front of her, put his hands on her shoulders and leaned down to kiss her forehead. "You should go back to the hotel. I will call an escort for you."

Celeste felt herself color at the unexpected tenderness of the gesture. "Thanks," she said.

Raul listened carefully as Celeste was escorted across the foyer and out of the police headquarters. Then he picked up the phone and dialed Miami again.

"Minot," he said, repeating the greeting in response to his call. "I'm helping because your Dr. Braun actually came up with some useful information. Of course, it would have been nice if we had known this earlier. She remembered that the passage from the museum was filled with cobwebs. That means the body came from inside the catacombs, as you had suspected.

"Good work," grunted Minot, feeling partially exonerated.

"There's something else you should know. She was being hunted by a dog. My men found it shot dead. The bullet looks to them like it came from the sort of gun that your agents often carry. I'm having a hard time figuring that one out unless your guys are interfering again. It certainly wasn't my men who shot the animal. They were looking for the person on the other end of the leash. Whoever it was shouldn't have been in the tunnels. That goes for your personnel, as well."

Minot sighed. He instantly knew the explanation and couldn't give it to Raul. "I'll look into it," he said. "When we talked last spring, I did give orders to our guys to clear out and leave things to your department, but maybe someone misunderstood. I'll do my best to make sure it doesn't happen again." Minot realized his credibility rating with the San Juan police was not exactly soaring and doubted that Raul was reassured.

But, thankfully, Raul had been helpful. He understood about the cobwebs and might be able to correlate it with additional evidence from their earlier investigation to connect the corpse to the clinic and ultimately to the Valentinos. Minot was ironically reassured by the fact that the dog was eliminated with a government bullet. Minot figured that the CIA must still be following Celeste, to be sure she backed off the case. There would be no way they could prove that she hadn't done this on her own, and it was their problem if they thought otherwise. In fact, she had, more or less, done it on her own. At least it wasn't the Valentinos who had been after her with the dog. So there was no reason that the aunt couldn't still be used to infiltrate their operation at the Taipei clinic. Minot hoped that Celeste had managed to arrange that, at least, before getting herself in trouble. He now awaited her report with considerably less annoyance than he had felt an hour earlier. Minot's only nagging worry was whether the mole had connections to what Raul knew. Minot had already reasoned that Raul himself was not a likely suspect for the mole, and Raul's own annoyance about who shot the dog supported Minot's reasoning. The real test, though, would be whether Minot was carpeted again.

11

Blackwater Blood

Sandra Lovett wondered how long she could keep the balancing act going. Sooner or later her family would figure out that she was sending her patients on other missions and there would be hell to pay. She had anglicized her name, but she couldn't escape the Valentino heritage. Recently one of her other clients had made it clear he was aware of her situation and, as she had feared, tried to use it to his advantage. His threat to expose her Mafia connections would trap her under his thumb as well as her family's. The next patient would have to be used for double duty.

Sandra had thought about it sufficiently to know it was theoretically possible for a patient to carry two messages at once. It wouldn't even change the treatment protocol, just the injection mixture. Sandra had half an hour before her double duty guinea pig showed up. It was time enough to prepare the injection and for her cigarette smoke to dissipate, or so she thought.

But she hadn't anticipated Audrey and her ex-smoker's keen nose. The minute Audrey entered Sandra's office she took a deep breath and said, "You can flaunt it now, honey, but if you don't quit soon you'll end up like me, a walking corpse.'' Indeed, Sandra could see that Audrey's skin was grey underneath the masque of her slightly uneven makeup and garish lipstick. Her bearing was that of someone who was just plain tired out and ready to be free of the fussing that accompanies chronic illness. Sandra wondered whether Audrey would even last long enough to be useful as a carrier pigeon. She would have to accelerate the treatment to maximize Audrey's utility.

''What can I do for you, Ms. Ruben?'' asked Sandra.

''My doctor in Miami found out that your clinic has beds at the Herbal Institute in Taipei,'' said Audrey, well-rehearsed. ''He was looking on the Web for experimental lung cancer treatments and saw that the Japanese trials were going on there. When he contacted them, they told him the beds were fully reserved but that bookings were available through your clinic. It would help me a lot to make the appointment through a U.S. clinic so I could get some insurance coverage for the treatment.''

Sandra assessed the sagging flesh of the woman in front of her and her pendulous gold jewelry. She understood that they both knew that the treatment was hopeless. Society was forcing this woman to grasp at straws. Her doctor benefited, Sandra and her clients benefited, but did Audrey benefit from this knee-jerk assumption that postponing her death was a good thing? Sandra couldn't afford to be philosophical, however.

''Yes, Ms. Ruben,'' she said. ''We do have beds available at the Taipei clinic. However, I will need to check with the director as to whether we can get you into the lung cancer treatment trials since my clinic normally specializes in neurological disorders. Fortunately, we have a good working relationship so I don't foresee any difficulties.''

''I'd like to go as soon as possible,'' said Audrey.

"At the rate things are progressing, I could be dead by the end of the year."

Sandra did some quick calculations. The minimum time needed between injections was two weeks and the minimum number of injections for making Audrey's journey useful was two. It was the week after Thanksgiving. If she were injected immediately, the second injection could be scheduled for mid-December, and the trip to Taipei could be scheduled for the end of the year. "If you are going to Taipei, you need some preparatory immunization. The clinic insists that all patients have booster shots for tetanus, one month in advance, and are given gamma globulin shots two weeks before accepting them as patients. Since you are in a hurry, we could give you the tetanus immunization today. If I am able to book the bed, you can come back in two weeks for the gamma globulin injection. Otherwise, a tetanus booster won't harm you anyway. It's only an injection of inactivated tetanus toxin to increase your protective antibody levels."

"It sounds okay to me," said Audrey. "Do I roll up my sleeves or drop my trousers?"

Sandra had to smile. She doubted she would be as spunky when confronting her own degeneration. She filled a syringe with the mix she had prepared prior to Audrey's arrival.

The period between Thanksgiving and Christmas was peaceful at BAU and Celeste appreciated it. Exams for the quarter were over by the first week in December and the medical, dentistry, and pharmacy students cleared out. Only the Ph.D. students were left and they had no classes or teaching assistant duties to distract them from working in the laboratories. Celeste's laboratory consisted of eight benches, two on either side of four islands projecting into the center of the room outside her office.

This was a lot of bench space for an assistant professor, particularly at BAU, where space wars were chronic. In fact, Celeste's laboratory consisted of nine personnel, but with Eric out of commission, there was enough bench space for everyone.

Celeste noticed that Eric's absence had coincided with a very productive period in the laboratory. Without his negative attitude and provocative questions, lab meetings were considerably more pleasant and constructive. It was remarkable how much difference one person's absence could make. She was anxious to have him back in the laboratory though, because the work he had initiated right before his accident had become indispensable for the success of another lab member's project.

Celeste tried to organize the work in her laboratory so that each person had a separate, but related problem to solve. This contrasted with the policy of a number of senior colleagues who assigned at least two people, and sometimes most of the lab, to the same project. Science progressed by both methods. In Celeste's case, she had to pick problems where her expertise could make a unique contribution so that there was not much competition with other laboratories. The labs where overlapping efforts were the norm were intensely competitive and usually in a race with several other labs to clone the trendy genes or characterize the hot proteins.

Recently, Meg, a quiet postdoctoral fellow in Celeste's laboratory, had uncovered a new pathway by which certain types of virus assemble in cells. If her observations turned out to be correct, they would have a significant impact on the development of anti-viral drugs. To confirm Meg's finding it would be very useful if she could compare the assembly of two different types of virus within the same cell. Eric had been studying virus variation and his goal had been to obtain antibodies that could distinguish between different virus strains.

These would be useful laboratory tools for locating virus particles inside cells. The role of antibodies in the immune system is to bind to infectious organisms and tag them for destruction. The same binding properties allow antibodies to tag infectious organisms in a laboratory experiment, making it possible to track them by attaching fluorescent dyes to the antibodies.

The anti-viral antibodies were being produced by rabbits that had been injected with proteins from the different virus strains. The injections had been initiated a few days before Eric's accident. He had provided enough material for booster injections to increase antibody production, which had been done while he was in the hospital. Blood had already been drawn from the injected rabbits and there was a phone message sitting on Eric's desk from the rabbit farm of the California Serum Company that the blood was ready for delivery. Meg approached Celeste about it. She stood stiffly in the doorway to Celeste's office, unaccustomed to asserting herself. "I don't see how I can wait until after Christmas, when Eric returns, to do the antibody experiments."

"I don't see how you can wait either. It won't be long before Pogue's lab or Churchill's group make the same observation, and we'd rather not be in a race to publish."

"Could you please ask Eric if he left enough material for me to test the antibodies and if he minds if I do it?"

"I think you should ask him," said Celeste. "He's certainly not going to mind if someone does his work for him. Especially if you make it clear he'll be a coauthor on your paper. Besides, if someone else is interested in the antibodies, it might even inspire him to see the value of having the rabbits injected. If I ask him, he'll just react negatively for the sake of it."

"Maybe," said Meg. She didn't look too happy about

having to take responsibility for her request.

Celeste thought, not for the first time, that teaching scientific principles was easy compared to teaching people how to get science done. If she negotiated everything for the people in her lab, they would never learn to fend for themselves.

The phone rang on Celeste's desk and she used it as a convenient excuse to end the discussion with Meg. Normally she let the tape answer if someone was in her office.

"Celeste darling, it's Audrey. I just got home from Washington."

"How did it go?"

"Fine, fine. She's taken me on and I go to Taipei at the end of the year. Even got my injection."

"What injection?"

"Um, you know, that shot they give you if you step on a nail or cut yourself."

"Tetanus?"

"Yeah, that's it."

"That seems strange."

"She said it was required by the clinic before sending anyone to Taipei. Also, I'll have to go back in two weeks for some other shot. Something to do with globs I think."

"Globs," said Celeste.

"Gummy globs, maybe?"

Celeste sat back in her swivel chair and looked around her office for inspiration. Her desk was piled with photocopied articles from scientific journals. Above the desk, which bordered two sides of the small room, the bookshelves were crammed with bound laboratory notebooks interspersed with a rainbow of colored looseleaf binders. Celeste's gaze rested on the diagram of a virus that was tacked to the bulletin board among schedules for various committee and class meetings and unreturned phone messages.

Audrey interrupted Celeste's puzzlement. "No, no it wasn't globs it was goblins. Gummy goblins. I remember because I was picturing goblins sticking to each other."

It could have been the image of the virus that made Celeste think of hepatitis and suddenly understand. "Gamma globulin, perhaps?"

"That's it!" said Audrey with enthusiasm.

It didn't help Celeste much, however. Gamma globulin is a type of immunoglobulin, the technical term for antibody. When isolated from the blood of patients who have been infected with hepatitis A and have developed immunity, the gamma globulin can protect against further infection and is injected into travelers who are visiting areas of high risk for contracting hepatitis. Neither of these prescribed injections, tetanus or gamma globulin, should have been necessary for preparing a patient for care at a high tech clinic of the calibre that Celeste had seen in Taipei.

"Celeste, are you there?"

"Yeah, sorry. I was just thinking about why you would need these particular injections."

"That's your department, dear."

"I'm sure that something about your treatment will give us a clue about how the clinics are using patients to transmit information. You'll have to keep your eyes open for more unusual procedures like this."

"Celeste, honey, I have to remind you that I didn't know this was unusual. To me whatever the doc says, goes. You see it's like you and fashion, dear. I can recognize fashion and I can recognize style. You can only recognize fashion because it's on the pages of a magazine. Lucky for you, you have style, which lasts, while fashion comes and goes."

"Audrey, what does that have to do with the price of eggs?" asked Celeste in frustration.

"Precisely my point, dear. You stick with what you know and I stick with what I know, and we make a good team."

Perhaps the lateral thinking was contagious. Celeste suddenly, incongruously, remembered her musings about messenger molecules. When she first saw the organic waste containers in Taipei she had considered the possibility that the clinic patients were injected with organic chemicals that could be detected in the blood as some kind of coded message. She had dismissed this as unlikely for several reasons, but here was potential evidence that information was transmitted by injection. It wouldn't hurt to do an analysis of Audrey's blood. If chemicals were being used, they should be detectable by chromatography.

"Okay, Audrey. I see your point," said Celeste. "You got me thinking about your injections. Do you think you could ask Dr. Kirshner to send me a blood sample?"

"Isn't he going to think that's a little strange?" asked Audrey.

"Just tell him we're doing a family study and need a sample of your blood in a red-topped tube."

"In a what?"

"Just tell him it doesn't matter if it clots. He can call me if he has any questions."

"That's disgusting," said Audrey.

"Audrey, please. Remember this is my department, as you said, and to me it's not disgusting."

"Whatever," said Audrey. "I'll call Dr. Kirshner in the morning. I assume you want the clot sent by some kind of courier."

"Please," said Celeste.

"All right, dear." Audrey sounded ready to hang up,

then startled both of them. "Oh! I almost forgot to tell you. I had a nice surprise waiting when I got home."

"What was that?"

"I had my own bouquet of white roses waiting at the door of my apartment. You must have told your police chief friend how much I enjoyed yours. Apparently he had some business in Miami and came around to see how I was doing. Left his card and the flowers when I wasn't there. Isn't that sweet?"

This was a bit too coincidental, thought Celeste. "Did any of your neighbors know where you were?" she asked Audrey.

"I'm not that stupid," said Audrey. "If I'm going on a secret mission, I'm not about to announce it to all my friends. I told Muriel that I was going on a buying trip."

"Good thinking," said Celeste, but she was uncomfortable about Raul checking up on Audrey nonetheless. "When do you go back for the gamma globulin injection?"

"Anytime after two weeks from today. Then I have to wait for two more weeks until I can go to Taipei."

"I'll meet you in Washington for the next appointment. Maybe we can go to some exhibitions while we're there." Given Raul's apparent interest in Audrey, Celeste wasn't sure who else might be interested. Under these circumstances, Celeste felt she should at least be nearby during Audrey's next clinic visit.

"That would be lovely, dear. I can take you shopping."

"Fine," said Celeste, already distracted by trying to figure out her schedule and by the sudden possibility of seeing Stash in Washington. This trip to meet Audrey would provide a perfect excuse. "I'll call you back as soon as I sort out the dates that I can leave here. Don't forget to send the blood in the meantime."

"How could I?" asked Audrey and hung up.

Celeste had tried hard to ignore the occasional thoughts of Stash, but she had been unable to get him out of her mind completely. She didn't think of him when she was busy in the lab and hadn't thought about him much during the trip to San Juan. But the recollection of their lovemaking and his evident intense need for whatever she was fulfilling was not easily dismissed. She knew that it was best to let him sort out his fatherhood situation and that it was best achieved by not giving him any options but to work things out with Jill. But what about Celeste? What about her needs as a woman? He wouldn't serve them in the long term but he filled a temporary gap for her as well, probably too satisfactorily for her own good. Celeste had been in situations like this before and had caught herself just in time. Such was the danger of dallying with men who were forbidden fruit. But there was no denying that the forbidden aspect contributed to their appeal. And maybe the certainty of their long term unavailability also appealed. Was this the logical behavior of a scientist?

Celeste decided that logic was irrelevant when Stash responded to her phone call. They arranged to meet for the weekend before Audrey's appointment. When Celeste hung up, she was satisfied that she had done the right thing in giving in to their mutual attraction. She anticipated that the intervening two weeks would crawl by.

Fortunately, within three days, a blood sample from Audrey arrived, and Celeste was absorbed by the analysis. The result, however, was disappointing but not surprising. It showed that nothing unusual was present in Audrey's blood. Celeste hadn't really expected that organic chemicals in non-toxic levels could provide a detectable system of communication, but at least she had ruled it out. She remained stuck with the puzzle of how the injections were connected to the generation of or-

ganic waste and how either of those processes could relate to the illicit passing of information. Out of long
habit, Celeste divided the remains of Audrey's blood
sample into several equal portions and stuck the vials
holding them in the freezer. Experience told her that, at
some point, she might think of something else to test
for.

Except for Celeste and Stash, the beach at Chincoteague
National Wildlife Refuge was deserted of human beings.
They shared the overcast afternoon with busy sander-
lings, who carried out the shore birds' comic choreography in their approach-avoidance dance with the tide
line. Watching the birds, Celeste and Stash did not
speak, nor did they touch. They were wrapped in an
adult, solemn intimacy different from the cuddling affection of domestic couples. Holding hands or reassuring
hugs were not in the repertoire of their interaction, yet
they were at that moment undefinably close.

Celeste had detected a sense of finality in Stash's
lovemaking, as though he could not get enough of her
and did not expect to have the chance again. It seemed
as if he had been a party to her conversation with herself
about what was best for him and, of course, for her. Two
days earlier they had met at the Baltimore–Washington
airport where Celeste rented a car. Kissing chastely at
the arrival gate, as old friends greeting each other, they
made small talk during the early evening drive across
the two bridges spanning the Chesapeake Bay toward
their destination, an old coaching inn near Cambridge
on the eastern shore of Maryland. Only once, after they
crossed the third bridge, over the Choptank River, did
Stash put his hand on the back of Celeste's neck. The
touch was electrifying, though Celeste felt shy about returning it.

It wasn't until their friendly landlady had shut the

door to their room and firmly shut the outside door to the inn, returning to her apartment in the carriage house, that Celeste and Stash could embrace. It was an embrace that locked out the rest of the world and was so filled with yearning that they couldn't remove their clothes fast enough.

The slow lovemaking should have come later, but they only had to begin again when the same fervor aroused them both. Ultimately they exhausted each other, slept, made love again and finally, ravenously hungry, ventured out the next morning in search of breakfast.

Their first day together had been an idyll, a day stolen from both their lives. They walked over the entire Black-water Wildlife Refuge and counted at least a dozen bald eagles soaring around their nesting area. Stash took several rolls of film, though no shots of Celeste. Celeste observed snow geese at close range for the first time. Refugees from their breeding ground in the Arctic tundra, they reminded Celeste of Audrey and her friends in Miami with their busy social interaction and incessant honking. A late afternoon drizzle had sent Celeste and Stash back through the boarded up factory town of Cambridge, with its single lunch counter and pool parlor, and back to bed. As if prescribed, they did not touch each other until they had returned to the privacy of their room. They had shared little except their bed, but their separate, quiet observations were companionable. Each was escaping from concerns that they wished to forget and they had found refuge in not exploring each other's psyche too deeply.

On the way back from Chincoteague, on their second day together, Stash seemed distracted and Celeste could sense that his thoughts of the outside world were encroaching on their self-styled neutral zone. She had a feeling that something was going to interfere with their last night together and thought it might be Stash himself. As she drove, Celeste watched him out of the corner of her eye. His gaze was directed straight ahead through the windshield. He was absentmindedly rubbing his forearm, which bore a serious-looking scar.

"It's funny I didn't remember your scar from last time," said Celeste. "We must have been pretty distracted."

"War wound," said Stash. "I'd rather not talk about it."

As soon as they got back to the inn, Stash excused himself to make a call from the phone in the sitting room on the ground floor. He suggested that Celeste might want to run a bath. His tone of practicality reminded Celeste of his managerial status in another world.

Celeste certainly did not want to hear him speak to Jill, so she was sitting obligingly in the steaming bathtub when Stash came in and sat down, fully dressed, on the edge. It could have been a sexy situation, but it wasn't. His manner was stiff and he didn't look at Celeste while he talked, as though respecting her privacy.

"I'm going to have to go back tonight. Jill's not coping with Damian very well and I . . ."

Celeste did not want to hear the rest of his excuse and interupted him. "I thought you might. Never mind. We've had a good couple of days."

"Yes, we have," said Stash and sighed. He put his hand on Celeste's shoulder and leaned down and kissed her forehead. It was a regretful, but indulgent gesture, not one of concern like Raul's had been. "Let's get dressed and get something to eat down at the waterfront. I'll leave from there."

"Fine," said Celeste, and stepped out of the tub to dry off. Stash washed up quickly and packed his bag, without even a look in her direction.

They had a simple dinner of beer and fried local

clams, overlooking the wintry harbor at the effluence of the Choptank into Chesapeake Bay. Evidently Stash had arranged for a shuttle ride to the Baltimore–Washington airport and planned to take the train into Washington from there. Celeste was meeting Audrey the following morning at the Baltimore–Washington airport where they would do the same after returning the car. Celeste offered to let Stash return the car that evening and to take the shuttle herself in the morning, since he might get home more quickly that way.

"That's not necessary, but thanks," said Stash, almost as though Celeste had said something out of line. "You might need the car to drive your aunt into Washington if she's not feeling up to taking the train. I've been getting the impression from you that she's quite frail."

Frail was never a word that Celeste could or would associate with Audrey. She realized that Stash meant ill and was being polite, but she couldn't suppress a smile. "If you knew her, you probably wouldn't use that exact word," she said, and then lost the humor of it to reality. "It's hardly a joking matter, though, and I certainly don't mean to make light of it. There's nothing funny about lung cancer."

"I realize," said Stash. "I'm so sorry. I didn't know the details of her illness. I had hoped there was a better prognosis since she was undergoing treatment." Celeste was slightly taken aback by his realistic assumption of Audrey's inevitable demise.

After Stash left the restaurant, Celeste drove back to the inn feeling a familiar numbness. She knew that it would pass in a few days and that the time with Stash would evolve into an occasional pleasant daydream. That night they were the only guests booked at the inn and the landlady had left the front door unlocked for them. Celeste let herself in, feeling more than ready for a good night's sleep. She appreciated the fact that the landlady had shut off the lights downstairs but left the stairway and upstairs corridor illuminated.

The door to the room that Stash and Celeste had been sharing was slightly ajar, though Celeste remembered shutting it. Stash had been amused at her concern that they should lock it. The landlady must have also done a turndown, something she hadn't had a chance to do the two previous evenings. Celeste pushed the door open and heard the tap dripping. The landlady must have tidied up the bathroom, too. Then, in the low light of the bedside lamp, Celeste saw what was dripping. The white bedspread was awash with blood, which had collected into a stream dripping steadily off the bed onto the braided rag carpet. In the middle of the bed lay a freshly butchered snow goose. Its belly had been ripped open in a V-shaped slash.

12

Rest Cure

The dormitory of the Taipei Medical College for Women
was not exactly the Grand Palace Hotel. However, it was
a less likely place for Celeste's presence in Taipei to be
discovered. Celeste shivered awake in the middle of her
first night there and pulled on a pair of pantyhose underneath her nightgown, already topped with a sweatshirt, then got back into bed. The cold damp was not
compatible with sleep, which was only reluctantly com-
peting with Celeste's tense anxiety.

Celeste did not want to be in Taipei, but Audrey had
been adamant about continuing her so-called treatment.
In fact, it seemed to Celeste that Audrey's stubborn in-
sistence was perversely increased when she heard about
the snow goose. The horror of finding the carcass, followed by dealing with the mess and confronting the inn-
keeper, had the desired effect on Celeste. The Valentino
family had made it clear they still had an eye on her.
She could feel their collective breath on her neck and
wanted out.

It wasn't just Audrey who was stubborn about completing the mission. Jack Minot supported Audrey all the
way in a protracted three-way debate between them.

Since the snow goose butchering, Celeste had avoided being with Audrey and hoped that she had managed to divert the presumed surveillance from having an interest in Audrey's activities. Instead of meeting Audrey at the airport after the weekend with Stash, Celeste had arranged for a driver and car to meet Audrey and take her into Washington. Celeste drove herself to her parents' place in New York, where she spent an edgy night before flying back to San Francisco. She had only communicated with Audrey using purchased phone cards and pay phones, clocking useless hours of trying to dissuade Audrey from their original plan.

Then Celeste approached Jack Minot, who was equally resistant. Minot's rationale for continuing was that nothing had connected Audrey to Celeste's work for the FBI. She was a bystander in San Juan, but that incident was fully explained by CIA interference. There had been no repercussion to Minot either, so the mole appeared to be uninformed about Celeste's tunnel exploration. What Celeste did not know was that Minot had also independently checked on Audrey and had taken the risk of communicating with her. He knew how ill she was, and he knew how little she desired to persist through her own deterioration. Minot and Audrey both decided that their collusion was their own business and that it was too risky to speak to Celeste about it over the phone anyway. If they had, collusion was hardly the word that Minot would have used, even though he was ever-conscious of Celeste's influence on his vocabulary.

Finally, outnumbered, Celeste insisted that she would not let Audrey go alone to Taipei. Celeste flew to Taipei via Japan, spending a few days with Kazuko en route. Kazuko arranged for Nan Shin to meet Celeste at the Taipei airport and to fix up the accommodation in the dormitory where she now lay. Even if the Valentinos had followed Celeste to Taipei on her ostensible consultancy trip for Fukuda, there would be no reason for them to connect her with Audrey or Audrey's simultaneous visit to the clinic.

Celeste finally slept, having put on most of the bed-compatible clothing she had brought with her. She woke with a desperate need to pee, exacerbated by sleeping in pantyhose. The small, cold bedroom connected to a minute, cold private bathroom with a corner that could be curtained off to run the shower, which drained into the floor. Celeste discovered that running a hot shower for a few minutes generated enough steam throughout both rooms that it was possible to undress, shower quickly and get dressed in relative comfort. She realized that this heating method may have been responsible for the overall feeling of damp that seemed to pervade the accommodation.

Celeste was scheduled to see Nan Shin at the clinic in the early afternoon, at which point Nan Shin would have already seen Audrey and could pass on details about Audrey's treatment to Celeste. The National Palace Museum wasn't open to the public that morning, so Celeste took a guidebook to breakfast to see what else she could do to pass the time. After all, this trip was as close to a Christmas vacation as she would get this year. Breakfast was served in a huge cafeteria and only a few tables were occupied since most of the students were home for the holidays. To get to where the food was served Celeste walked past an African gentleman in national garb who appeared to be having curried something with rice for his breakfast. Indeed, the selection at the serving counter included this dish. There was also a metal pan full of tired-looking fried eggs adjacent to a second pan full of soggy, toasted white bread. In front of these were small dishes with chopped up green vegetables, onions, tomatoes, and Chinese pickles. Celeste plopped an egg on top of a piece of toast and passed up the condiments, choosing a small plastic bottle of chemical orange juice. By the time she sat down with her tray, her stomach had uncooperatively knotted, as much from the unusual odors emanating from the food counter as from the prospect of a cold egg on soggy toast. She went back to the counter for a mug of tea, forgoing artificial creamer, and settled down to look at the guidebook hoping that her stomach would relent in a few minutes.

Celeste decided that a visit to the Botanical Gardens, which was also a home to the National Museum of History, would provide a good ceramic experience with potential birding opportunities. She gave up trying to consume the now-congealed eggy toast and headed back up to her room to collect her binoculars and bird book. As she walked past the reception desk, the guard called out to her.

"Doctor, you have message."

Celeste walked up to the desk, and he handed her a piece of paper with Chinese characters. She looked at it, perplexed. Then she looked up at the receptionist, who was smiling with amusement at his little prank.

"Call Dr. Nan Shin at the clinic," he said.

"Can you connect the call to my room?" asked Celeste.

"Yes, you phone from room and I connect."

Back in the room, Celeste stuffed the accessories she needed for her excursion into her handbag while she stood waiting for the call to go through.

"Nan Shin, speaking" she heard at last. Celeste identified herself and Nan Shin got straight down to business.

"Dr. Lovett has a lunch appointment outside the clinic and asked me to call a car for her to leave at 10:30. I also called for a car to pick you up at 10:15 at the dormitory. I gave them instructions to follow Lovett's car. I thought you might want to know her business."

Celeste looked at her watch. It was five minutes past ten. "Won't my driver say something to Lovett's driver?"

"Two different companies," said Nan Shin.

"Thanks a million," said Celeste.

"Don't mention it," said Nan Shin. "I do not like being taken advantage of."

Celeste hurried downstairs and had waited only a few minutes on the steps of the dormitory when a small, slate-colored sedan with a taxi sign on its roof pulled up. She peered through the window.

"Are you here for Dr. Braun?" she asked.

She was acknowledged with a nod. Evidently the driver didn't speak English.

Celeste got into the back, not feeling very confident. As soon as she shut the door, the driver sped away from the dormitory entrance toward the clinic. The clinic was only about a mile from the dormitory along the main road, which passed through the large medical center campus, but the driver was presumably demonstrating that he understood his instructions. They positively hurtled over the small bridge above yellow-green rice paddies belonging to the department of nutrition and, just short of the clinic, the driver stopped the car abruptly and cut the engine.

There were some scraggly bushes shielding the clinic steps from the spot where they were parked. Celeste looked at her watch. It was twenty minutes past ten. They sat in silence for a few minutes, the taxi driver was staring ahead at the clinic entrance. Then a white taxi cab pulled up at the clinic entrance and Celeste's driver started his engine. He grunted something in Chinese and put on a pair of sunglasses. Getting into the spirit, Celeste did likewise. They only had to wait a few more minutes before Dr. Lovett came down the steps, spoke to her waiting driver through the window, and got into the back of his taxi. The two cabs took off into the streets of Taipei.

Because the streets of Taipei are perpetually clogged with traffic, the average speed never exceeds twenty miles per hour. Driving consists of jockeying for position to make it through the next traffic light. Celeste's driver seemed to be in his element, grunting and exclaiming as he kept two to three cars behind the white taxi bearing Sandra Lovett. There was a rhythmic jerkiness to the chase, which took them past dusty arrays of storefronts plastered with neon signs and symbols. It was like one pulsating, commercial enterprise and Celeste wondered whether the people of Taipei had homes to rest in or were caught in an endless round of shopping and driving that kept them from settling down. She noted the regularity of the butterfly signs, identifying brothels, and it occurred to her that the symbol might represent the tenuousness of being able to alight anywhere in the moving city, in addition to the obvious connotation of fleeting pleasure.

Celeste thought they had entered a neighborhood she recognized and several minutes later the taxis turned onto a more open road that led past the Grand Hotel and onto the Sun Yat-sen freeway. Lovett's car was evidently headed for the Chiang Kai-shek International Airport. On the freeway, the traffic flow picked up slightly and within twenty minutes, the two taxis were caught up in the slowdown funneling past the terminal. Then the jam came to a dead standstill and Celeste lost sight of the white taxi ahead of them.

But her driver had seen the taxi pull into a curbside pickup lane and began to maneuver his way over toward the terminal building. Just as he pulled in, two cars behind the white taxi, it pulled out.

"There it is," exclaimed Celeste. "And someone's in there with her."

Her observation was rewarded with a grunt as they pulled out to resume their pursuit.

The taxi with Lovett and her passenger retraced the route they had taken to the airport. Celeste tapped her driver on the shoulder and tried to indicate in sign language that they should get closer. She had a gut feeling that it was important for her to get a look at the passenger. Each time her driver reduced the number of cars between them, the white taxi found a niche in the next lane over and gained a car. It was a classic, steady-state situation. Celeste had never before considered the possibility that Le Chatelier's principle of chemical equilibrium also applied to car chases. Finally, the white taxi took the exit off the Sun Yat-sen freeway from which they had come and Celeste was convinced that they must be heading back toward the clinic. Perhaps Lovett was just picking up another patient. Celeste's driver appeared to be convinced of the same thing since he didn't seem to be making more of an effort to catch up.

Just as they were about to pass the Grand Hotel, the white taxi turned off in front of them and proceeded up the drive to the hotel. Celeste's driver couldn't cross over the lanes in time to take the same turnoff and turned into the next ramp, which diverted the taxis around the back of the hotel into the pickup queue instead of the drop-off queue. Celeste's driver sped up this road, and when he reached the tail end of the queue, snaking down the steep ramp up to the hotel entrance, he started honking and gesturing to Celeste in the back to indicate to the other drivers that he had someone to drop off and to let him by. Celeste was concerned that this frantic behavior might catch the attention of Lovett and her passenger, but she needn't have worried since she saw Lovett's navy-blue jacketed back disappear into the hotel entrance just as the taxi reached a height in the ramp that the entrance became visible. There were a group of Caucasian tourists entering the hotel at the same time as Lovett, and Celeste could not distinguish whether Lovett's companion might have been caught up in that group.

Two minutes later, Celeste's taxi arrived at the hotel door and she got out, making gestures to the taxi driver to go back around the circular drive and rejoin the taxi queue. He seemed to understand what she was saying. She certainly hoped he did since he knew the way back to the clinic, and it was unlikely she would be able to explain her destination to another driver. On an earlier visit to Taipei she'd already had the disconcerting experience of getting into a taxi and being completely unable to communicate where she wanted to go.

The hotel lobby was packed with groups of tourists milling about and Celeste did not spot Lovett immediately. From her previous stay in the hotel, she knew that the promenade balcony on the seventh floor, where the main restaurant was located, would give her a bird's-eye view. Lovett and her companion were not among the group that Celeste joined to wait for the elevators on the right-hand side of the lobby. They were hopefully stuck in some registration queue that would move slowly and keep them visible until Celeste reached the seventh floor.

At least the elevators were more efficient than those back home in Celeste's laboratory at BAU, where she seemed to pass half of her working day waiting for a lift to the fifteenth floor. Within a few minutes, Celeste was on the seventh floor promenade, standing behind an elaborately carved wooden balustrade scanning the crowd below. As she looked out for Lovett's blazer and black hair, she fished around in her handbag for her bird-watching binoculars. Her hand closed on the small leather case just as she spotted what she thought was the top of Lovett's head. Lovett was standing in the registration queue in close conversation with a blond-haired

man. Celeste barely needed to look through the binoculars to confirm her recognition of Stash's familiar re-
ceding hairline. As she focused his features into view,
she realized she had been a complete fool.

But there was no time for self-recrimination. Whatever the connection between Stash and Lovett was, Celeste understood that he must have been the source of
the Valentino family's ability to find her at will. He
knew that Audrey was in the clinic. He knew her connection to Celeste. Audrey was undoubtedly in danger.

From the moment of revelation on the seventh floor
of the Grand Hotel to the minute she burst into Nan
Shin's office at the clinic, Celeste was seized by panic.
Much to the irritation of the patiently queuing taxi drivers waiting outside the hotel, Celeste had run halfway
down the ramp, found her driver, and jumped into the
backseat of his taxi. He peeled out of the queue with a
shrug of his shoulders to the other drivers and a pur-
poseful grunt. During the entire jerky ride back to the
clinic, Celeste anxiously canvassed the streets for land-
marks to reassure herself that her directions of ''Clinic,
clinic, Nan Shin!'' had been understood. Arriving at the
clinic, she ordered the receptionist to pay the taxi,
whereupon she marched behind the reception desk,
knocked perfunctorily on Nan Shin's office door, and
opened it.

Nan Shin looked up from her desk, startled and annoyed. ''Oh, it's you,'' she said. ''You wouldn't know
anything about my missing knife would you?''

Celeste was momentarily taken aback by the abrupt
question. She glanced at the wall behind Nan Shin's
desk where the bejeweled dagger was normally suspended. The curved mark on the wall where it had hung
was visible as a shadowy outline in the paint. She did
not want to think about where the dagger might be. A
dreadful feeling gripped her stomach.

"I hope I'm wrong," said Celeste, "but I think we should look in Audrey's room right away. Can you let us in? I'll explain later."

Nan Shin rose quickly from her chair and gestured to Celeste to follow her. She pulled out a bunch of keys from the pocket of her examination smock and sorted through them as they walked up the central staircase to the patient rooms on the second floor.

"I haven't checked on her since early this morning," said Nan Shin. "She was scheduled for some tests from Dr. Lovett's people all morning and, as you know, I was going to see her just after lunch."

"When did you find the dagger missing?" asked Celeste, as they hurried down the corridor.

"I'd been on my own rounds until lunchtime, so not until I went back to the office to get a bite to eat. I only just called security when you walked in."

They had reached the door to Audrey's room. Nan Shin knocked on the door and fit her key in the lock. It struck Celeste as rather unusual for a clinic to have the patients' rooms locked. Nan Shin knocked again on the partially open door. "May we come in," she called into the room.

There was no answer. Nan Shin pushed the door fully open. Celeste was standing behind her, but could easily see over her shoulder. The bed was shielded by a white cloth screen on wheels with only the foot of the bed visible. Covering the surface of the screen was a crude V-shape drawn in blood. Celeste gasped and remained frozen in the doorway. Nan Shin bustled into the room and stood at the foot of the bed, taking in the full view behind the screen.

"I have found the dagger," she said tersely. "You should not see this." She picked up Audrey's patient chart from a hook on the bedpost and turned away from the butchered corpse in front of her toward Celeste in the doorway. Nan Shin studied the chart before she spoke again. "She was heavily drugged before this happened. She would not have felt a thing. I can be absolutely sure of that."

Celeste tried to speak but couldn't.

"We will do a full autopsy," said Nan Shin, gesturing Celeste to be quiet as though she had said something. "Among other things, I think it will show that this was a merciful death compared to what your aunt was facing with her cancer. Furthermore, it could give you the information you seek. Let's go back to the office." Nan Shin gently but firmly propelled Celeste out the door and clicked it shut behind her. She then used a key from her ring to lock a dead bolt on the door. "Director's privilege," she said to Celeste. "No one except me has the key to the bolt. It should keep the corpse from going anywhere before the autopsy."

Celeste wanted to wail, to tell this autocratic doctor that the corpse couldn't go anywhere, that Audrey was no more. But her grief was too great to give voice to it. Her only action was to withdraw her arm from Nan Shin's grip. They walked in silence back down the corridor and down the central staircase to Nan Shin's office.

Celeste knew she should have been afraid for herself, but she only felt sick at heart. Should she suspect Nan Shin's motives? She hadn't yet come to grips with her own stupidity in falling for Stash and wondered whether she had any trustworthy instincts. She didn't actually care. She was responsible for Audrey's death. She would somehow have to live with the misery of that knowledge.

"Celeste," said Nan Shin sharply.

Celeste gave a start and realized she was seated on a couch in Nan Shin's office with Nan Shin standing over her, holding a cup of tea. "Sorry, Nan Shin," she said.

"I think I must be in some kind of shock." Only a few blank minutes had passed since their discovery of Audrey's body, but to Celeste it seemed hours later.

"I'm sure you are," said Nan Shin. "It's understandable. Here, drink this. It will make it easier to cope."

Like a child, Celeste took the cup from Nan Shin and drank obediently. The tea had an undefinable herbal fragrance. The warmth brought Celeste to her senses but also gave her a feeling of well-being that surprised her, under the circumstances.

"You're right, that's better," Celeste acknowledged.

"I don't think you should stay in Taipei any longer than necessary," said Nan Shin. "I will call a taxi to take you back to the dormitory to pack and will make sure that you have a seat on the evening flight out. My autopsy team is now doing their prep in the pathology lab. I will oversee the work myself. We should have the results before you leave."

"Thanks," said Celeste. She had to trust someone.

Back in the dormitory room, the microclimate had warmed up considerably. A sunny afternoon outside had helped erase the damp, and a feeble sunbeam was poking through the single window, which looked out over one of the experimental rice paddies. Celeste stood for a moment at the window, contemplating the wands of rice poking out of the muddy water. The first tears she would shed for Audrey welled up, and she let them flow unchecked down her face to drip on the floor. The tears stopped as abruptly as they had started, and Celeste turned back into the room. She found a tissue in her handbag, wiped her eyes and blew her nose, and felt the comforting release that comes after a good cry.

Celeste didn't have much to pack and most of what she had brought with her, she had worn in bed the previous night. It didn't take much effort to gather these things together and squish them into her carry-on bag.

But suddenly she felt absolutely depleted of energy and desperately wanted to sleep. She zipped up the bag and thought that she would just lie down for a few minutes since Nan Shin hadn't phoned yet. Kicking off her shoes and lying down fully dressed on the bed, Celeste felt herself drop off almost instantaneously. As she succumbed, she realized that she had been drugged. It must have been the tea in Nan Shin's office.

13

Bunny Business

The prick of the syringe needle was not sufficient to rouse Celeste from her inadvertent nap. But the antidote took hold within minutes, and Celeste opened her eyes to see Nan Shin sitting beside her bed, holding a syringe. In Celeste's experience, the sight of a syringe was as threatening as the sight of a gun. She mobilized herself to make a move, trying not to reveal that she was fully awake.

As soon as Nan Shin started to speak, Celeste reared up from her prone position and, with a blow to Nan Shin's forearm, she knocked the syringe out of Nan Shin's hand onto the floor.

"Well!" exclaimed Nan Shin. "Thank goodness, I'd already injected the antidote or we'd never have got you to the airport on time."

"What?" Celeste was inclined to be rude.

Nan Shin spoke patiently. "I gave you a sedative in my office because I knew you needed to rest and wouldn't be able to because of your distress. I thought some rest would make it easier to cope. I've just given you the antidote, so you should be fine. You've had a good sleep."

Celeste was livid. She understood that Nan Shin had tried to do her a favor. She supposed she should be grateful. But Celeste didn't like the idea of someone manipulating her states of consciousness. Even if it was for her own good. She was also wary of Nan Shin. These thoughts must have revealed themselves in her expression.

"I'm sorry you don't trust my judgement," said Nan Shin. "If you like we can phone Kazuko in Japan and she will—"

Celeste cut her off. "No, no. Never mind. I'm just trying to deal with it all." Her voice rose at the end of this last sentence and she swallowed quickly. Thoughts of Audrey had flooded back and a lump had formed in her throat.

"I have the autopsy report," said Nan Shin. She adopted a businesslike tone with the intent of pushing Celeste into professional mode. "I'll send it with you on the plane, but there are a few things I wanted to point out, to make sure you don't overlook them."

"Okay," said Celeste, checking her watch and thinking about the traffic in Taipei. "Should we talk about it in the taxi?" Celeste didn't care about the autopsy results anymore. She just wanted to get home and prove to the Valentino family that she wasn't meddling anymore, whatever she was meddling in.

"You're probably right," said Nan Shin. "We should leave for the airport. We can go in my car."

Nan Shin drove her compact Ford hatchback with confidence, weaving in and out of the pulsating mass of vehicles. As soon as they were in the midst of this familiar crush, Celeste felt more comfortable, particularly since she could now recognize features of the route to the airport.

"First of all," said Nan Shin, "I was right about your aunt's illness. Less than a quarter of her lung tissue was still functioning and the cancer had begun to spread to surrounding organs. Within the month, she would have died of kidney failure if she didn't suffocate first. She was too far gone for our treatments or anyone else's to reverse that degree of metastasis. Frankly, her murder was a far better way to go. We also did a blood analysis and confirmed that she was heavily drugged, so heavily that with her condition she might not have woken up anyway. But with that heavy a dosage, she would not have felt anything.''

''Thanks for telling me,'' said Celeste, stonily. Logically, she understood what Nan Shin was saying. She was, however, too emotionally involved to even consider the concept of euthanasia that Nan Shin was apparently promoting.

''That's not all,'' said Nan Shin. ''There were two other features of the autopsy that I'm trying to put in the picture. First, Audrey's spleen was very enlarged, although there was no evidence of tumor metastasis to that organ. Second, from the blood serum analysis we noticed an unusual pattern of antibodies. Commonly, the antibody fraction will appear as a smooth peak of gamma globulins. But in Audrey's serum there were spikes within the antibody peak. I've included a normal serum analysis along with the report, so you can see the difference.''

When they stopped at the next traffic light, Nan Shin withdrew the autopsy report from the folder she had been carrying and leafed through to find the two analyses. ''This Chinese character here means normal serum and this one means patient serum,'' Nan Shin explained.

The cars behind them started honking, and Nan Shin made a comment under her breath in Chinese. As her car leapt to fill the void in front of them, she said in English, ''You would know better than I do, but could these features suggest an infection?''

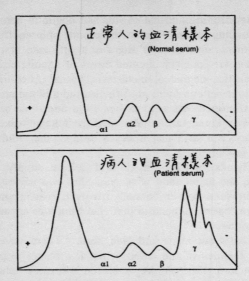

These are the blood analysis data Nan Shin showed to Celeste. The translation of the Chinese characters is in parentheses. Serum is the liquid component of blood and the peaks show the levels of the different kinds of proteins in the blood. The peak on the farthest left is albumin and the four proteins designated with Greek letters are called globulins. γ-globulin is another name for antibodies. The proteins are separated by their electric charge.

"Possibly," said Celeste, not very convinced. "An enlarged spleen certainly might, since the spleen is where populations of antibody-producing cells multiply when infectious agents are present. But this spiky pattern of antibody production doesn't fit a typical response to an infection. Normally, in an infected person, the antibody peak would be larger than in an uninfected individual. But, the peak would still be smooth because many different kinds of antibodies are produced to bind to the many foreign proteins that are present on any particular infectious organism. It's not common for single types of antibody to be increased out of proportion to the others, which would give rise to spikes.''

''Yes, I thought it seemed unusual,'' said Nan Shin. ''Could it be related to what Lovett is up to? I was unable to find any record of the procedures she ordered. The chart was changed before your aunt was infused with morphine. One hope is that the night nurse might remember what she was asked to do when your aunt was admitted. She won't be back on duty until later this evening, but I'll let you know if she can recollect any useful details.''

Nan Shin seemed so keen to help Celeste figure out what Lovett was up to that Celeste couldn't admit her sudden indifference to the whole enterprise. As far as Celeste was concerned, she was clearly out of her league and planned to stay out. She should have listened to Minot's warning when he had first told her to drop the case. And whatever Stash was up to, she didn't want to know. She knew she had been taken advantage of, and she had willingly collaborated. Nan Shin's reaction to being taken advantage of might be one of revenge, but Celeste's inclination at this juncture was to give up. The professionals could sort themselves out among themselves. She was no match for the Mafia, the FBI, and the presumably ex-CIA.

When they finally reached the airport, Celeste took the autopsy report from Nan Shin and stuffed it in her briefcase without any intention of looking at it again. It was part of the ballast she planned to toss overboard to resume her existence as Celeste Braun, mild-mannered scientist. Principal investigator perhaps, but not private investigator.

Celeste spent her first morning back in the laboratory on the telephone to Audrey's friends and relatives. There should have been some therapeutic value in making calls and discussing arrangements for Audrey's memorial service. Celeste was excruciatingly sensitive to the devastation expressed by so many whom she called, who had expected a miracle cure from the clinic in Taipei. It seemed that not only was she spreading news of Audrey's death but, to them, Celeste was confessing that science didn't yet have all the answers. This was, of course, true and a point that Celeste had often tried to explain. She was the only person who knew, however, that in this case the limitations of science were not the fundamental cause of Audrey's death. The reaction Celeste encountered exacerbated her feeling of helplessness and her own grief. And there was no question in her mind that she alone was responsible.

The only pleasant moment of Celeste's morning was reading an E-mail message from Harry, saying that he would be arriving in San Francisco later in the week to work on a story and wondered if Celeste would be there. He wasn't sure if Cammy would come with him, but he was trying to convince her. Celeste thought about how nice it would be to see Harry and had to admit to herself that she hoped Cammy would decide not to come. She could use some of Harry's sympathy all to herself, even if it was no longer dispensed physically. Maybe she could suggest that Cammy visit with her mathematician colleagues one evening if she did come to San Francisco with Harry.

Celeste had to smile when she thought about their evening at Bubba's. She'd enjoyed meeting Cammy's colleagues far more than Cammy herself, that was for sure. What was it they had called themselves? Celeste racked her brain, and she appreciated the distraction. It was something do with being from the South. Finally it came to her, the Queer Homeboys' Mathematician Project—QHMP. Celeste tried to compose a diplomatic E-mail message in response to Harry, and after a few minutes, she put it off until later since diplomacy was not coming to her fingertips.

Celeste was diverted from reading further E-mail by a timid knock on her office door. Celeste knew that it had to be Meg. She was the only person in the lab who knocked when Celeste's door was open.

"Come in, Meg," said Celeste. She swiveled around in her chair, turning her back on the computer, which displayed a long list of unanswered E-mail messages.

"I hate to bother you," said Meg, "but I've got a problem with Eric's antibodies."

"Yes?"

"Well, Eric told me I could go ahead and analyze them. He told me where the samples are, but he didn't know where the code to the experiment design was."

"What do you mean?"

"He isn't sure which rabbits were injected with which proteins, and some of the rabbits were injected with mixtures of protein."

"Well, it should be pretty easy to decode," said Celeste. "Test all the antibodies for their binding to each protein using an ELISA."

"I was afraid you would say that," said Meg. "I was hoping there might be some easier method like, I don't know, maybe an electrophoretic analysis to look at the gamma globulin peak."

Celeste was surprised, and at first taken aback by Meg's suggestion. Electrophoretic analysis of blood was strictly a clinical lab technique and even in the clinical setting was largely replaced by the ELISA procedure. The ELISA can detect antibody binding to individual proteins, so has the advantage of establishing the target as well as the presence of an antibody reaction. It also has universal appeal because it detects antibody binding by color. An ELISA-reading machine even had a cameo appearance in the film *E.T.* Celeste herself was far more familiar with interpretation of ELISA data than with understanding the significance of electrophoretic analysis of antibody fractions. Her puzzlement over Audrey's blood data that Nan Shin had shown her the previous day was a case in point. Meg, however, had done her doctoral work in a traditional clinical lab, where human blood was still analyzed by the electrophoretic method. It suddenly dawned on Celeste that Meg was likely to be aware of subtleties in this type of data that Celeste had dismissed. Meg might even be able to provide some insight regarding the data on Audrey's blood. Although Celeste had convinced herself that she had officially abandoned the case, her curiosity was getting the better of her. It was a matter of intellectual satisfaction.

"Meg," she said, slowly formulating her question. "Would spikes in a gamma globulin peak be diagnostic of having been injected with a particular antigen?"

"If the antigen is a single protein, I would think so. Our work in the lab where I did my thesis research analyzed the antibody reponse in patients who had been injected with the recombinant hepatitis B vaccine. That vaccine is a single protein, and we could see a characteristic spike of antibody that appeared within two weeks of injection."

"Amazing," said Celeste. "I wouldn't have thought it would be detectable. But you still can't correlate a particular spike with an antibody response to a particular protein if you are dealing with a mixture of proteins. So, to sort out Eric's antibodies you can't avoid doing an ELISA analysis."

"No, I guess you're right. My method won't work in this case." Meg hesitated for a moment. "Would you mind going over the ELISA procedure with me? Though I know the principle, I haven't actually done it before. I want to make sure I don't make a mistake and waste the proteins that Eric purified. He told me how important it was for his environmental concerns that he use purified proteins so he wouldn't have to make synthetic peptides. I guess he was unhappy about generating the organic waste."

Celeste did not appreciate being reminded of Eric's stubbornness. "If he had made synthetic peptides, then we wouldn't have to worry about wasting his precious purified protein. There would be plenty of sample to work with," she snapped, and then instantly regretted it. It wasn't fair for Celeste to penalize Meg for Eric's idiosyncracies, even though Meg seemed to be accepting them without comment. In fact, it was quite unusual for one laboratory member to be so concerned about wasting another's sample. Meg's cautious nature might be a disaster for professional advancement but, ironically, it ensured careful and precise science.

"I'm sorry," said Celeste to Meg, as she picked up a pencil and pad of paper. She hesitated before she explained herself. Celeste found it difficult making a personal excuse to someone whom she was trying to train to behave professionally. She continued slowly, in a measured voice, "I've been dealing with a death in the family. I guess I'm more upset than I realized. I'd be happy to go over the ELISA procedure with you."

Celeste gestured for Meg to sit down and placed the pad of paper on an empty chair between them. Celeste began to draw and explain at the same time. "First of all, the procedure is completely described by the acronym ELISA, which stands for Enzyme-Linked ImmunoabSorbant Assay. Antibodies in a blood sample are detected for their ability to bind to a known protein that has been stuck to a solid plastic surface. The binding of an antibody to the immobilized protein is revealed using an enzyme that produces a colored reaction. The binding test is performed in a plastic plate which has

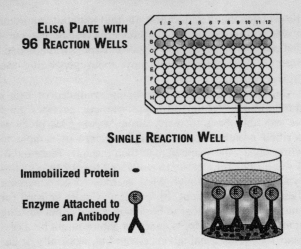

ELISA PLATE WITH 96 REACTION WELLS

SINGLE REACTION WELL

Immobilized Protein

Enzyme Attached to an Antibody

ninety-six small depressions in it, which serve as test tubes for the target protein immobilization and antibody binding and detection. The results of the reactions are rapidly measured by scanning the plate with a machine which measures ninety-six reactions at one time by light absorption through the colored liquid.''

While Celeste outlined the steps in the ELISA, her mind was trying to fathom the significance of Audrey's autopsy results in light of what Meg had explained. When she finally left Celeste's office, Meg was wondering how many years of being a principal investigator it took to evolve from being single-minded and focused to being absentminded and distracted.

Actually, Celeste's thoughts were quite focused, but not on her explanation to Meg. Based upon what Meg had said Celeste understood that Audrey's blood profile indicated she had been injected with a number of distinct proteins. The fact that prominent spikes of gamma globulin appeared and that they were limited in number demonstrated that the immunization had been deliberate and that she had probably received at least one secondary immunization, which would have exaggerated the antibody response. The data could not have been generated as a result of a passing infection, nor as a result of being injected with an infectious organism.

Then Celeste remembered that Audrey's first visit to Lovett's clinic had started with an injection and that when they had planned to meet in D.C., Audrey was keeping an appointment for another injection. Audrey had understood from Lovett that she was receiving prophylactic injections for her visit to Taipei, but it was conceivable that she was actually being injected with something else. So what was being injected?

Perhaps more to the point was the question of whether these injections could be related to the non-clinical activities at the clinics. Minot had been convinced that the patients themselves were being used as carrier pigeons between clinics, transmitting coded information. The FBI had no evidence that anything was actually carried by these patients, and yet the information always seemed to get through.

Celeste began to sift through the evidence. She had already eliminated the possibility that the patients were carrying chemical messengers in their blood. That theory hadn't been very viable anyway since chemical messengers would be eliminated too rapidly by urination or would be toxic. Small chemicals would also not stimulate an antibody response since the immune system primarily recognizes foreign proteins and carbohydrates. Whatever was being injected was causing an immune response, as indicated by the unusual spikes of antibody in Audrey's blood, but otherwise its presence wasn't obvious. Then it dawned on Celeste. It was so simple and so much a part of their routine procedures in the laboratory. It was the antibodies themselves that were conveying the coded messages.

A person's profile of antibodies is like a unique fingerprint, revealing what infectious organisms they have been exposed to. In fact, an antibody profile is often used by physicians to decode the history of a patient's previous infections. For example, detecting the presence of antibodies to the viruses causing German measles or HIV is the most reliable test for whether a patient has been previously exposed. An antibody profile could be easily manipulated by injecting known proteins that would stimulate antibody production. Furthermore, analysis of antibodies is done almost every day in molecular biology laboratories and in many, if not most, clinical laboratories. Decoding would be as straightforward as Meg trying to figure out which rabbits Eric had injected with which proteins.

Immunization was so common that using it to transmit information was brilliant. It was also completely harmless to the patient, as Celeste had explained many times to Eric during their endless arguments about using mice and rabbits to produce antibodies as tools to use in the laboratory. Evidence of the immunization could only be detected if the recipient of a blood sample knew what to look for. It made sense to Celeste that the presence of antibodies would be used to convey information instead of the proteins they bind to because injected proteins disintegrate rapidly in the blood while antibodies can last for weeks and often months. She then recalled that Lovett had been very specific about the timing of Audrey's visits, which correlated with maximizing the timing for a peak antibody response. Celeste began to consider whether she could detect further evidence of what she suspected in Audrey's blood.

Celeste's train of thought had been triggered by the spikes in Audrey's blood analysis that indicated that Audrey had been immunized and boosted with specific proteins. It would be impossible to guess what proteins had been used, but the code would have to depend on combinations of different proteins to be able to transmit a message with any complexity. This would require a varied supply of different proteins that could stimulate antibody production. Biologically, such a supply would be limited. Only proteins such as those derived from infectious organisms that are sufficiently different from human proteins could stimulate a vigorous antibody reaction in only one injection and one boost, as Audrey had received. But bacterial or viral proteins would not be useful for generating a coded message because many patients would already have existing antibodies against organisms that commonly infect humans. In addition, the proteins would have to be available in sufficient amounts for injection into the patient at the site of origination of the coded message and for blood analysis at the receiving end. If Celeste were advising the clinics, she would have given them the same advice she had given to Eric, to use synthetic peptides. These artificial pieces of protein can be generated chemically in unlimited supply. Eric had been resistant to the generation of organic waste by this procedure, but this would hardly bother someone developing a method to transmit code for criminal purposes. And, Celeste realized belatedly, it hadn't. Organic waste filling yellow barrels was abundant at both clinics. Synthetic peptides must be exactly what they were using.

Any student who had taken a basic immunology class would know how to test Celeste's reasoning. She was almost tempted to step into the lab area outside her office and pose the question to her students and fellows, but she resisted. Although synthetic peptides reproduce small pieces of proteins, they are too short to stimulate antibody production by themselves. They need to be attached chemically to a so-called carrier protein before injection. There is one common carrier protein that is used for this procedure. It is known as KLH, which stands for keyhole limpet cyanin, a protein found in the blood of the sea-dwelling limpet.[2] KLH is the universal carrier protein of choice because it is so different from a mammalian protein that it serves to stimulate an immune response in general and thereby helps to generate antibodies that bind to peptides that are attached to it. In the process, antibodies to KLH are generated as well. All that needed to be done to prove Celeste's theory was to find out whether Lovett had ordered ELISA tests on Audrey's blood and to establish whether Audrey had antibodies to KLH in her blood. This corroborative evidence would convince Celeste that she had found the answer to Minot's dilemma. His instincts had been right. Celeste did know enough to figure out how the code was working. Was she going to let him down now that she had?

For the second time that day Celeste thought about the Queer Homeboys' Mathematician Project. At the dinner at Bubba's, they had discussed the mathematics of code breaking and had raised the ghost of Alan Turing. Turing had worked with dedication for the British government in spite of its official attitude toward his sexual preference. His ultimate fate, suicide following imprisonment for homosexual practices, had been no better than Audrey's, and far more humiliating. Bearing the tragedy of Turing's sacrifice in mind, Celeste was moved to at least share her revelation with Minot, even if she stuck to her refusal to pursue the case further. She

[2]How this creature's blood came to be used by immunologists is another story!

wondered how Harry's Cammy would appreciate her choice of muse.

Celeste set about testing her theory. She knew there was a reason why she had saved the sample of Audrey's blood that initially failed to provide any evidence of chemical messengers. It would be the perfect test sample for Meg to learn how to set up the ELISA procedure. Within fifteen minutes she had found the frozen sample of Audrey's blood and located the laboratory stock of KLH protein. Having explained to Meg that she wanted to know if the blood sample contained antibodies to KLH, Celeste returned to her office to phone Nan Shin.

Nan Shin would be easily reached in her office since, in Taipei, it was already early morning the following day and before her clinic rounds started. Celeste picked up the telephone receiver and started to dial, but put it down. She wondered whether her phone was once again bugged.

This time there had been no mention of any mystery maintenance men visiting her office. But, without Eric around at odd hours, someone with determination could have gained access without detection in spite of the fact that Celeste had never replaced her office key in its public hiding place. It also struck Celeste that perhaps the identity of Eric's visitor was no longer a mystery now that Stash was implicated in this mess. If Celeste remembered correctly, Eric seemed to think that the imposter was blond. Hadn't Eric's accident occurred suspiciously within a day of Stash's first visit to San Francisco? Celeste recalled discussing it with Stash over their first dinner together. Stash had rolls of photographs of her, but did she have any of him that she could show Eric? It was probably not merely ironic coincidence that she did not.

Celeste sighed and stood up from her desk. She and Bill Clinton certainly had something in common. Sleeping around is never harmless, even in the most auspicious circumstances. And Celeste's affair had caused damage she couldn't have conceived of. But had the affair really been the problem? Or would Stash and whoever have chased her down anyway? There was no point in being needlessly moralistic, Celeste admonished herself. There was enough of that in the media between preachings of the radical right and fear of HIV. She needed to be practical.

Celeste wrote down Nan Shin's number on a yellow Post-It so she could make the call from another office. As she navigated her way around lab benches and pieces of equipment, through fire-marshall hell, Celeste saw that Meg was busily at work.

Celeste's nearest neighbor, Bill Webber, was on sabbatical leave in Australia, and his office was left open during the day so that members of his laboratory could use his computer and communicate with him by telephone. The office was empty, and Celeste walked in and shut the door. She sat down at the desk and dialed Nan Shin's number. Waiting for the phone connection, she looked around. This office, like hers, was filled with shelves containing the notebooks of former lab members and lined with file cabinets containing photocopies of articles from the scientific literature. Celeste had seen Bill ruffling through these files many times trying to find an article that would support some point he was making in a discussion. Unlike Celeste's office, Bill's was remarkably tidy and organized. Celeste stared at the photograph of Bill's freckle-faced twin daughters in a heart-shaped frame that sat on his desk. She figured that they must be in high school by now. There was something liberating about being on the phone in someone else's office, as though shedding one's own persona and taking on another one. Stable, Republican, Bill Webber, father of two strapping girls and pillar-of-the-community husband, was certainly a novel one for Celeste. The fact that he had pursued a Ph.D. to become a scientist must have been his one act of rebellion as a youth, shunning the M.D. tradition of his family.

The connection went through and Nan Shin's voice broke into Celeste's speculations. Their business was quickly transacted. The answers to Celeste's questions were as she had anticipated. Yes, the clinic had the equipment to do ELISA tests and, yes, the night nurse remembered being asked to draw blood when Audrey checked into the clinic. Celeste now only needed the word from Meg to be convinced that she had found the method for code transmission.

She looked at Bill Webber's daughters and the pen and pencil holder on his neat desk, possibly a Father's Day present, and once again had the reassuring feeling of being in disguise. She called Miami information and asked for the number of the office of the Federal Bureau of Investigation. Then she called the main number and asked for Jack Minot. This direct method of contact should have no problematic repercussions given that the call couldn't be traced to her.

"Minot, here," said the familiar, gruff voice.

"Uh, Mr. Minot, this is Celeste Braun from BAU calling."

There was silence at the other end, which Celeste felt she had to fill. "It's okay. This is a clandestine call."

There was no question in Minot's mind. It was vocabulary woman. He had to smile. "I guess I have to trust you. I'm all ears," he said.

"I've figured out your problem," Celeste told him. "I think it's something you probably want me to explain in person. Are you going to be in Miami in the next two days?"

"Babe, I don't go anywhere much."

Celeste could never quite get used to being called

babe. She wished she fit the description better. "Meet me at the espresso bar in the bookstore on the same street as Temple Emmanuel in Boca Raton, at 3 P.M. on Wednesday of this week. I can't remember which chain owns the bookstore, but I know it has a place to read and drink coffee." Celeste had once spent an hour in the bookstore waiting for Audrey to do a "quick" errand related to a fashion show she had organized for the temple's Hebrew school fund-raiser.

"I should be able to find it," said Minot.

"I'll be at the memorial service for my aunt at the temple before then, but you should definitely avoid the crowd there."

"I'm sorry to hear it," said Minot.

"You'll be more sorry when you hear what I have to say, I'm afraid."

"Hmph," grunted Minot. "See you the day after tomorrow, then."

"Okay, see you then," said Celeste and hung up.

14

Civil War

It wasn't raining the day of Audrey's funeral, but it had rained the night before and the cemetery was muddy. The day was chilly and damp, in spite of the Florida sunshine trying to exert itself. It took half an hour for those present at the funeral service to assemble in the cemetery, under the incongruously festive, striped tent. They constituted a straggling parade of Audrey's many friends in their pastel Florida-winter pantsuits, some using walkers, others with canes, negotiating the muddy path to the graveside.

While the memorial service was being held inside the temple, the gravediggers had produced a deep, casket-sized hole in the plot next to the stone engraved, NATHAN RUBENSTEIN. In a year, a new stone would be unveiled next to it engraved, ADA COHEN RUBENSTEIN. Audrey had written to Celeste that she had wanted to be remembered in death as she had been born.

Celeste stood under the tent between her parents. They had flown in that morning from New York for the service. Though Audrey was her mother's aunt, she had been much closer to her grandniece Celeste, and Celeste appreciated that her parents had made the trip as much for her sake as for theirs. Celeste wished her brother could have been there. When she'd finally reached him, on business in a remote part of South Africa, it wasn't possible for him to arrange the necessary flights to be able to join them.

Celeste spoke for the family at the service in the temple. She explained Audrey's wish to revert to being Ada Rubenstein née Cohen. During her life, Audrey was a purveyor of image. She had not been proud of her name change but had seen it as necessary for the success of her shop and her ability to help her clients. While image was her livelihood, what mattered in death was her legacy of providing others with self-images to respect. As Celeste stood at the graveside, she fingered Audrey's final letter in her pocket and drew comfort from it. The letter had arrived at Celeste's home the day after her return from Taipei. Audrey had posted it just before leaving for Taipei. Celeste had re-read the letter many times en route to the funeral. It was a remarkable last will and testament.

Darling Celeste, We both know that I am beyond treatment. I've known it for months now, and I think you've figured it out. You have given me a last chance to do something useful with this sickly bag of bones. The best I could hope for would be to help out on the case, but not make it home. If I do, so be it. But if I don't, I thank you from the bottom of my heart. I've seen enough of my own deterioration not to want to see the rest.

The letter went on to specify how she wanted her gravestone to be inscribed and why, and finished with the signature, "Your loving aunt and fashion-consultant, Audrey."

The freshly dug earth stood in a pile next to the open grave. It looked moist and heavy. Celeste felt her mother nudge her gently. The prayers at the graveside had stopped and the mourners were silent. The casket was lowered into the grave and the rabbi handed a shovel to

Audrey's surviving brother, the last of their generation. Each mourner would, in turn, walk up to the graveside and shovel some earth onto the casket.

When Celeste first encountered this tradition at her grandfather's funeral, she was initially horrified. It seemed that the mourners were contributing to the finality of his death. But she discovered that the process of carrying out the physical act of burial was a therapeutic one, an active channel to divert mental anguish. It also acknowledged the division between the physical corpse and the memory of the deceased. Celeste took the shovel from her father and picked up some earth from the pile. Before she dropped it on the casket, she looked down into the grave at the few clods of earth that had already been deposited there, lying on the polished wood casket. She could not think of Audrey's body as being there. What she was covering with dirt was the process that had resulted in all of this. She was burying her need for Stash. She was burying her unwillingness to commit. She was taking herself in hand, a process of which Audrey would approve.

Celeste and her mother and father went back to Grace's apartment together, where Audrey's friends catered a buffet lunch. Eating after the funeral was as much a part of the ceremony as the service at the temple. In the taxi, on the way to Grace's, Celeste sat between her parents and each had spontaneously taken one of her hands. It was a situation borrowed from time. And for a few moments Celeste felt the comfort and protection of childhood.

Ever since she had abandoned her parents' New York world to a life in the West that they couldn't understand, their adult relationship had never been comfortable. Her parents were busy and successful professionals, her mother in publishing and her father in investment. Celeste's interest in science and the world beyond New

York could only be explained by genetic mutation. Nonetheless, there was a blood tie between these three independent adults sitting in the back of the taxicab. They all felt it, but could only express it at times like this.

Celeste's parents were not much younger than the crowd at Grace's, but had aged extremely well and looked considerably younger. Their somber suits did not blend with the more relaxed wardrobe of the Florida residents, who had long since left the working world. Nor were they particularly at home in the frilly decor of Grace's living room. Celeste tried to make them comfortable by introducing them to Audrey's friends, but the end result was that Celeste's cheeks were peppered with red lipstick marks and her parents were clearly longing for a drink. All three suffered another hour of loud and vacuous conversation while they halfheartedly nibbled at canapes in stale pastry puffs and miniature brownies, accompanied by watery coffee. After what seemed like an eternity, Celeste and her parents finally left Grace's apartment in separate taxis.

Taking leave of one another, Celeste promised to visit her parents next time she had business in the East. There was no question that they would ever have business in the West. There was also no question of visiting without the excuse of a business trip. But that was what they had become accustomed to, and it didn't diminish the affection in the hugs with which they parted. Celeste's mother and father headed for the West Palm Beach Airport and, no doubt, the airport bar. Celeste headed for a stronger cup of coffee at the espresso counter in the bookstore near Temple Emmanuel.

It was a weekday afternoon and the bookstore was quiet. Celeste walked up and down the aisles checking out the other customers, pretending to be searching for a book. She never failed to experience a feeling of anticipation when entering a bookstore. It was a feeling that Celeste believed she could trace to her excitement at discovering the public library when she had just learned to read. Even though she was on a different mission today, the feeling grabbed hold of her momentarily. Celeste resisted the temptation to leaf through an enticing book or two. She then satisfied herself that the only other customers in the store were a teenaged girl dressed in gothic regalia and earphones in the music section, and an overweight man perched on a stool reading a computer manual.

Celeste had been inspired to perform this reconnaissance without consciously thinking about it. Ever since seeing Stash in Taipei she understood that he had been dogging her movements starting with their very first meeting. At least she had solved the mystery of why she had been invited to speak at that conference. Stash must have used some influence to get her on the program so that he could get to know her. Celeste figured that his interest had some relationship to her discovery of the body in Puerto Rico. This was where Minot could hopefully clarify the situation. Celeste realized that she needed to see Minot as much to restore her own sense of security as to fulfill her obligation to report on what she had deduced about code transmission between the clinics.

Having ascertained that the bookstore was a Stash-free zone, Celeste found a table in the coffee bar at the back of the store that had an oblique view of the door to the street. She removed the black jacket that matched her black, sleeveless funeral dress and slung it over the back of the chair with the view of the door. At the counter, Celeste bought a local newspaper and a cappuccino. Then she returned to her surveillance spot to wait the twenty minutes or so before her rendezvous with Minot.

Under the table, Celeste kicked off the high heels she had been wearing and wriggled her toes in relief.

Celeste stared at the front page of the newspaper without really taking it in, while thinking about how to explain herself to Minot. Disclosing her affair with Stash was not going to be easy. Celeste hoped she wouldn't have to tell him all the details. Then something in the newspaper caught her eye. The name Valentino jumped out at Celeste from the second paragraph of the lead story. She then read the headline, DRUG WAVE HAS PO- LICE MOBILIZED.

"We'll get 'em," said Minot, looking down at Celeste who was now absorbed in the article. "If you've really figured out the code."

Celeste raised her eyes from the paper. Minot stood solidly in front of the table. Her eyes were at the level of his stomach, which was clad in a black watch tartan shirt and expanded substantially above his belted trousers. Celeste held out her hand to shake his and when he took it, the wool of his jacket released a strong aroma of cigar smoke.

"I'm so glad to see you," said Celeste warmly.

Minot was suddenly made a little shy by this greeting. The young woman in front of him looked more sophisticated than he had recalled. In fact, she looked pretty damn classy. It wasn't everyday that he was greeted as a saviour by a good-looking babe. Then he recognized that her classy clothes were funeral duds. His shyness vanished.

"Sorry about your aunt," he said. "She was a good lady."

"You knew her?"

"Uh, yeah, well, we met once in Boca. I went to see her before your trip to Taiwan. She convinced me she could do the job."

"Audrey was pretty persuasive," said Celeste. She

left the rest unsaid, letting her silence acknowledge Minot's condolences.

Minot broke the spell. He seated himself noisily and said, "So tell me how it works."

With relief, Celeste started her tutorial. "This code is a real tour de force." Minot raised his eyebrows and suppressed a smile at Celeste's choice of words. "It's safe, transmission is achieved by a routine medical procedure, and it can only be detected if you know what to look for."

So far, Celeste hadn't told Minot anything he hadn't deduced already. "Go on," he encouraged, impatient to hear how much hard evidence Celeste had obtained.

"Basically, the message courier is a patient who is injected with synthetic peptides in one clinic. After two injections, about a month apart, the patient's immune system reacts to the injection by making antibodies. The antibodies show up in the patient's blood, so all that the clinic on the receiving end has to do is to take a blood sample. By testing the antibodies in the blood sample, the receiving clinic can determine what the patient was injected with in the first place. Are you following me?"

"More or less," said Minot. "But I don't see how knowing what the patient was injected with can transmit information."

"That's the really clever part. These synthetic peptides that are injected are essentially synthetic pieces of protein and like real proteins are strings of amino acids. There are twenty-three different amino acids, so you can think of it like a twenty-three letter code. The synthetic peptides can be formed from different combinations of the twenty-three amino acids and those combinations can be read as coded messages. The clinic on the receiving end determines which combinations were injected and can decode the information transmitted. With a twenty-three letter code, the messages could get quite complex.''

Minot sighed heavily. Complex appeared to be an understatement. ''And you have evidence of this?''

''I do,'' said Celeste. ''I know that injections, bleeding, and antibody tests are involved and can back that up with testimony from Dr. Nan Shin at the Taipei clinic. And there are two pieces of evidence that synthetic peptides have been injected. Both clinics have barrels of chemical waste that come from the procedure of synthesizing the peptides. I can tell you what chemicals you would find in those barrels if their contents were analyzed. There's also immunological evidence for the injections, which we found in my laboratory by testing Audrey's blood.'' Celeste paused to draw a breath to explain the antibodies against KLH. Minot interrupted her.

''You can give me the details on that later. I've heard enough to know that, in combination with this recent wave of junk in Miami, we've got our connection.'' He tapped the newspaper with his forefinger as he spoke about the drugs. ''This fits the pattern of all the recent releases of similar South American junk in both Miami and LA. Within a week of a carrier patient showing up at one of the clinics, a drug distribution order has gone out. This one had to be what Audrey was carrying and now you've got the evidence that she was carrying something. Her death by the Valentinos links them to the distribution.'' It was Minot's turn to pause and catch his breath. He resumed cautiously. ''I'm assuming that she was killed, and didn't die of natural causes.''

''You assume correctly,'' said Celeste tersely. ''I have the autopsy report with me. It confirms the V-shaped signature slash. This one was with an ancient, Chinese dagger.''

Minot visibly recoiled from the thought as the reality of Audrey's sacrifice struck him.

Though Celeste could still not forgive herself for being responsible, she took pity on Minot. "She was heavily drugged and wouldn't have felt it. And she was dying anyway."

"I knew that," said Minot. "That was how she persuaded me to let her go, which I suppose you've guessed."

Celeste simply nodded. She needed to tell Minot the rest of the story. "I know you've got what you need to link the Valentinos to the clinics and to the drug distribution ring, but I think there may be more going on than that."

Minot's face registered his surprise. "What makes you say that?"

"There's someone associated with Dr. Lovett who knows me. I think he's been passing on information about my activities to Lovett, which is getting to the Valentinos. The only part of this I know for sure is that I saw him with Lovett in Taipei. I was hoping you could explain it."

"Who is it?" Minot was suspecting Celeste may have found his mole.

"A guy named Stash Romanicz. Stash stands for Stanislaus. All I know about him is that he used to work for the CIA. Now he's retraining to run their conference center at a converted safe house. Have you heard of him?"

"Not in practice," said Minot, truthfully. "But certainly in theory."

"What do you mean?"

Minot didn't want to alarm Celeste and he, himself, wasn't sure what this guy was up to. It wasn't clear which side of the several fences that seemed to be materializing in the case, the mole was on. One thing was for sure. This smelled of the same CIA interference that had caused his boss, Navarro, to order him off the case. It also smelled of mole activity and seemed to correlate the two. For Celeste, at this point in time, Minot chose the simplest explanation.

"What I mean is that we were aware of some CIA interest in the case. It sounds like this guy, what's he call himself? Stash?" Celeste nodded for Minot to continue. "Well, it's likely Stash is still working for the CIA."

"But what do they have to do with the Valentinos?" asked Celeste. "I thought narcotics were FBI business."

"So did I," said Minot. "But there's some reason, unclear to me, that the CIA feels this case is their business, too."

"Well, I guess that would explain why Stash has, uh, made an effort to get to know me. I guess my impression that he's been helping the Valentinos keep track of me could just be an illusion. What's the connection between Lovett and the Valentinos, anyway. Have you guys figured it out?"

Minot's elation at having made the code connection was rapidly diminishing as he considered what could be going on. He was also annoyed by Celeste's last question since he hadn't satisfactorily come up with a connection between Lovett and the Valentinos, besides the fact that she was obviously collaborating with them.

"We don't know," Minot answered brusquely. His mind was racing with what needed to be done. "I think my boss, George Navarro, needs to hear what you've told me." He looked at his watch, it was already four. "I'll give him a call and if I can catch him at the bureau, could you come down to Miami with me?"

"I suppose so. My flight back isn't until after nine tonight," said Celeste.

"Good," said Minot. He realized he'd have to explain

to Navarro why he was still working on the case. However, since it looked to Minot like the CIA was screwing things up royally, he figured that Navarro would be sympathetic and willing to intervene. Minot punched out Navarro's number on his cellular phone. The phone was answered by Navarro's secretary, whom Minot considered a useless bimbo.

"Oh, hi, Jack," she said in response to his demand to speak to Navarro. "George had a meeting in Washington this afternoon. He won't be back until late tomorrow morning."

"Well, book me two hours with him tomorrow morning as soon as he's due to come in. It's urgent." Minot terminated the call before she could protest that Navarro had other appointments. Minot knew the other appointments could be cancelled, even if she didn't.

"Can you stay until tomorrow afternoon?" Minot asked Celeste. "We won't be able to take your deposition until late morning."

"I suppose," said Celeste. "I think a funeral ticket is changeable."

"Don't worry about the cost," said Minot. "The bureau will pay if it has to." He was getting impatient as his anger toward the CIA was building. Minot was wondering why he had to wait for Navarro to mediate. Sure, Navarro had to hear the deposition to make things official, but Minot wanted to know what was going on now. The CIA had no business being in bed with the Mafia, and that's what it looked like from Minot's point of view. Minot knew where he could find this guy Romanicz. He'd heard about the conference center scheme. If he caught the five p.m. flight, he could be in the D.C. area by early evening and pay this guy a visit. Who knows, maybe he'd even run into Navarro on the flight back to Miami and could brief him.

Minot stood up abruptly. "I've got to get going," he

said to Celeste. He tapped the newspaper again as he spoke. ''There are things going on with this case that can't wait.'' Minot then reached inside his jacket pocket and took out a business card, flipping it onto the open newspaper. ''Here's the address of the bureau in Miami. I'll see you there at ten, tomorrow morning.'' Then, belatedly remembering his manners, Minot said, ''Uh, have a good evening.''

''Thanks,'' said Celeste. ''You, too. See you tomorrow.'' The last phrase was directed at Minot's retreating back.

Minot's sudden departure left Celeste feeling somewhat at a loss. She focused first on changing her flight using the payphone in the back of the bookstore. The airline was remarkably accommodating regarding her funeral ticket, confirming their policy of maximum flexibility, even for discount tickets, in such situations. Celeste supposed that it was one deal that was rarely abused given that people would be too superstitious to lie about death.

The phone call brought Celeste's thoughts back to the reason she was in Miami. She was still only just across the street from the temple. Celeste decided to return to the cemetery for a solitary, final tribute to Audrey. She left her overnight bag in the storage area behind the cashier's desk near the street door, where she had been asked to deposit it upon entering the store. She crossed the street and walked around the back of the temple to the cemetery gates.

The cemetery was empty of mourners, and the tent had been taken down. Celeste wandered between gravestones toward the spot where Audrey was buried. She passed the spirits of ''Fanny, beloved wife of Benjamin Goldman; Seth and his brother Amos Levy; Natalee Chernick; Stella and Israel Kapstein; Mimi and David Weisbluth.'' The women had names of assimilation. The men's names were staunchly biblical. Celeste wondered if there was any significance to this.

Celeste reached the resting place of Nathan Rubenstein. Audrey's adjacent grave had been filled and she was cozily covered with freshly laid sod and several bouquets of flowers. The anonymity of the grave without a gravestone made Celeste feel sad. According to Jewish tradition, Audrey would have to wait a year before her memory could be advertised. Celeste thought of a graveyard she had visited in a hill town in the Spanish countryside. The dead were "buried" in raised, drawerlike stone caskets, stacked one on top of the other with the ends facing the aisles for mourners. Each was inscribed with the name of the occupant and had a photograph of the deceased attached to a spray of artificial flowers. Celeste felt that Audrey would have preferred this type of blatant memorial to an inexpressive stone, but a stone would be better than nothing.

In touch with Audrey's spirit, Celeste imagined the meeting between Audrey and Minot. They probably got on brilliantly. Celeste considered whether she should mind that they had used her, each in their own ways. Relatively speaking though, their offenses paled compared to the outrageous extent that Stash had evidently used her, the significance of which was still unclear. Celeste was grateful though that it hadn't been necessary to describe the extent of her relationship with Stash to Minot.

After further thought, Celeste decided she didn't mind about Audrey and Minot. She was glad she had decided to contact Minot about the code. It was the least she could do for Audrey's memory short of revolutionizing the gravestone culture at the Temple Emmanuel cemetery.

Celeste felt a crepuscular chill setting in and considered her next move, which was to find a hotel room for the night. As she turned away from Audrey's grave, a white rose from one of the funereal bouquets taunted Celeste with another loose end in the case. She had forgotten to ask Minot about the role of Police Chief Raul de Leon in all of this. There were several things about him that gave Celeste cause to think he had his own agenda, and she wondered if Minot trusted him fully. Celeste found herself wishing that Minot hadn't rushed off so suddenly. She'd have to remember to bring up her concern about Raul during their meeting the following morning.

Almost four hours after Celeste contemplated the issue of memorials at Audrey's graveside, Minot, driving a car he had rented at Dulles Airport, passed another memorial. It was a bronze plaque set into a boulder of local stone. The boulder sat on top of a grassy hill. It was visible from the road, even in the dark, because it was floodlit from below. A white-lettered sign informed passing traffic that they were driving by a CIVIL WAR BATTLEFIELD. Many battles of the Civil War were fought in the vicinity of Langley, Virginia, and Minot thought to himself with irony that he was about to engage in another one, between the FBI and the CIA.

Minot drove fast along the two-lane country highway toward the conference center. He hadn't been hungry when he landed at Dulles, and it was easy to pass up the fast-food concessions at the airport. Now, he regretted his abstention as he hurtled past the darkened countryside, his stomach rumbling. He was slowed by a blinking yellow light marking a crossroad with another country highway and noted a 7-11 store on the opposite side of the intersection. It was the only illuminated storefront in a row of colonial-style white, brick, commercial buildings that, according to the sign hanging by the road, also housed a real estate agent and a dental practice.

Minot slowed the car and swung across the intersection into the driveway in front of these buildings.

As he shut off the engine the lights in the 7-11 went out. This was followed by the emergence of a pimply young man in blue jeans wearing a Baltimore Orioles' baseball cap, who set about locking the dead bolt to the front door from the outside.

"Hey," said Minot. "Aren't you supposed to be open until eleven?"

"Not around here we ain't," said the young man with a thick Virginia drawl. "Ain't nobody comes to the store after six and it's just gone eight."

Minot sighed. "I don't suppose you know where I could get something to eat around here."

"Well, there's The Crab House, up the road about two—three miles."

"No kidding," said Minot. "Thanks, bud."

And sure enough, in the middle of absolute nowhere, Minot came upon The Crab House, like a shining beacon of blue neon light at the side of the road. There he quickly stuffed down an exquisitely creamy crabcake sandwich and thanked God for the poor patronage of the 7-11 that caused its premature closure. He also confirmed his directions to the conference center and set off for his confrontation feeling like a new man.

The turnoff to the conference center, named for the original plantation Skylie Mansion, led to a road that was even darker than the highway if that was possible, and much more winding. Finally, Minot reached the driveway to the center. He deduced that there was no conference in session because the first few buildings that he passed were completely dark. A few hundred yards ahead of him, Minot saw a single illuminated house, and he drove on until he reached it.

The house was small and situated next to what looked like a stable barn. In front of it two cars were parked.

One was a dark-colored, four-wheel drive vehicle splattered with road mud. The other was a pale sedan, fairly clean and, from its bumper, Minot saw that it was a rented car. Minot checked the holster inside the front of his jacket to make sure his gun was accessible before he got out of his own rented car and rang the doorbell.

Stash opened the door. He was holding a tumbler of ice and what looked like whiskey in his left hand.

"Jack Minot, FBI," said Minot, flashing his ID.

Stash smiled. "Stash Romanicz, CIA," he said, holding out his right hand. "Sorry, I'm not carrying my badge. Come on in, Jack."

They shook hands tentatively and Stash shut the door behind Minot as soon as he had stepped over the threshold. He motioned for Minot to follow him down the corridor toward the back of the house. Minot couldn't help but notice the framed black and white photographs lining the walls as he followed his host. Toward the end of the corridor, Minot thought he recognized one of Celeste in a state of semiundress. But before he had time to think about the significance of this or look at the photo more closely, Stash glanced back over his shoulder and said, "I think you'll find you know my visitor."

Minot turned his attention to the sitting room ahead of them and saw George Navarro, standing awkwardly in the center of the room, also holding a glass with brown liquid and ice cubes. Minot knew that Navarro, a lifelong teetotaler, was drinking iced tea.

"Jack," acknowledged Navarro. He shook his head slowly back and forth, as though grinding out his voice. "Never very good at following orders. Usually I can look the other way, but this time, I'm afraid you'll have to."

Minot's first reaction was not a rational one. If that bimbo of a secretary had been more specific about Navarro's whereabouts, Minot thought he might have been prepared for something like this. Now it was he who had to explain himself. His second thought was more rational. Navarro's presence didn't negate the fact that the information from Celeste still pointed to an association between the CIA and the Mafia.

"Since when does the CIA collaborate with the Mafia?" Minot demanded of Stash. "And for that matter, since when do we?" he asked of Navarro.

"Cool it, Jack," warned Navarro in his gravelly voice. "You've stepped in deeper shit than you realize, and it's not ours to evaluate."

"Have a seat, Jack," said Stash, in a friendly tone. "Can I get you a drink."

"Make it a double," said Minot. "It sounds like I'll need it."

Navarro sat down heavily in the armchair opposite the one where Minot had tensely perched. While Stash went out into the kitchen to pour Minot's drink, Navarro said, in a tone that was as apologetic as a growl could be, "I wish you'd laid off when I warned you. You know the pecking order. If it's a matter of national security, the FBI has to give way."

"What's national security got to do with a mob drug distribution scheme and several murders?"

"Can't you figure that one out?" asked Stash, returning with an almost full tumbler of whiskey and ice that he handed to Minot. "Your field agent, Dr. Braun, could tell you in a minute."

"What about Dr. Braun?" asked Minot defensively.

"She's too smart," said Stash. "I'll wager she's figured out how the code transmission works by now. But that's not why you're here. You wouldn't be here if she hadn't also figured out that I was involved."

"Damn right on both accounts," confirmed Minot. He took a gulp of his whiskey. The familiar burn did not soothe him. It made him more angry. "You're gonna have to do some fast talking to convince me that I shouldn't blow the whistle on this operation. You've been fucking around with a federal case that I've been working on for the past three years. The string of bodies alone is enough to nail the Valentinos, not to mention the junk dealing.''

"That's not all I've been 'fucking around with.' If your pet scientist had been a little less sex starved, your 'case' might have solved itself differently,'' said Stash smugly, making himself comfortable on the couch opposite the two FBI agents.

Minot's brief glimpse of Celeste's nudity made him imagine more than he wanted to, and he had a physical reaction to the thought of Celeste and Stash together that surprised him. The obvious seduction of Celeste enraged him further, and he glared at Stash, trying to think of a suitable retort.

"What it comes down to,'' said Stash, ''is that the code's too good for us to give it up. In this day of post–Cold War surveillance, the CIA needs to be extra discreet. Jack, you simply can't blow the whistle on a top secret protocol. I helped develop the code from a cruder version that the good doctor Lovett was trying to market to save her practice. I can't be responsible for her family commitments.''

"So that's the connection,'' said Minot.

"I'm surprised the clever Dr. Braun didn't pick that one up,'' said Stash. ''Lovett's a sort of anglicized version of Valentino.''

Minot's indignation now found its voice. "The CIA can't just ignore the fact that you've been sharing facilities with the mob. It makes a joke of everything the government stands for. And, personally, I can't let you get away with it.''

Navarro gave Stash an I-told-you-so look.

"It's all right, Jack,'' Stash said indulgently to Minot.

"You can calm down. George warned me that you have integrity." Stash took a sip of his drink. "I think there's a way we can make a deal without breaching the national security."

"I have no reason to want to make a deal," Minot pointed out pugnaciously.

Navarro corrected him. "I'm afraid you're wrong, Jack." He hated being in the position of saying what he had to say to his best agent, the one who had essentially made the reputation of the Miami branch of the bureau. "As I said earlier, I'm not going to be able to look the other way this time. Your breach of orders is already sufficient grounds for dismissal. Interference with CIA business would result in loss of your government pension on top of dismissal. If you stop now, I'm willing to overlook the insubordinance so far. But it's got be now, and it's got to be on our terms."

Minot was beyond furious, but he knew he was up against a wall. He turned to Stash. "All right, lover boy, what's the deal?"

"Maybe you won't be so annoyed when you hear it. George thinks very highly of you and helped me work this out, so you'll still get credit for your excellent work," said Stash. He sounded more condescending than conciliatory. "My colleagues and I, here in Virginia, feel we've exhausted the physical utility of Lovett's clinic, and we can now take our code system elsewhere. We've actually got much more use for it in the spas of Europe, where it's even harder to carry on our business of surveillance in the countries of longtime allies. Therefore, as far as we're concerned, Lovett is dispensable. Her connection with the Valentinos won't be that hard to verify. You can pin two murders on her, your foolish courier in Puerto Rico and the aunt. Of course, you won't be able to reveal the existence of the code or how it was being used. But we figure that Valentino will have to find another way to run his drug operation once his niece is out of business. Then it's only a matter of time before you nail him for the narcotics traffic. Of course, you'll have to break off contact with Celeste Braun and keep her from making any official statements.''

''She's got a mind of her own,'' said Minot. ''How do you propose I manage that?''

''All you have to do is tell her that everything is taken care of and that you'll make sure the information gets to the right place,'' said Stash. ''She's very trusting.'' He smiled knowingly.

It took all the self-control that Minot could muster to keep his hands to himself and away from his piece. He had an overwhelming urge to blast the self-satisfied bastard's smile off his face.

Navarro saw that Minot was struggling with himself. He stood up, walked over to where Minot was sitting, and put his hand on Minot's shoulder. Minot jerked away, as though he had been touched by something contaminated.

''Come see me tomorrow morning,'' said Navarro.

''I was going to anyway,'' said Minot in a defeated tone. He rose from his chair, took a large swallow of whiskey, and set the glass down on a side table. He didn't trust himself to behave in the presence of these scum any longer. Wordlessly, Minot turned his back on Stash and Navarro and walked past the photograph of Celeste without a second glance, down the corridor to the front door. He would be less miserable sleeping in the rented car or the airport lounge than accepting any further hospitality at Skylie Mansion.

When they heard Minot roar away from the front door, Stash asked, ''Can we trust him to keep quiet?''

''You'll have no problem with him,'' Navarro replied.

"It's this Dr. Braun I'm worried about. Can we trust her?"

"Don't worry," said Stash. "I've considered how to deal with her already. I'll take care of it. Just leave it to me."

15

Cold Shoulders

Celeste made her way to downtown Miami from Boca
Raton using a combination of taxi rides and the shuttle
service between the West Palm Beach and the Miami
International airports. By the time she'd arrived, she was
too tired to do anything but check into one of the large
downtown hotels where she had once stayed while attending a conference. The hotel was as characterless as
Celeste remembered. After a solitary, unsatisfactory dinner and a restless night, Celeste was anxious to finish
her business with the FBI and return to San Francisco.
It was the last day of the year and Celeste looked forward to starting the next year back home and free of
obligation.

Taking a taxi from the hotel, Celeste arrived at FBI
headquarters, shortly before 10 A.M. The tall, spindly
palm trees in the forecourt of the building and the gran-
diose staircase gave Celeste the impression that she was
approaching a colonial outpost of the federal government. The trees made her think of a high school botany
experiment in which plants were forced to grow toward
the light and became unnaturally elongated. Etiolated,

thought Celeste, dredging up the technical word from the depths of her brain.

Entering the building, Celeste stood for a moment in the large foyer to get her bearings. She watched as suited government officials navigated their way purposefully around knots of confused immigrants. A bank of elaborately decorated, guilded elevators stood in front of her, the kind with arrows and numbered half moons at the top showing the progress of each car as it ascended and descended. On the left was a battered wooden teacher's desk of the type seen in public school classrooms. It bore the sign RECEPTION.

Celeste approached the desk. Behind it sat a large black woman who was wearing a Christmas tree pin on one lapel of her bulky cardigan sweater and, on the other, a badge reading M. CRAWFORD. Celeste recognized her name as the woman who had been the recipient of her report to Minot. "I'm looking for Jack Minot, at the FBI. Have you seen him yet this morning?" inquired Celeste.

"The FBI office is on the fifth floor," said Marjorie. "I think I saw him this morning. But it's been quite busy. You'd think things would quiet down on New Year's Eve. At least we close at noon today."

"Thanks," said Celeste. "Can I just go up there?"

"Sure, honey, it's only an office."

"Oh," said Celeste, surprised it was so accessible.

"Sorry to disappoint you," said Marjorie. "It's not the CIA, you know."

Celeste looked at her quizzically.

"Just an agency joke," said Marjorie. "Now, you get your business done and go have a Happy New Year."

"You, too," said Celeste.

Five minutes later she realized that Ms. Crawford was not typical of the other government staff. What Celeste encountered when she reached the FBI office on the fifth floor could only favorably be described as a bureacratic runaround.

Access to the offices of FBI personnel was shielded by a reception counter that spanned the entire width of the entrance to the Federal Bureau of Investigation, Miami Branch, as it was designated on the mirrored glass doors. Celeste could see that one segment of the counter could be raised, like a drawbridge, to get to the protected zone behind it. The small waiting area in front of the counter was furnished with a two person couch covered in turquoise vinyl, and bracketed by dull, chrome arms that looked like it had been rescued from a rummage sale. These were hardly salubrious headquarters and Celeste guessed that the salaries were hardly salubrious either, by the sullen attitude of the lackluster blond behind the counter. When Celeste asked to see Jack Minot, the receptionist asked for Celeste's name and for identification. She said she would find out if he was in and disappeared for almost ten minutes.

When the blond returned, she said, ''Minot's at an off-site meeting. He'll be tied up all day.''

Celeste said, ''But the receptionist downstairs saw him come in.''

''Well, he's not here now,'' said the woman behind the counter.

''I know he wanted me to meet his boss,'' explained Celeste. ''Could I talk to his boss?''

''The boss is away, too,'' said the woman. ''You'll have to get in touch after New Year's.''

''But I'm only here this morning,'' said Celeste. ''Are you sure Minot didn't leave a message for me?''

The receptionist rolled her eyes at Celeste's persistence. She then turned her back on Celeste and walked back into the rabbit warren of partitions behind the counter. Celeste first thought that she was just trying to escape from her enquiries. Then she saw the receptionist proceed down a corridor into what looked like real offices at the back of the partitioned area. Celeste's level of discomfort was rising. She sat down tentatively on the vinyl couch to wait. As Celeste correctly anticipated, it was another ten minutes before the receptionist reappeared.

"Here's a message," the blond said unapologetically and thrust a pink slip of paper, of the type used for phone messages, across the counter at Celeste. It said, "Thank Dr. Braun and tell her that everything is taken care of. She can go home." There was no signature and nothing official about the document.

"But," protested Celeste to the receptionist. "Do they want me to get in touch?"

"Sorry, honey. I can't help you," said the receptionist with finality.

Many things went through Celeste's mind at once. Obviously something had changed Minot's plans. Celeste had assumed that his abrupt departure the previous evening had something to do with the anticipated drug raid. Perhaps something had happened to him in that raid. But hadn't the receptionist in the building lobby said she had seen him that morning? Perhaps there had been a new break in the case this morning. Whatever had taken Minot and his boss off-site, it was obviously of more immediate importance than Celeste's small piece of the puzzle. But, Celeste didn't have a good feeling about the reception she had just experienced. Minot had always been extra courteous and respectful, and this communication did not emulate his previous behavior.

By this time the blond behind the counter had sat down and was filing her nails, having completely lost interest in watching a speechless Celeste standing in front of her. With a feeling of ultimate frustration, Celeste finally turned away from the counter. She decided that she would at least double-check with Ms. Crawford, downstairs, that Minot had been around earlier in the morning. But when she returned to the lobby, Ms. Crawford wasn't there.

The only course of action left for Celeste was to hail a taxi for the airport and head home.

Celeste was back at her condominium in San Francisco in time to celebrate New Year's Eve on her own. Over the course of the return journey, she had become increasingly uneasy. Unable to settle down to the welcome-home supper of canned soup and bread that she had prepared for herself, Celeste found herself alert to every small noise in the building. She opened a bottle of Cabernet Sauvignon and poured a generous glass to take the edge off her nervousness.

Celeste's discontent certainly had nothing to do with the fact that she was alone on an evening that most people spend with partners, family, or friends. On the contrary, she intensely disliked the false new start and pretence at resolutions that accompanied the long overdue end to the Christmas season. The ingrained hypocrisy of New Year's Eve was one that Celeste was relieved to be able to ignore. But it was a minor relief, and no match for her worries that had begun festering at the FBI headquarters and had reached the paranoia stage.

Celeste was convinced that she was dealing with hypocrisy and betrayal at every level of this case. She had already recognized that a major motivating factor in wanting to see Minot was the hope that he would provide some protection for her. Now he had apparently let her down. It wouldn't be long before the Valentinos knew that she knew what was going on in Lovett's clinics. Quite possibly they already knew and were just biding their time before perpetrating another "discouraging" act. It puzzled Celeste that the Valentinos had so far dealt with her lightly and relatively indirectly. At some point they would surely close in on her and deal with her in person. This realization increased Celeste's feeling of being frighteningly alone. There were three so-called law enforcement officers involved in this case, Raul, Jack Minot, and, evidently, Stash. Could any of them be trusted to help her?

Eventually exhausted with trying to sort through this conundrum, Celeste left her half-eaten supper on the dining room table and carried the wine bottle and glass into the bathroom. There she drew a hot bath. Accompanied by the sound of Dexter Gordon playing ballads on his saxophone, Celeste sat soaking in her oversized bathtub and finished the bottle of wine. This therapy had the desired effect, and she was asleep in bed by 10 P.M.

Just before midnight the telephone rang. Celeste woke in time to hear her answering machine message begin. Much as she hated listening to herself, she decided to wait to hear who was calling at this hour before picking up.

It was Stash, and she didn't pick up. He paused and took a deep breath before leaving his message. His voice and breathing were so close to Celeste that, for a fleeting moment, she had the impression he was in bed with her. "Celeste," said Stash to the message machine, "I was just thinking about you and wanted to wish you a Happy New Year." Another deep breath. "I'm sorry I'm not spending it with you, but we'll figure some way to meet soon, I hope." Another breath. "I'm missing you. Take care." The phone clicked and started to blink in the dark, alerting Celeste to her message. She lay in bed, fully awake, watching the blinking light.

Celeste's first reaction was absolute outrage. All that she could think of in her initial fury was that this guy had balls. Upon reflection, however, Celeste realized that Stash probably didn't know that she had seen him in

Taipei. So the call was business as usual for him, continuing to try to string her along, presumably to keep an eye on her investigation of Lovett. This insight didn't change Celeste's opinion much. He was still a bastard, and he still had balls.

Celeste thought about how easily she had fallen into bed with him. Their lovemaking, if you could call it that, had seemed so compatible. Even now the memory of it, of their bodies intimately linked, stirred her into physical longing, but not for him. It was that hollow, hungry feeling that was the ultimate punishment for sex without commitment. But Celeste had a foreboding that she was due for more punishment in this case.

New Year's Day dawned sunny and Celeste was up early, feeling somewhat restored by the sleep that had finally provided some temporary relief from her mental anguish. Before putting the kettle on to make tea, she wandered out to the living room and stood at the large windows overlooking the city. Surveying San Francisco in her dressing gown made her feel like she belonged to it. The inhabitants were still dozing while their city sparkled in the sun. Celeste relished the peacefulness of this brilliant view from her secret vantage point and wondered how many others were sharing this privilege of the city.

Celeste turned from the window, and retied the cord to her dressing gown, a cotton kimono sent to her by Kazuko for her birthday last year. Thinking of Kazuko always gave her strength, and Celeste realized that she was hungry. Practicality took over and Celeste set about starting the New Year with a poached egg, if not a firm resolution.

After breakfast, Celeste cleared a space for her Powerbook on the dining room table. This required disposing of a vase of faded chrysanthemums as well as the dishes from the previous evening's unappetizing supper. Celeste began to work on an outline for the manuscript describing Meg's work that would soon be submitted for publication. Whatever else was happening in her life, the needs of her science career took priority. Professional demands that she had recently resented as being relentless had their therapeutic aspects as well, providing a commitment with prescribed ways in which to fulfill it. Celeste worked with concentration and spent a satisfying hour thinking about the scientific significance of Meg's work and how best to present it. At eight-thirty a.m. she was interrupted by the telephone.

Once again Celeste listened to herself tersely invite the caller to leave a message. After she heard the beginning of the message, she picked up. It was Nick Coruna, the custodian and security guard for the floor where her laboratory was located.

"Hi, Nick. It's Celeste here," she said. She had a dreadful feeling in the pit of her stomach. Someone could do a lot of serious damage in the laboratory. "Is anything wrong?"

"Hi, Dr. Braun," said Nick. "It's the alarm on your deep freeze. I heard it going off when I made the rounds. The temperature looks okay, but I'd feel better if someone who knows about it took a look. I'm sorry to bother you, but I called all the names on the emergency list before yours and got no answers." The deep freeze held years of accumulated samples from Celeste's research. It was a sort of frozen archive and had almost sacred status in the laboratory. It was critical that the samples not be allowed to thaw.

"Thanks, Nick," said Celeste. "I'll be there in about half an hour."

"Happy New Year, Dr. Braun," said Nick.

"Same to you, Nick." She hoped it would be.

Celeste didn't bother to shower, just threw on a pair

of jeans and a T-shirt and sweater, and brushed her hair back into a ponytail. She drove over to the BAU campus as fast as possible. There was very little traffic, and she walked into the lab just before nine a.m.

Celeste went immediately to the freezer that Nick had identified. It was located in an inner corridor between her lab and Bill Webber's lab. The freezer's temperature gauge was registered at −85 degrees centigrade, and the compressor was working hard to bring the temperature down further. Normally the setting for the freezer was −80 degrees, but it had been reset to −90 degrees, a temperature that was really below the physical range of the instrument. Presumably the inability to lower the temperature consistently to the setting was what had triggered the alarm. Celeste bent down and reset the temperature for −80 degrees. As she stood up, she noticed that two of the four names on the emergency contact list pasted to the front of the freezer were people who no longer worked in the lab. It obviously hadn't been updated for a couple of years.

Celeste sighed. At least no harm had been done. The setting needle must have been bumped by cleaning personnel or some such accident, though it was a little difficult to imagine how that could have happened. Celeste decided to wait for an hour before returning home to make sure that the freezer could hold temperature at its proper level after so much strain had been put on the compressor.

Celeste let herself into her office with the intent of paging Nick to tell him everything seemed to be fine before she settled down to do some work. Her intent was completely forgotten, however, as soon as she walked in.

Stash was sitting at her desk. He was holding a small revolver pointed at Celeste. He gestured with the revolver for her to sit down on the couch.

''Happy New Year,'' he said. ''I'm sorry I had to get you here on false pretences to wish you well in person. It must be reassuring to know that your freezer alarm is in good working order.''

''That doesn't look like you're wishing me well,'' said Celeste, nodding at the revolver.

''Just to make sure you won't run off until you hear what I have to say,'' said Stash breezily. ''I'll put it away if you want.''

''Please,'' said Celeste. Her heart was pounding, but she was ironically gratified that seeing Stash in person now had a different physical effect on her.

Stash tucked the gun inside his jacket, restoring it to a holster.

''You're just too smart for your own good,'' began Stash. ''I suppose you've figured out by now that you have been interfering where you had no business. We realize that it's not your fault. It's that goon Minot who should have dropped the case when he was told to.''

''Who's we?'' asked Celeste.

''Haven't you figured that out by now?''

''I'm not sure,'' said Celeste, stalling.

''The CIA, of course,'' said Stash.

Celeste didn't know whether to believe him. She wasn't sure it would be wise to tip her hand that she had seen Stash with Lovett. She asked carefully, ''What does the CIA have to do with what is going on at Lovett's clinics?''

''You already figured that one out,'' said Stash. ''The coded transmissions are invaluable to us. The Cold War may be over, but our need to keep an eye on things abroad hasn't diminished.''

This explanation seemed far too pat, and it annoyed Celeste that Stash considered it satisfactory. She went out on a limb. ''All the evidence that I've seen suggests that the clinic operations were controlled by the Valentino family. That's what Minot was investigating.''

''The clinics are an independent operation. The CIA is a major client. If there are other clients, that's Lovett's business. Interfering in CIA business, however, is certainly not within the jurisdiction of the FBI and absolutely not within the jurisdiction of the Puerto Rican police force. Nor is it the business of an expert witness like you.''

Celeste did not like what she was hearing, but it was starting to make sense. If the CIA had precedence over the FBI, it explained her sudden dismissal by Minot, his apparent reluctance over dismissing her and, possibly, his recent disappearance. Furthermore, what Stash was telling her seemed to vindicate Raul.

Interrupting Celeste's thoughts, Stash said, ''I certainly didn't mind keeping an eye on you, though. But you've made it hell to keep the Valentinos off your back if it's any consolation. I promised them I would scare you off myself. I didn't think they would be as subtle about it.'' He held out his scarred arm. ''These police dogs can cause serious damage. At least I caused him more.''

So the scar on Stash's arm *was* a new scar. It had been Stash chasing her in the tunnel in San Juan. Celeste was momentarily glad he had been the victim of the dog's last bite. Then she thought of Audrey and was suddenly furious.

''I suppose murdering an old woman counts as 'scaring off' tactics,'' said Celeste accusingly.

''Celeste, my dear,'' Stash replied in a patronizing tone. ''You, yourself, told me so many times how ill Audrey was. We did her a favor. And, kept the Valentinos appeased.''

Celeste was on the verge of tears, but managed to control her voice. It came out in a low, harsh whisper.

"No one gave you permission to play God. Not even the CIA."

Taking a breath and finding a stronger voice, Celeste continued, "What's to keep me from blowing the whistle on you. Based on what I've found out, the FBI can put Lovett's clinic out of business for its collaboration with the Valentinos. There are two murders involved here. The newspapers would have a heyday with the CIA turning a blind eye to the Mafia."

"We've taken care of Minot. What you've told him won't go any further."

"You didn't . . . ?" Celeste couldn't even voice her fear that Minot might have been eliminated.

"It was hardly necessary," said Stash contemptuously. "Minot knows what side his bread is buttered on. He's a widower with only a small pension to look forward to. He knows he disobeyed orders. He won't talk."

"You can't pull the same stunt on me," said Celeste. "I'm a free agent."

"Oh, is that right?" asked Stash. "You should think hard about which side your bread is buttered on, too. It's my understanding that resesarch labs like yours would be dust without funding from the National Institutes of Health, which, you must realize, is a branch of the federal government. Those who can take away Minot's pension can easily pull strings at the NIH."

"Funding is decided by peer review, not by government gift."

"Wrong," said Stash. "Eligibility for funding is decided by peer review. Budgeting is still decided at the government level."

Celeste knew she was utterly helpless against a threat to withhold her lab funding. It wasn't just her career, the careers of all those whom she was training and supporting would be affected by financial loss to her research operation. She had been right. She was no match for the Mafia, the FBI, and the CIA. She could only draw consolation from the fact that even if funding to her lab was hush money, it would be spent peacefully and productively.

"I guess that's that," said Celeste.

Stash looked at Celeste carefully. She saw a hint of his personal interest in her in that look and it made her stomach turn. But his professional commitment was much stronger. "You're a tough lady," he said as he stood up. "There's more than one reason I'm sorry our business is over." He didn't dare to touch her before he left, shutting the office door behind him.

Celeste did not feel like a tough lady. She felt used up and wrung out. She sat for a long time at her desk, staring at nothing in particular and wondering whether she had any choice about succumbing to Stash's threat. There was a lot of inertia to overcome to start the new year.

Celeste ended up spending the rest of the morning in her office, working halfheartedly on Meg's manuscript. Finally she ventured out to grab a bite for lunch in the hospital cafeteria. The huge dining room, which was normally full of jostling people and trays of dirty dishes, was practically deserted.

Celeste helped herself to some limp lettuce and heaped onto it various chopped up bits of garnish from the metal receptacles sitting on the salad bar. As she smothered the pile in synthetic, blue cheese dressing, Celeste's stomach turned for the second time that day. She hoped that once she transported the salad back to her office, away from the residual smell of dishwashing and overcooked food, that it might magically become palatable. She chose a Diet Coke to accompany her meal.

Celeste set her cardboard tray down at the condiment station and looked around for a piece of foil to cover the salad for its journey through the hospital corridors, back to the laboratory. Not far from where she was standing sat an Hispanic family of several generations: grandparents, parents, and several small children. All were eating without saying a word to one another, enveloped by the silence of concern about someone in one of the hospital beds. Celeste found it too depressing to even try to figure out which one of the clan was missing and might be bedridden. Then, as she reached for a piece of foil, Celeste noticed a solitary figure lunching by himself at the far end of the cafeteria, near the window with a view of the trees from Golden Gate Park. Eric's fuzzy head was unmistakable.

Having been shut up in her office all morning, Celeste hadn't realized that Eric had been out in the laboratory working. She carried her tray over to join him.

Eric was reading a photocopy of an article from a scientific journal and didn't look up until Celeste arrived at the table. "Oh, hi, Celeste. Happy New Year," he said.

"Hi, Eric. Happy New Year to you. How's it going?"

"Well, fine really. I told Meg that I would finish off analyzing the antibodies while she was home for Christmas. It was my fault anyway for losing the records. I think I've figured it out, now." Then he launched into a detailed explanation of what he had been up to and what he planned to do now that he was back at the bench.

Celeste was only half listening to him, she was so struck by the change in his demeanor. Perhaps Eric's conversion would be the only good outcome of this whole wretched business. Celeste managed to eat her entire salad without being aware of it and walked back to the lab with Eric, slowing her pace to accommodate his residual limp. He assured Celeste that he would be back to normal in no time with the intensive physical therapy he was undergoing. She thought to herself that after such trauma, it was inevitable that one's concept of normal changes. In Eric's case, this was clearly a blessing.

Spirits boosted by this encounter, Celeste returned to her office to spend a much more productive afternoon. For a couple of hours she even managed to ignore the nagging feeling of defeat that Stash's visit had left behind. Shortly before five p.m., the phone in her office rang, and Celeste picked it up absentmindedly.

"Celeste!" came Harry's voice. "I've been trying to reach you all day at home. I guess I should have called the lab earlier. How's tonight for dinner?"

Celeste had completely forgotten that Harry was planning to be in town. She was thoroughly grateful for this distraction, even if it meant spending the evening with Cammy as well. "I'm up for it," she said. "Just tell me when and where to meet you."

"I'm staying at the Miyako, in Japantown," said Harry. "Why don't we meet in the lobby at eight and then wander around Fillmore to see what's open."

"That sounds fine," said Celeste. He had said I, not we, did that mean he was alone? She didn't want to offend him by asking, she would find out soon enough. "See you then."

Celeste hung up and looked at her watch. This was a windfall. She had felt dragged down all day and was glad to have an excuse to go home and freshen up. At least a pleasant social evening meant she could postpone confronting her conscience about what to do, if anything, about all that had occurred.

Celeste thought about how much Harry had changed in appearance when she last saw him and was suddenly inspired. Audrey had been agitating her about getting her hair cut into something more sophisticated than a bush that could only look professional when it was braided into a twist. Celeste telephoned her friend Madge, who had moved from salon cutting to freelance fashion work, but still cut her friends' hair at home in her kitchen. Celeste was in luck. Madge was *chez elle* and would be happy to see Celeste for a glass of wine and a trim.

Three hours later, Celeste was still getting used to the air on her neck and a literal feeling of light-headed freedom when she walked into the lobby of the Miyako Hotel. She had been happy to see her thick locks lying in a heap on the floor, gaining strength from the dramatic change in her appearance, a sort of reverse Samson experience.

Harry was slumped in a chair in the lobby. When he saw Celeste with her new short-cropped hair, dressed for the occasion, he stood up immediately with enthusiasm. "You look terrific," he said. "I hope you'll still go out with me."

Celeste took one look at Harry and had to laugh. He had at least two days' beard growth and was wearing a baggy corduroy jacket and one of his old knit ties with a plaid flannel shirt. Gone was the Brooks Brother's blazer and button down collar. Celeste assumed, correctly, that Cammy had gone as well.

"What happened?" she asked.

"Cold shoulder," said Harry. "I just didn't come up to snuff at Christmas with her family in Atlanta. Things deteriorated fast after that. The only good side is that I don't have to shave anymore."

"Well, never mind," said Celeste. "There are more fish in the sea."

"I suppose," said Harry with little enthusiasm. "You're looking good, at least. Life must be agreeing with you."

"I wouldn't quite put it like that," said Celeste.

They found that several of the restaurants on Fillmore were open, including Celeste's favorite fusion restaurant where the specialty of the house was "unaghetti," spaghetti with Japanese smoked eel. Sharing this consolation meal, Celeste realized how much she had missed Harry's friendship.

Over dinner, with a huge sense of relief, Celeste told Harry the story of her casework for the FBI. She knew she could trust both his opinion and his discretion. She asked him the question that had been bothering her all day. Did he think that, morally, she was obliged to go to the media with her story at the risk of her lab funding?

Harry listened wide-eyed to her tale. Then he said, "Rock, paper, scissors."

"What?" queried Celeste. She was about to follow up with her routine response to a nonsequitur and ask Harry what his remark had to do with the price of eggs. Then she realized exactly what Harry meant. He was referring to that school-yard game of guessing your opponent's choice of weapon and trying to select a more powerful one. Scissors could cut paper. Paper could cover rock. Rock could smash scissors. Harry was merely describing what Celeste had told him about the relationship between the Mafia, the FBI, and the CIA.

He started to explain this to Celeste, who interrupted him. "Never mind, I see what you're saying. So what do you think? Does the media overpower all?"

Harry was surprisingly dubious. Especially for a reporter who had benefited from Celeste's last misadventure with a Pulitzer prizewinning exclusive. But, he rationalized to himself, going for a second prize would be greedy. Furthermore, it seemed to Harry that this case had too many outstanding threatening aspects to it to tempt him beyond a promise to Celeste to do a little preliminary research. Celeste was relieved, but slightly disappointed that Harry didn't want to dive into action.

They finished the evening at the bar in the Miyako, examining the events of Harry and Cammy's relationship with a fine toothed comb. It was Celeste's turn to dispense therapy, big time. Harry drained his second Johnnie Walker and stood up. He looked down at Celeste.

"It's too soon for both of us," she said, rising herself. "I think it's time for me to get a taxi."

"You're still my best friend," said Harry.

"I know," said Celeste. "The best."

When she arrived home and opened the outer gate to the courtyard, Celeste saw that a florist's box was propped up against the inner gate leading to her upstairs condominium. When she got closer, she could see through the cellophane that the box contained long-stemmed white roses. The card read, "Happy New Year from San Juan." So that's what Raul had been up to all along. Seen in a different light, his little courtship was harmlessly flattering.

That night, Celeste dreamed of Harry and Raul and other fish in the sea.

16

Rock, Paper, Scissors

Stash was not happy about his last conversation with Celeste. Before their confrontation he had been confident that threatening her NIH funding would do the trick. Now, as he paced around his quiet house in Virginia the evening of his return from San Francisco, he wasn't so sure. It was the photograph of Celeste, half-naked, that got him thinking about how unpredictable she was. She'd been a tigress in bed. Not at all what one would have expected from the apparent phenotype.

Navarro and Minot were flying in the next morning to follow up on the fabrication of the Lovett case. Much as Stash disliked agents like Minot, he might have to enlist his help in getting Celeste to keep quiet. But it occurred to Stash that there was an alternative strategy. If something happened to Celeste, there would be no further worry about her discretion. Perhaps, Stash thought, he shouldn't be so eager to break with the Valentinos yet. All he would have to do is to tell them that his hands were tied in terms of keeping Dr. Braun under control. The simplicity of the solution was tempting.

Stash poured himself a small shot of Macallan malt whisky and stood in front of the photograph of Celeste, sipping it slowly. In this position, his back was turned on the photograph of his pregnant wife. The corridor to the front door extended to Stash's right. As he took a sip of whisky, he thought he heard a car drive up to the front of the house and cut the engine.

He wasn't expecting the FBI visitors until the morning, but there could have been a misunderstanding. It had happened before with Navarro's useless secretary. As a precaution, however, Stash put down the whisky glass and picked up his revolver from the holster lying on the couch in the sitting room. He held the gun ready as he walked to the front, expecting the bell to ring.

The bell did not ring, and when Stash reached the front door, he cautiously peered through the peephole to see whether a car had indeed pulled up outside. He saw nothing.

Stash considered whether the noise he had heard could have come from the main road. He didn't think so. Occasionally drivers from the main road turned down the conference center driveway when they were lost and needed to ask for directions. Stash supposed that one of these could have bypassed the house and would be backing up just about now.

Sure enough, when he opened the door and poked his head out, Stash saw the reflection of red taillights on the driveway where it rounded the corner of his house. When the itinerant car turned the corner, the driver would have noticed that Stash's house was the only illuminated building visible from the drive.

Stash stood in the doorway with his arms crossed over his chest, waiting for the car to back up and for the inevitable request for directions. His gun was tucked under the opposite armpit, accessible but not alarmingly visible to an innocent driver who had lost the way.

What Stash did not see was that Luigi, Jr. was standing in the bushes across the drive from the front door, with an eye on Stash and a cell phone connected to that of the driver's in the car.

"Pronto," whispered Luigi into the phone.

The car leapt into reverse and backed up with a screech so that the gunman perched on the backseat, with his automatic rifle poking out the window, was perfectly aligned with Stash. Stash didn't have time to even think about uncrossing his arms to release his gun before he was blasted.

Stash collapsed on the stoop, now wanting to uncross his arms, but felt they were glued to his chest by a warm, moist substance. He could just make out three tall, dark figures standing over him. They seemed a long way above him. As Stash faded from consciousness, he heard a strange hissing voice.

"Let Sss-stefano finish the job, Luigi. You'll have your turn tomorrow at the sss-swimming pool."

Two days later, Celeste received E-mail from Harry saying that he was transmitting by fax two articles from the *Washington Post* related to the research she had asked him to do. Celeste went downstairs to the department office and found that the articles had already arrived and were sitting in her mailbox. The first article was an obituary of Dr. Sandra Lovett, head of a successful neurology clinic in Washington, D.C. Dr. Lovett had drowned in a freak swimming accident in the pool at George Washington University gym, where she was a frequent user. The second article reported a fire at a new conference center near Langley, Virginia. It had occurred between conferences so no guests had been endangered. It was believed that the only casualty was the conference center manager, who had lived there alone, but the police were still searching the grounds, which had suffered extensive damage.

Celeste shivered. There were no loose ends. No bodies slashed with a signature V. No story. At least her lab funding would remain intact until the usual threat of budget cuts at grant renewal time.

B. B. Jordan

PRINCIPAL

Investigation

A Scientific Mystery

One man holds the cure to a mutant strain of the Eke virus—one of the most deadly of all. And for the sake of money and power, he's holding the whole world hostage. But there's an even greater problem:

No one knows if the cure will work.

Now virologist Dr. Celeste Braun must turn her scientific skills to the art of investigation—by solving the crime and finding the cure...

___0-425-16090-4/$5.99

BERKLEY
PRIME
CRIME

PENGUIN PUTNAM INC.
Online

Your Internet gateway to a virtual environment with
hundreds of entertaining and enlightening books from
Penguin Putnam Inc.

*While you're there, get the latest buzz on
the best authors and books around—*

Tom Clancy, Patricia Cornwell, W.E.B. Griffin,
Nora Roberts, William Gibson, Robin Cook,
Brian Jacques, Catherine Coulter, Stephen King,
Jacquelyn Mitchard, and many more!

Penguin Putnam Online is located at
http://www.penguinputnam.com

PENGUIN PUTNAM NEWS

Every month you'll get an inside look at our upcoming
books and new features on our site. This is an ongoing
effort to provide you with the most up-to-date
information about our books and authors.

Subscribe to Penguin Putnam News at
http://www.penguinputnam.com/ClubPPI